Dr. Nikola Returns
Boothby, Guy Newell

Published: 1896
Categorie(s): Fiction, Mystery & Detective, Occult & Supernatural
Source: Gutenberg Australia http://gutenberg.net.au/ebooks06/0601621h.html

About Boothby:

Guy Newell Boothby was an Australian novelist and writer, born in Adelaide, son of Thomas Wilde Boothby, who for a time was a member of the South Australian Legislative Assembly. Guy Boothby's grandfather was Benjamin Boothby (1803-1868), judge of the supreme court of South Australia from 1853 to 1867. When Boothby was six, he traveled to England with his mother. Around 1890, he took the position of private secretary to the mayor of Adelaide, Australia, but was not content with the work due to little opportunity for advancement. He turned to his writing talents, writing librettos for 2 comic operas and stories about Australian life. Boothby moved back to the United Kingdom in 1894. He wrote over 50 books in the course of a decade, before dying of pneumonia in Bournemouth. Some of Boothby's earlier works were non-fiction, but later he turned to writing novels. He was once well known for his series of five novels about Doctor Nikola, an occultist anti-hero seeking immortality and world domination. In *A Prince of Swindlers* he created the character of Simon Carne, a gentleman thief in the Raffles mold, with an alter ago as the eccentric detective Klimo: Carne first appeared in *Pearson's Magazine* in 1897, predating Raffles by two years. (http://en.wikipedia.org/wiki/Guy_Boothby)

Also available on Feedbooks for Boothby:
- *Dr. Nikola's Experiment* (1899)
- *The Lust of Hate* (1898)
- *A Bid for Fortune or Dr Nikola's Vendetta* (1895)
- *Farewell, Nikola* (1901)

Note: This book is brought to you by Feedbooks
http://www.feedbooks.com
Strictly for personal use, do not use this file for commercial purposes.

Introduction

My Dear William George Craigie—

I have no doubt as to your surprise at receiving this letter, after so long and unjustifiable a period of silence, from one whom you must have come to consider either a dead man or at least a permanent refugee. When last we met it was on the deck of Tremorden's yacht, in the harbour of Honolulu. I had been down to Kauai, I remember, and the day following, you, you lucky dog, were going off to England by the Royal Mail to be married to the girl of your heart. Since then I have heard, quite by chance, that you have settled down to a country life, as if to the manner born; that you take an absorbing interest in mangel-wurzels, and, while you strike terror into the hearts of poachers and other rustic evil-doers, have the reputation of making your wife the very best of husbands. Consequently you are to be envied and considered one of the happiest of men.

While, however, things have been behaving thus prosperously with you, I am afraid I cannot truthfully say that they have fared so well with me. At the termination of our pleasant South Sea cruise, just referred to, when our party dismembered itself in the Sandwich Islands, I crossed to Sydney, passed up inside the Barrier Reef to Cooktown, where I remained three months in order to try my luck upon the Palmer Gold Fields. This proving unsatisfactory I returned to the coast and continued my journey north to Thursday Island. From the last-named little spot I visited New Guinea, gave it my patronage for the better part of six months, and received in return a bad attack of fever, after recovering from which I migrated to Borneo, to bring up finally, as you will suppose, in my beloved China.

Do you remember how in the old days, when we both held positions of more or less importance in Hong-Kong, you used to rally me about my fondness for the Celestial character and my absurd liking for going fantee into the queerest company and places? How little did I imagine then to what straits that craze would ultimately conduct me! But we never know what the future has in store for us, do we? And perhaps it is as well.

You will observe, my dear Craigie, that it is the record of my visit to China on this particular occasion that constitutes this book; and you must also understand that it is because of our long friendship for each other, and by reason of our queer researches into the occult world together, that you find your name placed so conspicuously upon the forefront of it.

A word now as to my present existence and abode. My location I cannot reveal even to you. And believe me I make this reservation for the strongest reasons. Suffice it that I own a farm, of close upon five thousand acres, in a country such as would gladden your heart, if matrimony and continued well-being have not spoilt your eyes for richness of soil. It is shut in on all sides by precipitous mountain ranges, on the western peaks of which at this moment, as I sit in my verandah writing to you, a quantity of cloud, tinted a rose pink by the setting sun, is gathering. A quieter spot, and one more remote from the rush and bustle of civilization, it would be difficult to find. Once every six months my stores are brought up to me on mule-back by a trusted retainer who has never spoken a word of English in his life, and once every six weeks I send to, and receive from, my post office, four hundred miles distant, my mails. In the intervals I imitate the patriarchal life and character; that is to say, I hoe and reap my corn, live in harmony with my neighbour, who is two hundred odd miles away, and, figuratively speaking, enjoy life beneath my own vine and fig-tree.

Perhaps when the cool west wind blows in the long grass, the wild duck whistle upon the lagoons, or a newspaper filled with gossip of the outer world finds its way in to me, I am a little restless, but at other times I can safely say I have few regrets. I have done with the world, and to make my exile easier I have been permitted that greatest of all blessings, a good wife. Who she is and how I won her you will discover when you have perused this narrative, the compiling of which has been my principal and, I might almost say, only recreation all through our more than tedious winter. But now the snow has departed, spring is upon us, clad in its mantle of luscious grass and accompanied by the twitterings of birds and the music of innumerable small waterfalls, and I am a new man. All nature is busy, the swallows are working overtime beneath the eaves, and to-morrow, in proof of my remembrance, this book goes off to you.

Whether I shall ever again see Dr. Nikola, the principal character in it, is more than I can tell you. But I sincerely trust not. It is for the sake of circumstances brought about by that extraordinary man that I have doomed myself to perpetual exile; still I have no desire that he should know of my sacrifice. Sometimes when I lie awake in the quiet watches of the night I can hardly believe that the events of the last two years are real. The horror of that time still presses heavily upon me, and if I live to be a hundred I doubt if I shall outgrow it. When I tell you that even the things, I mean the mysteries and weird experiences, into which we thrust our impertinent noses in bygone days were absolutely as nothing compared with those I have passed through since in Nikola's company, you will at first feel inclined to believe that I am romancing. But I know this, that by the time you have got my curious story by heart all doubt on that score will have been swept away.

One last entreaty. Having read this book, do not attempt to find me, or to set my position right with the world. Take my word for it, it is better as it is.

And now, without further preamble, let us come to the story itself. God bless you, and give you every happiness. Speak kindly of me to your wife, and believe me until death finishes my career, if it does such a thing, which Dr. Nikola would have me doubt,

Your affectionate friend,
Wilfred Bruce.

Chapter 1

How I Came To Meet Dr. Nikola

It was Saturday afternoon, about a quarter-past four o'clock if my memory serves me, and the road, known as the Maloo, leading to the Bubbling Well, that single breathing place of Shanghai, was crowded. Fashionable barouches, C-spring buggies, spider-wheel dogcarts, to say nothing of every species of 'rickshaw, bicycle, and pony, were following each other in one long procession towards the Well. All the European portion of Shanghai, and a considerable percentage of the native, had turned out to witness the finish of the paper hunt, which, though, not exciting in itself, was important as being the only amusement the settlement boasted that afternoon. I had walked as far as the Horse Bazaar myself, and had taken a 'rickshaw thence, more from pride than because I could afford it. To tell the truth, which will pop out sooner or later, however much I may try to prevent it, I was keeping up appearances, and though I lay back in my vehicle and smoked my cheroot with a princely air, I was painfully conscious of the fact that when the ride should be paid for the exchequer would scarcely survive the shock.

Since my arrival in Shanghai I had been more than usually unfortunate. I had tried for every billet then vacant, from those choice pickings at the top of the tree among the high gods, to the secretaryship of a Eurasian hub of communistical tendencies located somewhere on the confines of the native city, but always without success. For the one I had not the necessary influence, for the other I lacked that peculiar gift of obsequiousness which is so essential to prosperity in that particular line of business.

In the meantime my expenditure was going remorselessly on, and I very soon saw that unless something happened, and that quickly too, I had every prospect of hiding myself deprived of my belongings, sleeping on the Bund, and finally figuring in that Mixed Court in the Magistrate's Yamen, which is so justly dreaded by every Englishman, as the debtor of a Cochin China Jew. The position was not a cheerful one, look at it in whatever light I would, but I had experienced it a good many times before, and had always come out of it, if not with an increased amount of self-respect, certainly without any *very* great degree of personal embarrassment.

Arriving at the Well, I paid off my coolie and took up a position near "the last jump," which I noticed was a prepared fence and ditch of considerable awkwardness. I was only just in time, for a moment later the horses came at it with a rush; some cleared it, some refused it, while others, adopting a middle course, jumped on the top of it, blundered over, and finally sent their riders spinning over their heads into the mud at the feet of their fairest friends. It was not exactly an aesthetic picture, but it was certainly a very amusing one.

When the last horse, had landed, imagining the sport to be over for the day, I was in the act of moving away when there was a shout to stand clear, and wheeling round again, I was just in time to see a last horseman come dashing at the fence. Though he rode with considerable determination, and was evidently bent on putting a good finish to his day's amusement, it was plain that his horse was not of the same way of thinking, for, when he was distant about half a dozen yards from the fence, he broke his stride, stuck his feet into the mud, and endeavoured to come to a standstill. The result was not at all what he expected; he slid towards the fence, received his rider's *quirt,* viciously administered, round his flank, made up his mind to jump too late, hit the top rail with his forehead, turned a complete somersault, and landed with a crash at my feet. His rider fell into the arms of the ditch, out of which I presently dragged him. When I got him on the bank he did not look a pretty sight, but, on the other hand, that did not prevent him from recognizing me.

"Wilfred Bruce, by all that's glorious!" he cried, at the same time rising to his feet and mopping his streaming face with a very muddy pocket-handkerchief. "This is a fortunate encounter, for do you know, I spent two hours this morning looking for you?"

"I am very sorry you should have had so much trouble," I answered; "but are you sure you are not hurt?"

"Not in the least," he answered, and when he had scraped off as much mud as possible, turned to his horse, which had struggled to his feet and was gazing stupidly about him.

"Let me first send this clumsy brute home," he said, "then I'll find my cart, and if you'll permit me I'll take you back to town with me."

We saw the horse led away, and, when we had discovered his dog-cart among the crowd of vehicles waiting for their owners, mounted to our seats and set off—after a few preliminary antics on the part of the leader—on our return to the settlement.

Once comfortably on our way George Barkston, whom, I might mention here, I had known for more than ten years, placed his whip in the bucket and turned to me.

"Look here, Bruce," he said, flushing a little in anticipation of what he was about to say, "I'm not going to mince matters with you, so let us come straight to the point; we are old friends, and though we've not seen as much of each other during this visit to Shanghai as we used to do in the old days when you were deputy-commissioner of whatever it was, and I was your graceless subordinate, I think I am pretty well conversant with your present condition. I don't want you to consider me impertinent, but I *do* want you to let me help you if I can."

"That's very good of you," I answered, not without a little tremor, however, as he shaved a well-built American buggy by a hair's breadth. "To tell the honest truth, I want to get something to do pretty badly. There's a serious deficit in the exchequer, my boy. And though I'm a fairly old hand at the game of poverty, I've still a sort of pride left, and I have no desire to figure in the Mixed Court next Wednesday on a charge of inability to pay my landlord twenty dollars for board and lodging."

"Of course you don't," said Barkston warmly; "and so, if you'll let me help you, I've an idea that I can put you on to the right track to something. The fact is, there was a chap in the smoking-room at the club the other night with whom I got into conversation. He interested me more than I can tell you, for he was one of the most curious beings who, I should imagine, has ever visited the East. I never saw such an odd-looking fellow in my life. Talk about eyes—well, his were—augh! Why, he looked you through and through. You know old Benwell, of the revenue-cutter *Y-chang?* Well, while I was talking to this fellow, after a game of pool, in he came.

"'Hallo! Barkston,' he said, as he brought up alongside the table, 'I thought you were shooting with Jimmy Woodrough up the river? I'm glad to find you're not, for I——' He had got as far as this before he became aware of my companion. Then his jaw dropped; he looked hard at him, said something under his breath, and, shaking me by the hand, made a feeble excuse, and fled the room. Not being able to make it out at all, I went after him and found him looking for his hat in the hall. 'Come, I say, Benwell, 'I cried;' what's up? What on earth made you bolt like that? Have I offended you?' He led me on one side, so that the servants should not hear, and having done so said confidentially: 'Barkston, I am not a coward; in my time I've tackled Europeans, Zulus, Somalis, Malays, Japanese, and Chinese, to say nothing of Manilla and Solomon boys, and what's more, I don't mind facing them all again; but when I find myself face to face with Dr. Nikola, well, I tell you I don't think twice, I bolt! Take my tip and do the same.' As he might just as well have talked to me in low Dutch for all I should have understood, I tried to question him, but I might have spared myself the trouble, for I could get nothing satisfactory out of him. He simply shook me by the hand, told the boy in the hall to call him a 'rickshaw, and as soon as it drew up at the steps jumped into it and departed. When I got back to the billiard-room Nikola was still there, practising losing hazards of extraordinary difficulty.

"'I've an opinion I've seen your friend before,' he said, as I sat down to watch him. 'He is Benwell of the *Y-chang,* and if I mistake not Benwell of the *Y-chang* remembers me.'

"'He seems to know you,' I said with a laugh.

"'Yes, Nikola continued after a little pause; 'I have had the pleasure of being in Mr. Benwell's company once before. It was in Haiphong.' Then with peculiar emphasis: 'I don't know what he thinks of the place, of course, but somehow I have an idea your friend will not willingly go near Haiphong again.' After he had said this he remained silent for a little while, then he took a letter from his pocket, read it carefully, examined the envelope, and having made up his mind on a certain point turned to me again.

"'I want to ask you a question,' he said, putting the cue he had been using back into the rack. 'You know a person named Bruce, don't you? a man who used to be in the Civil Service, and who has the reputation of being able to disguise himself so like a Chinaman that even Li Chang Tung would not know him for a European?'

"'I do,' I answered; 'he is an old friend of mine; and what is more, he is in Shanghai at the present moment. It was only this morning I heard of him.'

"'Bring him to me," said Nikola quickly. 'I am told he wants a billet, and if he sees me before twelve to-morrow night I think I can put him in the way of obtaining a good one. Now there you are, Bruce, my boy. I have done my best for you."

"And I am sincerely grateful to you," I answered. "But who is this man Nikola, and what sort of a billet do you think he can find me?"

"Who he is I can no more tell you than I can fly. But if he is not the first cousin of the Old Gentleman himself, well, all I can say is, I'm no hand at finding relationships."

"I am afraid that doesn't tell me very much," I answered. "What's he like to look at?"

"Well, in appearance he might be described as tall, though you must not run away with the idea that he's what you would call a big man. On the contrary, he is most slenderly built. Anything like the symmetry of his figure, however, I don't remember to have met with before. His face is clean shaven, and is always deadly pale, a sort of toad-skin pallor, that strikes you directly when you see him and the remembrance of which never leaves you again. His eyes and hair are as black as night, and he is as neat and natty as a new pin. When he is watching you he seems to be looking through the back of your head into the wall behind, and when he speaks you've just got to pay attention, whether you want to or not. All things considered, the less I see of him the better I shall like him."

"You don't give me a very encouraging report of my new employer. What on earth can he want with me?"

"He's Apollyon himself," laughed Barkston, "and wants a *maitre d'hotel.* I suppose he imagines you'll suit."

By this time we had left the Maloo and were entering the town.

"Where shall I find this extraordinary man?" I asked, as we drew near the place where I intended to alight.

"We'll drive to the club and see if he's there," said Barkston, whipping up his horses. "But, putting all joking aside, he really seemed most anxious to find you, and as he knew I was going to look for you I don't doubt that he will have left some message for one of us there."

Having reached the Wanderers' Club, which is too well known to need any description here, Barkston went inside, leaving me to look after the horses. Five minutes later he emerged again, carrying a letter in his hand.

"Nikola was here until ten minutes ago," he said, with a disappointed expression upon his handsome face; "unfortunately he's gone home now, but has left this note for me. If I find you he begs that I will send you on to his bungalow without delay. I have discovered that it is Fere's old place in the French Concession, Rue de la Fayette; you know it, the third house on the right hand side, just past where that renegade French marquis shot his wife. If you would care about it I'll give you a note to him, and you can dine, think it over quietly, and then take it on yourself this evening or not, as pleases you best."

"That would be the better plan," I said. "I should like to have a little time to collect my thoughts before seeing him."

Thereupon Barkston went back into the building, and when he returned, which was in something under a quarter of an hour, he brought the letter he had promised me in his hand. He jumped up and took the reins, the Chinese groom sprang out of the way, and we were off.

"Can I drive you round to where you are staying?" he asked.

"I don't think you can," I answered, "and for reasons which would be sure to commend themselves to you if I were to tell them. But I am very much obliged to you all the same. As to Nikola, I'll think the whole matter carefully out this evening, and, if I approve, after dinner I'll walk over and present this letter personally."

I thereupon descended from the dogcart at the corner of the road, and having again thanked my friend for the kindness he had shown me, bade him good-bye and took myself off.

Reaching the Bund I sat myself down on a seat beneath a tree and dispassionately reviewed the situation. All things considered it was a pretty complicated one. Though I had not revealed as much to Barkston, who had derived such happiness from his position of guide, philosopher, and friend, this was not the first time I had heard of Nikola. Such a strange personality as his could not expect to go unremarked in a gossip-loving community such as the East, and all sorts of stories had accordingly been circulated concerning him. Though I knew my fellow-man too well to place credence in half of what I had heard, it was impossible for me to prevent myself from feeling a considerable amount of curiosity about the man.

Leaving the Bund I returned to my lodgings, had my tea, and about eight o'clock donned my hat again and set off in the direction of the French Concession. It was not a pleasant night, being unusually dark and inclined towards showery. The wind blew in fitful gusts, and drove the dust like hail against one's face. Though I stood a good chance of obtaining what I wanted so much—employment, I cannot affirm with any degree of truth that I felt easy in my mind. Was I not seeking to become connected with a man who was almost universally feared, and whose reputation was not such as would make most people desire a closer acquaintance with him? This thought in itself was not of a reassuring nature. But in the face of my poverty I could not afford to be too squeamish. So leaving the Rue de la Paix on my left hand I turned into the Rue de la Fayette, where Nikola's bungalow was situated, and having picked it out from its fellows, made my way towards it.

The compound and the house itself were in total darkness, but after I had twice knocked at the door a light came slowly down the passage towards me. The door was opened, and a China boy stood before me holding a candle in his hand.

"Does Dr. Nikola live here?" I inquired, in very much the same tone as our boyhood's hero, Jack of Beanstalk climbing fame, might have used when he asked to be admitted to the residence of the giant Fee-fo-fum. The boy nodded, whereupon I handed him my letter, and ordered him to convey it to his master without delay. With such celerity did he accomplish his mission that in less than two minutes he had returned and was beckoning me to follow him. Accordingly I accompanied him down the passage towards a small room on the left hand side. When I had entered it the door was immediately closed behind me. There was no one in the apartment, and I was thus permitted an opportunity of examining it to my satisfaction, and drawing my own conclusions before Dr Nikola should enter.

As I have said, it was not large, nor was its furniture, with a few exceptions, in any way extraordinary. The greater part of it was of the usual bungalow type, neither better nor worse. On the left hand as one entered was a window, which I observed was heavily barred and shuttered; between that and the door stood a tall bookshelf, filled with works, standard and otherwise, on almost every conceivable subject, from the elementary principles of Bimetallism to abstract Confucianism. A thick matting covered the floor and a heavy curtain sheltered a doorway on the side opposite to that by which I had entered. On the walls were several fine engravings, but I noticed that they were all based on uncommon subjects, such as the visit of Saul to the Witch of Endor, a performance of the magicians before Pharaoh, and the converting of the dry bones into men in the desert. A clock ticked on the bookcase, but with that exception there was nothing to disturb the silence of the room.

I suppose I must have waited fully five minutes before my ears caught the sound of a soft footstep in an adjoining apartment, then the second door opened, the curtain which covered it was drawn slowly aside, and a man, who could have been none other than Dr. Nikola, made his appearance. His description was exactly what Barkston had given me, even to the peculiar eyes and, what proved to be an apt illustration, the white toad-coloured skin. He was attired in faultless evening dress, and its deep black harmonized well with his dark eyes and hair. What his age might have been I could not possibly tell, but I afterwards discovered that he was barely thirty-eight. He crossed the room to where I stood, holding out his hand as he did so and saying—

"Mr. Wilfred Bruce?"

"That is my name," I answered, "and I believe you are Dr. Nikola?"

"Exactly," he said, "I am Dr. Nikola; and now that we know each other, shall we proceed to business?"

As he spoke he moved with that peculiar grace which always characterized him across to the door by which he had entered, and having opened it, signed to me to pass through. I did so, and found myself in another large room, possibly forty feet long by twenty wide. Ac the further end was a lofty window, containing some good stained glass; the walls were hung with Japanese tapestry, and were ornamented with swords, battle-axes, two or three specimens of Rajput armour, books galore, and a quantity of exceedingly valuable china. The apartment was lit by three hanging lamps of rare workmanship and design, while scattered about the room were numberless cushioned chairs and divans, beside one of which I noticed a beautifully inlaid huqa of a certain shape and make that I had never before seen out of Istamboul.

"Pray sit down," said Dr. Nikola, and as he spoke he signed me to a chair at the further end. I seated myself and wondered what would come next.

"This is not your first visit to China, I am given to understand," he continued, as he seated himself in a chair opposite mine, and regarded me steadfastly with his extraordinary eyes.

"It is not," I answered. "I am an old resident in the East, and I think I may say I know China as well as any living Englishman."

"Quite so. You were present at the meeting at Quong Sha's house in the Wanhsien on the 23rd August, 1907, if I remember aright, and you assisted Mah Poo to evade capture by the mandarins the week following."

"How on earth did you know that?" I asked, my surprise quite getting the better of me, for I had always been convinced that no other soul, save the man himself, was aware of my participation in that affair.

"One becomes aware of many strange things in the East," said Nikola, hugging his knee and looking at me over the top of it, "and yet that little circumstance I have just referred to is apt to teach one how much one might know, and how small after all our knowledge is of each other's lives. One could almost expect as much from brute beasts."

"I am afraid I don't quite follow you," I said simply.

"Don't you?" he answered. "And yet it is very simple after all. Let me give you a practical illustration of my meaning. If you see anything in it other than I intend, the blame must be upon your own head."

Upon a table close to his chair lay a large sheet of white paper. This he placed upon the floor. He then took a stick of charcoal in his hand and presently uttered a long and very peculiar whistle. Next moment, without any warning, an enormous cat, black as his master's coat, leapt down from somewhere on to the floor, and stood swishing his tail before us.

"There are some people in the world," said Nikola calmly, at the same time stroking the great beast's soft back, "who would endeavour to convince you that this cat is my familiar spirit, and that, with his assistance, I work all sorts of extraordinary magic. You, of course, would not be so silly as to believe such idle tales. But to bear out what I was saying just now let us try an experiment with his assistance. It is just possible I may be able to tell you something more of your life."

Here he stooped and wrote a number of figures up to ten with the charcoal upon the paper, duplicating them in a line below. He then took the cat upon his knee, stroked it carefully, and finally whispered something in its ear. Instantly the brute sprang down, placed its right fore-paw on one of the numerals of the top row, while, whether by chance or magic I cannot say, it performed a similar action with its left on the row below.

"Twenty-four," said Nikola, with one of his peculiar smiles.

Then taking the piece of charcoal once more in his hand, and turning the paper over, he wrote upon it the names of the different months of the year. Placing it on the floor he again said something to the cat, who this time stood upon June. The alphabet followed, and letter by letter the uncanny beast spelt out "Apia."

"On the 24th June," said Nikola, "of a year undetermined you were in Apia. Let us see if we can discover the year."

Again he wrote the numerals up to ten, and immediately the cat, with fiendish precision, worked out 1895.

"Is that correct?" asked this extraordinary person when the brute had finished its performance.

It was quite correct, and I told him so.

"I'm glad of that. And now do you want to know any more?" he asked. "If you wish it I might perhaps be able to tell you your business there."

I did not want to know. And I can only ask you to believe that I had very good reasons for not doing so. Nikola laughed softly, and pressed the tips of his long white fingers together as he looked at me.

"Now tell me truthfully what you think of my cat?" said he.

"One might be excused if one endowed him with Satanic attributes," I answered.

"And yet, though you think it so wonderful, it is only because I have subjected him to a curious form of education. There is a power latent in animals, and particularly in cats, which few of us suspect. And if animals have this power, how much more may men be expected to possess it. Do you know, Mr. Bruce, I should be very interested to find out exactly how far you think the human intelligence can go; that is to say, how far you think it can penetrate into the regions of what is generally called the occult?"

"Again I must make the excuse," I said, "that I do not follow you."

"Well, then, let me place it before you in a rather simpler form. If I may put it so bluntly, where should you be inclined to say this world begins and ends?"

"I should say," I replied—this time without hesitation—"that it begins with birth and ends with death."

"And after death?"

"Well, what happens then is a question of theology, and one for the parsons to decide."

"You have no individual opinion?"

"I have the remnants of what I learned as a boy."

"I see; in that case you believe that as soon as the breath has forsaken this mortal body a certain indescribable part of us, which for the sake of argument we will denominate soul, leaves this mundane sphere and enters upon a new existence in one or other of two places?"

"That is certainly what I was taught," I answered.

"Quite so; that was the teaching you received in the parish of High Walcombe, Somersetshire, and might be taken as a very good type of what your class thinks throughout the world, from the Archbishop of Canterbury down to the farm labourer's child who walks three miles every seventh day to attend Sunday school. But in that self-same village, if I remember rightly, there was a little man of portly build whose adherents numbered precisely forty-five souls; he was called Father O'Rorke, and I have not the slightest doubt, if you had asked him, he would have given you quite a different account of what becomes of that soul, or essence, if we may so call it, after it has left this mortal body. Tobias Smallcombe, who preaches in a spasmodic, windy way on the green to a congregation made up of a few enthusiasts, a dozen small boys, and a handful of donkeys and goats, will give you yet another, and so on through numberless varieties of creeds to the end of the chapter. Each will claim the privilege of being right, and each will want you to believe exactly as he does. But at the same time we must remember, provided we would be quite fair, that there are not wanting scientists, admittedly the cleverest men of the day, who assert that, while all our friends are agreed that there *is* a life after death—a spirit world, in fact—they are all wrong. If you will allow me to give you my own idea of what you think, I should say that your opinion is, that when you've done with the solid flesh that makes up Wilfred Bruce it doesn't much matter what happens. But let us suppose that Wilfred Bruce, or his mind, shall we say?—that part of him at any rate which is anxious, which thinks and which suffers—is destined to exist afterwards through endless aeons, a prey to continual remorse for all misdeeds: how would he regard death then?"

"But before you can expect an answer to that question it is necessary that you should prove that he does so continue to exist," I said.

"That's exactly what I desire and intend to do," said Nikola, "and it is to that end I have sought you out, and we are arguing in this fashion now. Is your time very fully occupied at present?"

I smiled.

"I quite understand," he said. "Well, I have got a proposition to make to you, if you will listen to me. Years ago and quite by chance, when the subject we are now discussing, and in which I am more interested than you can imagine, was first brought properly under my notice, I fell into the company of a most extraordinary man. He was originally an Oxford don, but for some reason he went wrong, and was afterwards shot by Balmaceda at Santiago during the Chilian war. Among other places, he had lived for many years in North-Western China. He possessed one of the queerest personalities, but he told me some wonderful things, and what was more to the point, he backed them with proofs. You would probably have called them clever conjuring tricks. So did I then, but I don't now. Nor do I think will you when I have done with you. It was from that man and an old Buddhist priest, with whom I spent some time in Ceylon, that I learnt the tiny fact which put me on the trail of what I am now following up. I have tracked it clue by clue, carefully and laboriously, with varying success for eight long years, and at last I am in the position to say that I believe I have my thumb upon the key-note. If I can press it down and obtain the result I want, I can put myself in possession of information the magnitude of which the world—I mean the European world, of course—has not the slightest conception. I am a courageous man, but I will confess that the prospect of what I am about to attempt almost frightens *me.* It is neither more nor less than to penetrate, with the help of certain Chinese secret societies, into the most extraordinary seat of learning that you or any other men ever heard of, and when there to beg, borrow, or steal the marvellous secrets they possess. I cannot go alone, for a hundred reasons, therefore I must find a man to accompany me; that man must be one in a thousand, and he must also necessarily be a consummate Chinese scholar. He must be plucky beyond the average, he must be capable of disguising himself so that his nationality shall never for a moment be suspected, and he must go fully convinced in his own mind that he will never return. If he is prepared to undertake so much I am prepared to be generous. I will pay him £5,000 down before we start and £5,000 when we return, if return we do. What do you say to that?"

I didn't know what to say. The magnitude of the proposal, to leave the value of the honorarium out of the question, completely staggered me. I wanted money more than I had ever done in my life before, and this was a sum beyond even my wildest dreams; I also had no objection to adventure, but at the same time I must confess this seemed too foolhardy an undertaking altogether.

"What can I say?" I answered. "It's such an extraordinary proposition."

"So it is," he said. "But as I take it, we are both extraordinary men. Had you been one of life's rank and file I should not be discussing it with you now. I would think twice before I refused if I were you; Shanghai is such an unpleasant place to get into trouble in, and besides that, you know, next Wednesday will see the end of your money, even if you do sell your watch and chain, as you proposed to yourself to-night."

He said this with such an air of innocence that for the moment it did not strike me to wonder how he had become acquainted with the state of my finances.

"Come," he said, "you had better say yes."

"I should like a little more time to think it over," I answered. "I cannot pledge myself to so much without giving it thorough consideration. Even if it were not folly on my part it would scarcely be fair to you."

"Very good then. Go home and think about it. Come and see me to-morrow night at this time and let me have your decision. In the meantime if I were you I would say nothing about our conversation to any one."

I assured him I would not, and then he rose, and I understood that our interview was at an end. I followed him into the hall, the black cat marching sedately at our heels. In the verandah he stopped and held out his hand, saying with an indescribable sweetness of tone—

"I hope, Mr. Bruce, you will believe that I am most anxious for your companionship. I don't flatter you, I simply state the truth when I affirm that you are the only man in China whose co-operation I would ask. Now good-night. I hope you will come to me with a favourable answer to-morrow."

As he spoke, and as if to emphasize his request, the black cat, which up to that time had been standing beside him, now

19

came over and began to rub its head, accompanying its action with a soft, purring noise, against my leg.

"I will let you know without fail by this time tomorrow evening," I said. "Good-night."

Chapter 2

Nikola's Offer

After I had bidden Dr. Nikola good-night in the verandah of his house, I consulted my watch, and discovering that it was not yet eleven o'clock, set off for a long walk through the city in order to consider my position. There were many things to be reckoned for and against his offer. To begin with, as a point in its favour, I remembered the fact that I was alone in the world. My father and mother had been dead some years, and as I was their only child, I had neither brother nor sister dependent upon my exertions, or to mourn my loss if by ill-chance anything desperate should befall me. In the second place, I had been a traveller in strange lands from my youth up, and was therefore the more accustomed to hard living. This will be better understood when I say that I had run away from home at the age of fifteen to go to sea; had spent three years in the roughest life before the mast any man could dream of or desire; had got through another five, scarcely less savage, as an Australian bushman on the borders of the Great Desert; another two in a detachment of the Cape Mounted Police; I had also held a fair appointment in Hong-Kong, and had drifted in and out of many other employments, good, bad, and indifferent. I was thirty-five years of age, had never, with the exception of my attack of fever in New Guinea, known what it was to be really sick or sorry, and, if the information is of any use to the world, weighed thirteen stone, stood close upon six feet in my stockings, had grey eyes and dark-brown hair, and, if you will not deem me conceited for saying so, had the reputation of being passably good-looking.

My position at that moment, financially and otherwise, was certainly precarious in the extreme. It was true, if I looked long enough I might find something to do, but, on the other hand, it was equally probable that I should not, for, as I knew to my cost, there were dozens of men in Shanghai at that moment, also on the look-out for employment, who would snap up anything that offered at a moment's notice. Only that morning I had been assured by a well-known merchant, upon whom I had waited in the hope of obtaining a cashiership he had vacant in his office, that he could have filled it a hundred times over before my arrival. This being so, I told myself that I had no right to neglect any opportunity which might come in my way of bettering my position. I therefore resolved not to reject Nikola's offer without the most careful consideration. Unfortunately, a love of adventure formed an integral part of my constitution, and when a temptation, such as the present, offered it was difficult for me to resist it. Indeed, this particular form of adventure appealed to me with a voice of more than usual strength. What was still more to the point, Nikola was such a born leader of men that the mysterious fascination of his manner seemed to compel me to give him my co-operation, whether I would or would not. That the enterprise was one involving the chance of death was its most unpleasant feature; but still, I told myself, I had to die some time or other, while if my luck held good, and I came out of it alive, £10,000 would render me independent for the rest of my existence. As the thought of this large sum came into my mind, the sinister form of my half-caste landlord rose before my mind's eye, and the memory of his ill-written and worse-spelled account, which I should certainly receive upon the morrow, chilled me like a cold douche. Yes, my mind was made up, I *would* go; and having come to this decision, I went home.

But when I woke next morning Prudence sat by my bedside. My dreams had not been good ones. I had seen myself poisoned in Chinese monasteries, dismembered by almond-eyed headsmen before city gates, and tortured in a thousand terrible ways and places. Though these nightmares were only the natural outcome of my anxiety, yet I could not disabuse my mind of the knowledge that every one was within the sphere of probability. Directly I should have changed into Celestial dress, stained my face and sewn on my pigtail, I would be a Chinaman pure and simple, amenable to Chinese laws and liable to Chinese penalties. Then there was another point to be considered. What sort of travelling companion would Nikola prove? Would I be able to trust him in moments of danger and difficulty? Would he stand by me as one comrade should by another? And if by any chance we should get into a scrape and there should be an opportunity of escape for one only, would Nikola, by virtue of being my employer, seize that chance and leave me to brave the upshot, whatever it might be? In that case my £5,000 in the Shanghai Bank and the £5,000 which was to be paid to me on my return would be little less useful than a worn-out tobacco pouch. And this suggested to my mind another question: Was Nikola sufficiently rich to be able to pay £10,000 to a man to accompany him on such a harebrained errand? These were all matters of importance, and they were also questions that had to be satisfactorily answered before I could come to any real decision. Though Barkston had informed me that Nikola was so well known throughout the East, though Benwell, of the Chinese Revenue Service, had shown himself so frightened when he had met him face to face in the club, and though I, myself, had heard all sorts of queer stories about him in Saigon and the Manillas, they were none of them sufficiently definite to be any guarantee to me of his monetary stability. To set my mind at rest, I determined to make inquiries about Nikola from some unbiassed person. But who was that person to be? I reviewed all my acquaintances in turn, but without pitching upon any who would be at all likely to be able to help me in my dilemma. Then, while I was dressing, I remembered a man, a merchant, owning one of the largest *hongs* along the Bund, who was supposed to know more about people in general, and queer folk in particular, than any man in China.

I ate my breakfast, such as it was, received my account from my landlord with the lordly air of one who has £10,000 reposing at his banker's, lit an excellent cigar in the verandah and then sauntered down town.

Arriving at the Bund, I walked along until I discovered my friend's office. It overlooked the river, and was as fine a building as any in Shanghai. In the main hall I had the good fortune to discover the merchant's chief *comprador,* who, having learned that his master was disengaged, conducted me forthwith to his presence.

Alexander McAndrew hailed from north of the Tweed—this fact the least observant would have noticed before he had been five minutes in his company. His father had been a night watchman at one of the Glasgow banks, and his own early youth was spent as a ragged, barefooted boy in the streets of that extraordinary city. Of his humble origin McAndrew, however, was prouder than any De la Zouch could have been of friendship with the Conqueror; indeed, he was wont, when he entertained friends at his princely bungalow in the English Concession, to recall and dwell with delight upon the sordid circumstances that brought about the happy chance which, one biting winter's morning, led him to seek fame and fortune in the East.

"Why, Mr. Bruce," he cried, rising from his chair and shaking me warmly by the hand, "this is a most unexpected pleasure! How long have you been in Shanghai?"

"Longer than I care to remember," I answered, taking the seat he offered me.

"And all that time you have never once been to see me. That's hardly fair treatment of an old friend, is it?"

"I must ask your pardon for my remissness," I said, "but somehow things have not gone well with me in Shanghai this time, and so I've not been to see anybody. You observe that I am candid with you."

"I am sorry to hear that you are in trouble," he said. "I don't want to appear impertinent, but if I can be of any service to you I sincerely hope you will command me."

"Thank you," I answered. "I have already determined to do so. Indeed, it is to consult you that I have taken the liberty of calling upon you now."

"I am glad of that. Upon what subject do you want my advice?"

"Well, to begin with, let me tell you that I have been offered a billet which is to bring me in £10,000."

"Why, I thought you said things were not prospering with you?" cried my friend. "This doesn't look as if there is much wrong. What is the billet?"

"That, I am sorry to say, I am not at liberty to reveal to any one."

"Then in what way can I be of use to you?"

"First, I want to know if you can give me any information about my employer?"

"Tell me his name and I'll see what I can do," the merchant answered, not without a show of pride. "I think I know nine out of every ten men of any importance in the East."

"Well," I said, "this man's name is Nikola."

"Nikola!" he cried in complete astonishment, wheeling round to face me. "What possible business can you have with Nikola that is to bring you in £10,000?"

"Business of the very utmost importance," I answered, "involving almost life and death. But it is evident you know him?"

In reply the old man leant over the table and sank his voice almost to a whisper.

"Bruce," he said, "I know more of that man than I dare tell you, and if you will take my advice you will back out while you have time. If you can't, why, be more than careful what arrangements you make with him."

"You frighten me," I said, more impressed by his earnestness than I cared to own. "Is he not good for the money, then?"

"Oh, as for the money, I don't doubt that he could pay it a dozen times over if he wanted to," the worthy merchant replied. "In point of fact, between ourselves, he has the power to draw upon me up to the extent of £50,000."

"He's a rich man, then?"

"Immensely!"

"But where on earth does his money come from?"

"Ah! that's a good deal more than I can tell you," he replied. "But wherever he gets it, take my advice and think twice before you put yourself into his power. Personally, and I can say it with truth, I don't fear many men, but I *do* fear Nikola, and that I'm not the only man in the world who does I will prove to you by this letter."

As he spoke he opened a drawer in his writing-table and took out a couple of sheets of notepaper. Spreading them upon the table before him, he smoothed the page and began to read.

"This letter, you must understand," he said, "is from the late Colonial Secretary of New South Wales, the Hon. Sylvester Wetherell, a personal friend of mine. I will skip the commencement, which is mainly private, and come to the main issue. He says:

"'... Since I wrote to you in June last, from London, I have been passing through a time of terrible trouble. As I told you in a letter some years ago, I was brought, quite against my will, into dealings with a most peculiar person named Nikola. Some few years since I defended a man known as China Pete, in our Central Criminal Court, against a charge of murder, and, what was more, got him off. When he died, being unable to pay me, he made me a present of all he had to leave, a peculiar little stick, covered with carved Chinese characters, about which he told me a mad rigmarole, but which has since nearly proved my undoing. For some inscrutable reason this man Nikola wanted to obtain possession of this stick, and because I refused to let him have it has subjected me to such continuous persecution these few years past as to nearly drive me into a lunatic asylum. Every method that a man could possibly adopt or a demoniacal brain invent to compel me to surrender the curio he tried. You will gather something of what I mean when I tell you that my house was twice broken into by Chinese burglars, that I was garrotted within a hundred yards of my own front door, that my wife and daughter were intimidated by innumerable threatening letters, and that I was at length brought to such a pitch of nervousness that after my wife died I fled to England to escape him. Nikola followed me, drew into the plot he was weaving about me the Duke of Glenbarth, his son, the Marquis of Beckenham, Sir Richard Hatteras, who has since married my daughter, our late Governor, the Earl of Amberley, and at least a dozen other persons. Through his agency Beckenham and Hatteras were decoyed into a house in Port Said and locked up for three weeks, while a spurious nobleman was sent on in his lordship's place to Sydney to become acquainted with my daughter, and finally to solicit her hand in marriage. Fortunately, however, Sir Richard Hatteras and his friend managed to make their escape from custody in time to follow the scoundrels to Sydney, and to warn me of the plot that was hatching against me. The result was disastrous. Foiled in his endeavours to revenge himself upon me by marrying my daughter to an impostor, Nikola had the audacity to abduct my girl from a ball at Government House and to convey her on a yacht to an island in the South Pacific, whence a month later we rescued her. Whether we should have been permitted to do so if the stick referred to, which was demanded as ransom, had not fallen, quite by chance, into Nikola's possession, I cannot say. But the stick *did* become his property, and now we are free. Since then my daughter has married Sir Richard Hatteras, and at the present moment they are living on his estate in England. I expect you will be wondering why I have not prosecuted this man Nikola, but to tell you the honest truth, McAndrew, I have such a wholesome dread of him that since I have got my girl back, and have only lost the curio, which has always been a trouble to me, I am quite content to say no more about the matter. Besides, I must confess, he has worked with such devilish cunning that, trained in the law as I am, I cannot see that we should stand any chance of bringing him to book.'"

"Now, Bruce, that you have heard the letter, what do you think of Dr. Nikola?"

"It puts rather a different complexion on affairs, doesn't it?" I said. "But still, if Nikola will play fair by me, £10,000 is £10,000. I've been twenty years in this world trying to make money, and this is the sum total of my wealth."

As I spoke I took out of my pocket all the money I had in the world, which comprised half a dozen coins, amounting in English to a total of *6s. 10d.* I turned to the merchant.

"I don't know what you will think, but my own opinion is that Nikola's character will have to be a very outrageous one to outweigh 10,000 golden sovereigns."

"I am afraid you are a little bit reckless, aren't you, Bruce?" said the cautious McAndrew. "If you will take my advice I should say try for something else, and what is more, I'll help you to do so. There is a billet now open in my old friend Webster's office, the salary is a good one and the duties are light. When I saw him this morning it was still unfilled. Why not try for it? If you like I'll give you a letter of introduction to him, and will tell him at the same time that I shall consider it a personal favour if he will take you into his employ."

"I'm sure I'm very much obliged to you," I answered warmly. "Yes, I think I will try for it before I give Nikola a reply. May I have the letter now?"

"With pleasure," he said. "I will write it at once."

Thereupon he dipped his pen in the ink and composed the epistle. When it was written and I had taken it, I thanked him warmly for his kindness, and bade him good-bye.

Mr. Webster's *hong* was at the far end of the Bund, and was another fine building. As soon as I had gained admittance I inquired for the merchant, and after a brief wait was conducted to his office. He proved to be Mr. McAndrew's opposite in every way. He was tall, portly, and intensely solemn. He seldom laughed, and when he did his mirth was hard and cheerless like his own exterior. He read my letter carefully, and then said—

"I am exceedingly sorry, Mr. Bruce, that you should have had all this trouble. I should have been only too glad for my friend McAndrew's sake to have taken you into my employ; unfortunately, however, the position in question was filled less than an hour ago."

"I regret to hear that," I said, with a little sigh of disappointment. "I really am most unfortunate; this makes the thirteenth post I have tried for, as you see, unsuccessfully, since I arrived in Shanghai."

"Your luck does not seem propitious," was the reply. "But if you would like to put your applications up to an even number I will place you in the way of another. I understand that the Red and Yellow Funnel Steamer Company have a vacancy in their office, and if you would care to come along with me at once I'll take you up and introduce you to the manager myself. In that case he will probably do all he can for you."

I thanked him for his courtesy, and when he had donned his *topee* we accordingly set off for the office in question. But another disappointment was in store for me. As in Mr. Webster's own case the vacant post had just been filled, and when we passed out of the manager's sanctum into the main office the newly-appointed clerk was already seated upon his high stool making entries in a ledger.

On leaving the building I bade my companion good-bye on the pavement, and then with a heavy heart returned to my abode. I had not been there ten minutes before my landlord entered the room, and without preface, and with the smallest modicum of civility, requested that I would make it convenient to discharge my account that very day. As I was quite unable to comply with his request, I was compelled to tell him so, and when he left the room there was a decidedly unpleasant coolness between us. For some considerable time after I was alone again. I sat wrapped in anxious thought. What was I to do? Every walk of life seemed closed against me; my very living was in jeopardy; and though, if I remained in Shanghai, I might hear of other billets, still I had no sort of guarantee that I should be any more successful in obtaining one of them than I had hitherto been. In the meantime I had to live, and what was more, to pay my bill. I could not go away and leave things to take care of themselves, for the reason that I had not the necessary capital for travelling, while if I remained and did not pay, I should find myself in the Mixed Court before many days were over.

Such being the desperate condition of my affairs, to accept Dr. Nikola's offer was the only thing open to me. But I was not going to do so without driving a bargain. If he would deposit, as he said, £5,000 to my credit in the bank I should not only be saved, but I should then have a substantial guarantee of his solvency. If not, well, I had better bring matters to a climax at once. Leaving the house I returned to the Bund, and seating myself in a shady spot carefully reviewed the whole matter. By the time darkness fell my mind was made up—*I would go to Nikola.*

Exactly at eight o'clock I reached his house and rang the bell. In answer to my peal the native boy, the same who had admitted me on the previous occasion, opened the door and informed me that his master was at home and expecting me. Having entered I was conducted to the apartment in which I had waited for him on the preceding evening. Again for nearly five minutes I was left to myself and my own thoughts, then the door opened and Dr. Nikola walked into the room.

"Good evening, Mr. Bruce," he said. "You are very punctual, and that is not only a pleasant trait in your character, but it is also a good omen, I hope. Shall we go into the next room? We can talk better there."

I followed him into the adjoining apartment, and at his invitation seated myself in the chair I had occupied on the previous night. We had not been there half a minute before the black cat made his appearance, and recognizing me as an old friend rubbed his head against my leg.

"You see even the cat is anxious to conciliate you," said Nikola, with a queer little smile. "I don't suppose there are five other men in the world with whom he would be as friendly as that on so short an acquaintance. Now let me hear your decision. Will you come with me, or have you resolved to decline my offer?"

"Under certain conditions I have made up my mind to accompany you," I said. "But I think it only fair to tell you that those conditions are rather stringent."

"Let me hear them," said Nikola, with that gracious affability he could sometimes assume. "Even if they are overpowering, I think it will go hard with me if I cannot effect some sort of a compromise with you."

"Well, to begin with," I answered, "I shall require you to pay into a bank here the sum of £5,000. If you will do that, and will give me a bill at a year for the rest of the money, I'm your man, and you may count upon my doing everything in my power to serve you."

"My dear fellow, is that all?" said Nikola quickly. "I will make it £10,000 with pleasure to secure your co-operation. I had no idea it would be the money that would stop you. Excuse me one moment."

He rose from his chair and went across to a table at the other end of the room. Having seated himself he wrote for two or three moments; then returning handed me a small slip of paper, which I discovered was a cheque for £10,000.

"There is your money," he said. "You can present it as soon as you like, and the bank will cash it on sight. I think that should satisfy you as to the genuineness of my motives. Now I suppose you are prepared to throw in your lot with me?"

"Wait one moment," I said. "That is not all. You have treated me very generously, and it is only fair that I should behave in a similar manner to you."

"Thank you," answered Nikola. "What is it you have to say to me now?"

"Do you know a man named Wetherell?"

"Perfectly," replied Nikola. "He was Colonial Secretary of New South Wales until about six months ago. I have very good reasons for knowing him. I had the honour of abducting his daughter in Sydney, and I imprisoned his son-in-law in Port Said. Of course I know him. You see I am also candid with you."

"Vastly. But pardon the expression, was it altogether a nice transaction?"

"It all depends upon what you consider a *nice* transaction," he said. "To you, for instance, who have your own notions of what is right and what is wrong, it might seem a little peculiar. I am in a different case, however. Whatever I do I consider right. What you might do, in nine cases out of ten, I should consider wrong. Whether I might have saved himself all trouble by selling me the stick which China Pete gave him, and about which he wrote to McAndrew, who read the letter to you this morning!"

"How do you know he did?"

"How do I know anything?" inquired Nikola, with an airy wave of his hand. "He *did* read it, and if you will look at me fixedly for a moment I will tell you the exact purport of the rest of your conversation."

"I don't know that it is necessary," I replied.

"Nor do I," said Nikola quietly, and then lit a cigarette. "Are you satisfied with my explanation?"

"Was it an explanation?" I asked.

Nikola only answered with a smile, and lifted the cat on to his knee. He stroked its fur with his long white fingers, at the same time looking at me from under his half-closed eyelids.

"Do you know, I like you," he said after a while. "There's something so confoundedly matter-of-fact about you. You give me the impression every time you begin to speak that you are going to say something out of the common."

"Thank you."

"I was going to add that the rest of your sentence invariably shatters that impression."

"You evidently have a very poor impression of my cleverness."

"Not at all. I am the one who has to say the smart things; you will have to do them. It is an equal distribution of labour. Now, are we going together or are we not?"

"Yes, I will go with you," I answered.

"I am delighted," said Nikola, holding out his hand. "Let us shake hands on it."

We shook hands, and as we did so he looked me fairly in the face.

"Let me tell you once and for all," he said, "if you play fair by me I will stand by you, come what may; but if you shirk one atom of your responsibility—well, you will only have yourself to blame for what happens. That's a fair warning, isn't it?"

"Perfectly," I answered. "Now may I know something of the scheme itself, and when you propose to start?"

Chapter 3

Nikola's Scheme

"By all means," said Dr. Nikola, settling himself down comfortably in his chair and lighting a cigarette. "As you have thrown in your lot with me it is only right I *should* give you the information you seek. I need not ask you to keep what I tell you to yourself. Your own common-sense will commend that course to you. It is also just possible you may think I over-estimate the importance of my subject, but let me say this, if once it became known to certain folk in this town that I have obtained possession of that stick mentioned in Wetherell's letter, my life, even in Shanghai, would not be worth five minutes' purchase. Let me briefly review the circumstances of the case connected with this mysterious society. Remember I have gone into the matter most thoroughly. It is not the hobby of an hour, nor the amusement of an idle moment, but the object of research and the concentrated study of a lifetime. To obtain certain information of which I stood in need, I have tracked people all over the world. When I began my preparations for inducing Wetherell to relinquish possession of what I wanted, I had followed a man as far as Cuyaba, on the Bolivian frontier of Brazil. During the earlier part of his career this person had been a merchant buying gold-leaf in Western China, and in this capacity he chanced to hear a curious story connected with the doings of a certain sect, whose monastery is in the mountains on the way up to Thibet. It cost me six months' continuous travel and nearly a thousand pounds in hard cash to find that man, and when I did his story did not exceed a dozen sentences; in other words, I paid him fully £10 per word for a bit of information that you would not, in all probability, have given him tenpence for. But I knew its value. I followed another man as far as Monte Video for the description of an obscure Chinese village;

another to the Gold Coast for the name of a certain Buddhist priest, and a Russian Jew as far as Nijni Novgorod for a symbol he wore upon his watch-chain, and of the value of which he had not the slightest conception. The information I thus obtained personally I added to the store I had gathered by correspondence, and having accumulated it all I drafted a complete history of my researches up to that time. When that was done I think I may say without boasting that, with the exception of three men—who, by the way, are not at liberty to divulge anything, and who, I doubt very much, are even aware that a world exists at all beyond their own monastery walls—I know at least six times as much about the society in question as any man living. Now, having prefaced my remarks in this fashion, let me give you a complete summary of the case. As far as I can gather, in or about the year 288 b.c., in fact at the time that Devenipiatissa was planting the sacred Bo tree at Anuradhapura, in Ceylon, three priests, noted for their extreme piety, and for the extent of their scientific researches, migrated from what is now the island of Ceylon, across to the mainland of Asia. Having passed through the country at present called Burmah, and after innumerable vicissitudes and constant necessary changes of quarters, they brought up in the centre of the country we now call Thibet. Here two of the original trio died, while the remaining one and his new confreres built themselves a monastery, set to work to gather about them a number of peculiar devotees, and to continue their researches. Though the utmost secrecy was observed, within a few years the fame of their doings had spread itself abroad. That this was so we know, for we find constant mention made of them by numerous Chinese historians. One I will quote you."

Dr. Nikola rose from his chair and crossed the room to an old cabinet standing against the further wall. From this he took a large book, looking suspiciously like a scrap-album, in which were pasted innumerable cuttings and manuscripts. He brought it across to his chair and sat down again. Then, having turned the leaves and found what he wanted, he prepared to read.

"It may interest you to know," he said, looking up at me before he began, "that the paragraph I am about to read to you, which was translated from the original with the utmost care by myself, was written the same year and month that William the Conqueror landed in England. It runs as follows:—

"'And of this vast sect, and of the peculiar powers with which they are invested, it is with some diffidence that I speak. It is affirmed by those credulous in such matters that their skill in healing is greater than that of all other living men, also that their power in witchcraft surpasses that of any others the world has known. It is said, moreover, that they possess the power of restoring the dead to life, and of prolonging beyond the ordinary span the days of man. But of these things I can only write to you as they have been told to me.'"

Dr. Nikola turned to another page.

"After skipping five hundred years," he said, "we find further mention made of them; this time the writer is Feng Lao Lan, a well-known Chinese historian who flourished about the year 1500. He describes them as making themselves a source of trouble to the kingdom in general. From being a collection of a few simple monks, installed in a lonely monastery in the centre of Thibet, they have now become one of the largest secret societies in the East, though the mystic powers supposed to be held by them are still limited to the three headmen, or principal brothers. Towards the end of the sixteenth century it is certain that they exercised such a formidable influence in political affairs as to warrant the Government in issuing orders for their extermination. Indeed, I am inclined to believe that the all-powerful Triad Society, with its motto, 'Hoan Cheng Hok Beng,' which, as you know, exercised such an enormous influence in China until quite recently, was only an offshoot of the society which I am so eager to explore. That the sect *does* possess the scientific and occult knowledge that has been attributed to it for over two thousand years I feel convinced, and if there is any power which can assist me in penetrating their secrets I intend to employ it. In our own and other countries which we are accustomed to call 'civilized' it has long been the habit to ridicule any belief in what cannot be readily seen and understood by the least educated. To the average Englishman there is no occult world. But see what a contradictory creature he is when all is said and done. For if he be devout, he tells you that he firmly believes that when the body dies the soul goes to Heaven, which is equivalent to Olympus, Elysium, Arcadia,

Garden of Hesperides, Valhalla, Walhalla, Paradise, or Nirvana, as the case may be. He has no notion, or rather, I think, he will not be able to give you any description, of what sort of place his Heaven is likely to be. He has all sorts of vague ideas about it, but though it is part of his religion to believe beyond question that there is such a place, it is all wrapped in shadow of more or less impenetrable depth. To sum it all up, he believes that, while, in his opinion, such a thing as—shall we say Theosophy?—is arrant nonsense, and unworthy of a thought, the vital essence of man has a second and greater being after death. In other words, to put my meaning a little more plainly, it is pretty certain that if you were to laugh at him, as he laughs at the Theosophist and Spiritualist, he would consider that he had very good grounds to consider his intelligence insulted. And yet he himself is simply a contradiction contradicted. You may wonder towards what all this rigmarole is leading. But if I were to describe to you the curious things I have myself seen in different parts of the East, and the extraordinary information I have collected first hand from others, I venture to think you would believe me either a wizard myself or an absurdly credulous person. I tell you, Bruce, I have witnessed things that would seem to upset every known law of nature. Though there was occasionally trickery in the performance I am convinced in the majority of cases the phenomena were genuine. And that brings us to another stumbling-block—the meaning of the expression, 'trickery.' What I should probably call 'trick' you would, in nine cases out of ten, consider blackest magic. But enough talking. Let me give you an illustration of my meaning."

As he spoke he went across to a sideboard and from it he took an ordinary glass tumbler and a carafe of water, which he placed upon the table at his elbow. Then seating himself again in his chair he filled the glass to overflowing. I watched him carefully, wondering what was coming next.

"Examine the glass for yourself," he said. "You observe that it is quite full of water. I want you to be very sure of that."

I examined the glass and discovered that it was so full that it would be impossible to move it without spilling some of its contents. Having done so I told him that I was convinced it was fully charged.

"Very well," he said; "in that case I will give you an example of what I might call 'Mind *versus* Matter.' That glass is quite full, as you have seen for yourself; now watch me."

From a tray by his side he took a match, lit a wax candle, and when the flame had burnt up well, held it above the water so that one drop of wax might fall into the liquid.

"Now," he said, "I want you to watch that wax intently from where you are while I count twenty."

I did as he ordered me, keeping my eyes firmly fixed upon the little globule floating on the surface of the water. Then as I looked, slowly, and to the accompaniment of Nikola's monotonous counting, the water sank lower and lower, until the tumbler was completely empty.

"Get up and look for yourself, but don't touch the glass," said my host. "Be perfectly sure, however, that it is empty, for I shall require your affidavit upon that point directly."

I examined the glass most carefully, and stated that, to the best of my belief, there was not a drop of water in it.

"Very well," said Nikola. "Now be so good as to sit down and watch it once more."

This time he counted backwards, and as he did so the water rose again in the glass until it was full to overflowing, and still the wax was floating on the surface.

For a moment we were both silent. Then Nikola poured the water back into the jug, and having done so handed the glass to me.

"Examine it carefully," he said, "or you may imagine it has been made by a London conjuring firm on purpose for the trick. Convince yourself of this, and when you have made sure give me your explanation of the mystery."

I examined the glass with the most searching scrutiny, but no sign of any preparation or mechanism could I discover.

"I cannot understand it at all," I said; "and I'm sure I can give you no explanation."

"And yet you are not thoroughly convinced in your mind that I have not performed a clever conjuring trick, such as you might see at Maskelyne and Devant's. Let me give you two more examples before I finish. Look me intently in the face until that clock on the mantelpiece, which is now standing at twenty-eight minutes past nine, shall strike the half-hour."

I did as I was ordered, and anything like the concentrated intensify of his gaze I never remember to have experienced before. I have often heard men say that when persons gifted with the mesmeric power have looked at them (some women have this power too) they have felt as if they had no backs to their heads. In this case I can only say that I not only felt as if I had no back to my head, but as if I had no head at all.

The two minutes seemed like two hours, then the clock struck, and Nikola said:

"Pull up your left shirt cuff, and examine your arm."

I did as he ordered me, and there in red spots I saw an exact reproduction of my own signature. As I looked at it it faded away again, until, in about half a minute from my first seeing it, it was quite gone.

"That is what I call a trick; in other words, it is neither more nor less than hypnotism. But you will wonder why I have put myself to so much trouble. In the first place the water did not go out of the glass, as you supposed, but remained exactly as when you first saw it. I simply willed that you should imagine it did go, and your imagination complied with the demand made upon it. In the last experiment you had a second proof of the first subject. Of course both are very easily explained, even by one who has dabbled in the occult as little as yourself. But though you call it hypnotism in this airy fashion, can you give me an explanation of what you mean by that ambiguous term?"

"Simply that your mind," I answered, "is stronger than mine, and for this reason is able to dominate it."

"That is the popular theory, I grant you," he answered; "but it is hardly a correct one, I fancy. Even if it were stronger, how could it be possible for me to transmit thoughts which are in my brain to yours?"

"That I cannot attempt in any way to explain," I answered. "But isn't it classified under the general head of thought transference?"

"Precisely—I am prepared to admit so much; but your description, hypnotism, though as involved, is quite as correct a term. But let me tell you that both these illustrations were given to lead up to another, which will bring us nearer than we have yet come to the conclusion I am endeavouring to arrive

38

at. Try and give me your complete attention again; above all, watch my finger."

As he spoke he began to wave his first finger in the air. It moved this way and that, describing figures of eight, and I followed each movement so carefully with my eyes that presently a small blue flame seemed to flicker at the end of it. Then, after perhaps a minute, I saw, or thought I saw, what might have been a tiny cloud settling in the further corner of the room. It was near the floor when I first noticed it, then it rose to about the height of a yard, and came slowly across the apartment towards me. Little by little it increased in size. Then it assumed definite proportions, became taller, until I thought I detected the outline of a human figure. This resemblance rapidly increased, until I could definitely distinguish the head and body of a man. He was tall and well-proportioned; his head was thrown back, and his eyes met mine with an eager, though somewhat strained, glance. Every detail was perfect, even to a ring upon his little finger; indeed, if I had met the man in the street next day I am certain I should have known him again. A strange orange-coloured light almost enveloped him, but in less than a minute he had become merged in the cloud once more; this gradually fell back into the corner, grew smaller and smaller, and finally disappeared altogether. I gave a little shiver, as if I were waking from some unpleasant dream, and turned to Nikola, who was watching me with half-closed eyes.

After I had quite recovered my wits, he took an album from the table and handed it to me.

"See if you can find in that book," he said, "the photograph of the man whose image you have just seen."

I unfastened the clasp, and turned the pages eagerly. Near the middle I discovered an exact reproduction of the vision I had seen. The figure and face, the very attitude and expression, were the same in every particular, and even the ring I had noticed was upon the little finger. I was completely nonplussed.

"What do you think of my experiment?" asked Nikola.

"It was most wonderful and most mysterious," I said.

"But how do you account for it?" he asked.

"I can't account for it at all," I answered. "I can only suppose, since you owned to it before, that it must also have been hypnotism."

"Exactly," said Nikola. "But you will see in this case that, without any disc or passes, I not only produced the wish that you should see what I was thinking of, but also the exact expression worn by the person in the photograph. The test was successful in every way. And yet, how did I transfer the image that was in my mind to the retina of your eyes? You were positively certain you saw the water decrease in the glass just now; you would have pledged your word of honour that you saw your name printed upon your arm; and under other circumstances you would, in all probability, have ridiculed any assertion on my part that you did not see the vision of the man whose photograph is in that book. Very good. That much decided, do you feel equal to doubting that, though not present in the room, I could wake you in the night, and make you see the image of some friend, whom you knew to be long dead, standing by your bedside. Shall I make myself float in mid-air? Shall I transport you out of this room, and take you to the bottom of the Pacific Ocean? Shall I lift you up into heaven, or conduct you to the uttermost parts of hell? You have only to say what you desire to see and I will show it to you as surely and as perfectly as you saw those other things. But remember, all I have done is only what I call trickery, for it was done by hypnotism, which is to my mind, though you think it so mysterious, neither more nor less than making people believe what you will by the peculiar power of your own mind. But answer me this: If hypnotism is only the very smallest beginning of the knowledge possessed by the sect I am trying to discover, what must their greatest secret be? Believe me when I tell you that what I have shown you this evening is as a molehill to a mountain compared with what you will learn if we can only penetrate into that place of which I have told you. I pledge you my word on it. Now answer me this question: Is it worth trying for, or not?"

"It is worth it," I cried enthusiastically. "I will go with you, and I will give you my best service; if you will play fair by me, I will do the same by you. But there is one further question I must ask you: Has that stick you obtained from Mr. Wetherell anything at all to do with the work in hand?"

"More than anything," he answered. "It is the key to everything. Originally, you must understand, there were only three of these sticks in existence. One belongs, or rather *did* belong, to each of the three heads of the sect. In pursuit of some particular information one of the trio left the monastery, and came out into the world. He died in a mysterious manner, and the stick fell into the possession of the abbot of the Yung Ho Kung, in Pekin, from whom it was stolen by an Englishman in my employ, known as China Pete, who risked his life, disguised as a Thibetan monk, to get it. Having stolen it, he eluded me, and fled to Australia, not knowing the real value of his treasure. The society became cognizant of its loss, and sent men after him. In attempting to obtain possession of it one of the Chinamen was killed off the coast of Queensland, and China Pete was arrested in Sydney on a charge of having murdered him. Wetherell defended him, and got him off; and, not being able to pay for his services, the latter made him a present of the stick. A month later I reached Sydney in search of it, but the Chinese were there before me. We both tried to obtain possession of it, but, owing to Wetherell's obstinacy, neither of us was successful. I offered Wetherell his own price for it; he refused to give it up. I pleaded with him, argued, entreated, but in vain. Then I set myself to get it from him at any hazard. How I succeeded you know. All that occurred six months ago. As soon as it was in my possession I returned here with the intention of penetrating into the interior, and endeavouring to find out what I so much wanted to know."

"And where is the stick now?" I asked.

"In my own keeping," he answered. "If you would care to see it, I shall have very much pleasure in showing it to you."

"I should like to see it immensely," I answered.

With that he left the room, to return in about five minutes. Then, seating himself before me, he took from his pocket a small case, out of which he drew a tiny stick, at most not more than three inches long. It was a commonplace little affair, a deep black in colour, and covered with Chinese hieroglyphics in dead gold. A piece of frayed gold ribbon, much tarnished, and showing evident signs of having passed through many hands, was attached to it at one end.

He handed it to me, and I examined it carefully.

"But if this stick were originally stolen," I said, "you will surely not be so imprudent as to place yourself in the power of the society with it in your possession? It would mean certain death."

"If it were all plain sailing, and there were no risk to be run, I doubt very much if I should pay you £10,000 for the benefit of your company," he answered. "It is because there *is* a great risk, and because I must have assistance, though I am extremely doubtful whether we shall ever come out of it alive, that I am taking you with me. I intend to discover their secret if possible, and I also intend that this stick, which undoubtedly is the key of the outer gate, so to speak, shall help me in my endeavours. If you are afraid to accompany me, having heard all, I will allow you to forego your promise and turn back while there is time."

"I have not the slightest intention of turning back," I answered. "I don't know that I am a braver man than most, but if you are willing to go on I am ready to accompany you."

"And so you shall, and there's my hand on it," he cried, giving me his hand as he spoke.

"Now tell me what you intend to do," I said. "How do you mean to begin?"

"Well, in the first place," said Nikola, "I shall wait here until the arrival of a certain man from Pekin. He is one of the lay brethren of the society who has fallen under my influence, and as soon as he puts in an appearance and I have got his information we shall disguise ourselves, myself as an official of one of the coast provinces, you as my secretary, and together we shall set out for the capital. Arriving there we will penetrate the Llama-serai, the most anti-European monastery in all China, and, by some means or another, extract from the chief priest sufficient information to take the next step upon our journey. After that we shall proceed as circumstances dictate."

"And when do you intend that we shall start?"

"As soon as the man arrives, perhaps to-night, probably to-morrow morning."

"And as to our disguises?"

"I have in my possession everything we can possibly need."

"In that case I suppose there is nothing to be done until the messenger arrives?"

"Nothing, I think."

"Then if you will allow me I will wish you good-bye and be off to bed. In case I do not hear from you tonight, at what hour would you like me to call tomorrow?"

"I will let you know before breakfast-time without fail. You are not afraid, are you?"

"Not in the least," I answered.

"And you'll say nothing to anybody, even under compulsion, as to our mission?"

"I have given you my promise," I answered, and rose from my seat.

Once more I followed him down the main passage of the bungalow into the front verandah. Arriving there we shook hands and I went down the steps into the street.

As I turned the corner and made my way in the direction of the road leading to the English Concession, I saw a man, without doubt a Chinaman, rise from a corner and follow me. For nearly a quarter of a mile he remained about a hundred yards behind me, then he was joined by a second, who presently left his companion at a cross street and continued the march. Whether their espionage was only accidental, or whether I was really the object of their attention, I was for some time at a loss to conjecture, but when I saw the second give place to a third, and the third begin to decrease the distance that separated us, I must own I was not altogether comfortable in my mind. Arriving at a more crowded thoroughfare I hastened my steps, and having proceeded about fifty yards along it, dodged down a side lane. This lane conveyed me into another, which eventually brought me out within half a dozen paces of the house I wanted.

That the occupants of the dwelling had not yet retired to bed was evident from the lights I could see moving about inside. In response to my knock some one left the room upon the right hand of the passage and came towards the door where I waited. When he had opened it I discovered that it was Mr. McAndrew himself.

"Why, Bruce!" he cried in surprise, as soon as he discovered who his visitor was. "You've chosen a pretty late hour for calling; but never mind, come along in; I am glad to see you." As he spoke he led me into the room from which he had just emerged. It was his dining-room, and was furnished in a ponderous, but luxurious, fashion. In a chair beside the long table—for Mr. McAndrew has a large family, and twelve sat down to the morning and evening meal—was seated a tiny grey-haired lady, his wife, while opposite her, engaged upon some fancy work, was a pretty girl of sixteen, his youngest daughter and pet, as I remembered. That the lateness of my visit also occasioned them some surprise I could see by their faces; but after a few commonplace remarks they bade me good-night and went out of the room, leaving me alone with the head of the house.

"I suppose you have some very good reason for this visit, or you wouldn't be here," the latter said, as he handed me a box of cigars. "Have you heard of a new billet, or has your innocent friend Nikola commenced to blackmail you?"

"Neither of these things has happened," I answered with a laugh."

"But as I am in all probability leaving Shanghai to-morrow morning before banking hours, I have come to see if I may so far tax your kindness as to ask you to take charge of a cheque for me." I thereupon produced Nikola's draft and handed it to him. He took it, glanced at it, looked up at me, returned his eyes to it once more, and then whistled.

"This looks like business," he said.

"Doesn't it," I answered. "I can hardly believe that I am worth £10,000."

"You are to be congratulated. And now what do you want me to do with it?" inquired McAndrew, turning the paper over and over in his hand as if it were some uncanny talisman which might suddenly catch him up and convert him into a camel or an octopus before he could look round.

"I want you to keep it for me if you will," I answered "To put it on deposit in your bank if you have no objection. I am going away, certainly for six months, possibly for a year, and when I return to Shanghai I will come and claim it. That's if I *do* return."

"And if not?"

"In that case I will leave it all to you. In the meantime I want you to advance me £20 if you will; you can repay yourself out of the amount. Do you mind doing it?"

"Not in the very least," he answered; "but we had better have it all in writing, so that there may be no mistake."

He thereupon produced from a drawer in a side table a sheet of notepaper. Having written a few lines on it he gave it to me to sign, at the same time calling in one of his sons to witness my signature. This formality completed he handed me £20 in notes and English gold, and our business was concluded. I rose to go.

"Bruce," said the old gentleman in his usual kindly fashion, putting his hand upon my shoulder as he spoke, "I don't know what you are up to, and I don't suppose it will do for me to inquire, but I am aware that you have been in pretty straitened circumstances lately, and I am afraid you are embarking on some foolishness or other now. For Heaven's sake weigh carefully the pros and cons before you commit yourself. Remember always that one moment's folly may wreck your whole afterlife."

"You need have no fear on that score," I answered. "I am going into this business with my eyes open. All the same I am obliged to you for your warning and for what you have done for me. Good-night and good-bye."

I shook hands with him, and then passing into the verandah left the bungalow.

I was not fifty yards from the gate when a noise behind me induced me to look round. A man had been sitting in the shadow on the other side of the road. He had risen now and was beginning to follow me. That it was the same individual who had accompanied me to McAndrew's house I had not the slightest doubt. I turned to my right hand down a side street in order to see if he would pursue me; he also turned. I doubled again; he did the same. I proceeded across a piece of open ground instead of keeping on in the straight line I had hitherto been following; he imitated my example. This espionage was growing alarming, so I quickened my pace, and having found a side street with a high fence on one side, followed the palisading along till I came to the gate. Through this I dashed, and as soon as I was in, stooped down in the shadow. Half a minute later I heard the man coming along on the other side. When he could no longer see me ahead of him he came to a halt within half a dozen paces of where I crouched. Then having made up

45

his mind that I must have crossed the road and gone down a dark lane opposite, he too crossed, and in a few seconds was out of sight.

As soon as I had convinced myself that I had got rid of him I passed out into the street again and made my way as quickly as possible back to my abode.

But I was not to lose my mysterious pursuer after all, for just as I was entering my own compound he put in an appearance. Seeing that I had the advantage I ran up the steps of the verandah and went inside. From a window I watched him come up the street and stand looking about him. Then he returned by the way he had come, and, for the time being, that was the last I saw of him. In less than a quarter of an hour I was in bed and asleep, dreaming of Nikola, and imagining that I was being turned into an elephant by his uncanny powers.

How long I remained snoozing I cannot say, but I was suddenly awakened by the feeling that somebody was in my room. Nor was I mistaken. A man was sitting by my bedside, and in the dim moonlight I could see that he was a Chinaman.

"What are you doing here?" I cried, sitting up in bed.

"Be silent!" my visitor whispered in Chinese. "If you speak it will cost you your life."

Without another word I thrust my hand under the pillow intending to produce the revolver I had placed there when I went to bed. But it was gone. Whether my visitor had stolen it or I had imagined that I had put it there and forgotten to do so, it was beyond my powers to tell. At any rate the weapon, upon which it would seem my life depended, was gone.

"What is your business with me?" I asked, resolved to bring my visitor to his bearings without loss of time.

"Not so loud," he answered. "I am sent by Dr. Nikola to request your honourable presence. He desires that you will come to him without a moment's delay."

"But I've only just left him," I said. "Why does he send for me again?"

"I cannot say, but it is possible that something important has occurred," was the man's answer. "He bade me tell you to come at once."

With that I got up and dressed myself as quickly as possible. It was evident that the expected messenger from Pekin had arrived, and in that case we should probably be setting off for the capital before morning. At any rate I did not waste a moment, and as soon as I was ready went out into the verandah, where the man who had come to fetch me was sitting. He led me across the compound into the street and pointed to a chair which with its bearers was in waiting for me.

"Your friend is in a hurry," said the man who had called me, by way of explanation, "and he bade me not lose a moment."

"In that case you may go along as hard as you like," I answered; "I am quite ready."

I took my place in the chair, which was immediately lifted by the bearers, and within a minute of my leaving the house we were proceeding down the street at a comparatively fast pace. At that hour the town was very quiet; indeed, with the exception of an occasional Sikh policeman and a belated 'rickshaw coolie or two, we met no one. At the end of a quarter of an hour it was evident that we had arrived at our destination, for the chair came to a standstill and the bearers set me down. I sprang out and looked about me. To my surprise, however, it was not the house I expected to see that I found before me. We had pulled up at the entrance to a much larger bungalow, standing in a compound of fair size. While I waited my messenger went into the house, to presently return with the information that, if I would be pleased to follow him, Dr. Nikola would see me at once.

The house was in total darkness and as silent as the grave. I passed into the main hall, and was about to proceed down it towards a door at the further end, when I was, without warning, caught by the back of the neck, a gag of some sort was placed in my mouth, and my hands were securely fastened behind me. Next moment I was lifted into the air and borne into a room whence a bright light suddenly streamed forth. Here three Chinamen were seated, clad in heavy figured silk, and wearing enormous tortoiseshell spectacles upon their noses. They received me with a grunt of welcome, and bade my captors remove the gag from my mouth. This done the elder of the trio said quietly—but it seemed to me somewhat inconsequently:

"We hope that your honourable self is enjoying good health?"

I answered, with as much calmness as I could possibly assume at so short a notice, that, "For such an utterly insignificant personage I was *in* the enjoyment of the best of health." Whereupon I was requested to say how it came about that I was now in China, and what my business there might be. When I had answered this the man on the right leant a little forward and said:

"You are not telling us the honourable truth. What business have you with Dr. Nikola?"

I summoned all my wits to my assistance.

"Who is Dr. Nikola?" I asked.

"The person whom you have visited two nights in succession," said the man who had first spoken. "Tell us what mischief you and he are hatching together."

Seeing that it would be useless attempting to deny my association with Nikola I insinuated that we were interested in the purchase of Chinese silk together, but this assertion was received with a scornful grunt of disapproval.

"We must have the truth," said the man in the biggest spectacles.

"I can tell you no more," I answered.

"In that case we have no option," he said, "but to extract the information by other means."

With that he made a sign to one of the attendants, who immediately left the room, to return a few moments later with a roll of chain, and some oddly-shaped wooden bars. A heavy sweat rose upon my forehead. I had seen a good deal of Chinese torture in my time, and now it looked as if I were about to have a taste of it.

"What do you know of Dr. Nikola?" repeated the man who had first spoken, and who was evidently the principal of the trio.

"I have already told you," I repeated, this time with unusual emphasis.

Again he asked the same question without change of tone.

But I only repeated my previous answer.

"For the last time, what do you know of Dr. Nikola?"

"I have told you," I answered, my heart sinking like lead. Thereupon he raised his hand a little and made a sign to the men near the door. Instantly I was caught and thrown on my back upon the floor. Before I could expostulate or struggle a curious wooden collar was clasped round my neck, and a screw was turned in it until another revolution would have choked me. Once more I heard the old man say monotonously.

"What do you know of Dr. Nikola?"

I tried to repeat my former assertion, but owing to the tightness of the collar I found a difficulty in speaking. Then the man in the centre rose and came over to where I lay; instantly the collar was relaxed, my arms were released, and a voice said:

"Get up, Mr. Bruce. You need have no further fear; we shall not hurt you."

It *was Dr. Nikola!*

Chapter 4

We Set Out For Tientsin

I could scarcely believe the evidence of my senses. Nikola's disguise was so perfect that it would have required almost superhuman cleverness to penetrate it. In every particular he was a true Celestial. His accent was without a flaw, his deportment exactly what that of a Chinaman of high rank would be, while his general demeanour and manner of sustaining his assumed character could not have been found fault with by the most fastidious critic. I felt that if he could so easily hoodwink me there could be little doubt that he would pass muster under less exacting scrutiny. So as soon as I was released I sprang to my feet and warmly congratulated him, not a little relieved, you may be sure, to find that I was with friends, and was not to be tortured, as I had at first supposed.

"You must forgive the rough treatment to which you have been subjected," said Nikola. "But I wanted to test you very thoroughly. Now what do you think of my disguise?"

"It is perfect," I answered. "Considering your decided personality, I had no idea it could possibly be so good. But where are we?"

"In a bungalow I have taken for the time being," he replied. "And now let us get to business. The man whom you saw on my right was Laohwan, the messenger whom I told you I expected from Pekin. He arrived half an hour after you had left me this evening, gave me the information I wanted, and now I am ready to start as soon as you are."

"Let me go home and put one or two things together," I answered, "and then I'm your man."

"Certainly," said Nikola. "One of my servants shall accompany you to carry your bag, and to bring you back here as soon as your work is completed."

With that I set off for my abode, followed by one of Nikola's boys. When we reached it I left him to wait for me outside, and let myself into my bedroom by the window. Having lit a candle, I hastened to put together the few little odds and ends I wished to take with me on my journey. This finished I locked my trunks, wrote a letter to my landlord, enclosing the amount I owed him, and then another to Barkston, asking him to be good enough to send for, and take charge of my trunks until I returned from a trip into the interior. This done I passed out of the house again, joined the boy who was waiting for me at the gate, and returned to the bungalow in which I had been so surprised by Nikola an hour or so before. It was long after midnight by the time I reached it, but I had no thought of fatigue. The excitement of our departure prevented my thinking of aught else. We were plunging into an unknown life bristling with dangers, and though I did not share Nikola's belief as to the result we should achieve, I had the certain knowledge that I should be well repaid for the risk I ran.

When I entered the house I found my employer awaiting my coming in the room where I had been hoaxed that evening. He was still in Chinese dress, and once again as I looked at him I felt it difficult to believe that this portly, sedate-looking Chinaman could be the slim European known to the world as Dr. Nikola.

"You have not been long, Mr. Bruce," he said, "and I am glad of it. Now if you will accompany me to the next room I will introduce you to your things. I have purchased for you everything that you can possibly require, and as I am well acquainted with your power of disguise, I have no fear at all as to the result."

On reaching the adjoining room I divested myself of my European habiliments, and set to work to don those which were spread out for my inspection. Then with some mixture from a bottle which I found upon the table, I stained my face, neck, and arms, after which my pigtail, which was made on a cleverly contrived scalp wig, was attached, and a large pair of tortoiseshell glasses of a similar pattern to those worn by Nikola, were placed upon my nose. My feet were encased in sandals, a stiff round hat of the ordinary Chinese pattern was placed upon my head, and this, taken with my thickly-padded robe of yellow silk, gave me a most dignified appearance.

When Nikola returned to the room he examined me carefully, and expressed himself as highly pleased with the result; indeed, when we greeted each other in the Chinese fashion and language he would have been a sharp man who could have detected that we were not what we pretended to be.

"Now," said Nikola, "if you are ready we will test the efficiency of our disguises. In half an hour's time there is a meeting at the house of a man named Lo Ting. The folk we shall meet there are members of a secret society aiming at the overthrow of the Manchu dynasty. Laohwan has gone on ahead, and, being a member of the society, will report to them the arrival of two distinguished merchants from the interior, who are also members. I have got the passwords, and I know the general idea of their aims, so, with your permission, we will set off at once. When we get there I will explain my intentions more fully."

"But you are surely not going to attend a meeting of a secret society to-night?" I said, astonished at the coolness with which he proposed to run such a risk. "Wouldn't it be wiser to wait until we are a little more accustomed to our dresses?"

"By no means," answered Nikola. "I consider this will be a very good test. If we are detected by the folk we shall see to-night we shall know where the fault lies, and we can remedy it before it is too late. Besides, there is to be a man present who knows something of the inner working of the society, and from him I hope to derive some important information to help us on our way. Come along."

He passed into the passage and led the way through the house out into the compound, where we found a couple of chairs, with their attendant coolies, awaiting us. We stepped into them, and were presently being borne in a sedate fashion down the street.

In something under twenty minutes our bearers stopped and set us down again; we alighted, and after the coolies had disappeared Nikola whispered that the password was "Liberty," and that as one said it it was necessary to place the fingers of the right hand in the palm of the left. If I should be asked any questions I was to trust to my mother wit to answer them satisfactorily.

We approached the door, which was at the end of a small alley, and when we reached it I noticed that Nikola rapped upon it twice with a large ring he wore upon the first finger of his right hand. In answer a small and peculiar sort of grille was opened, and a voice within said in Chinese:

"Who is it that disturbs honest people at this unseemly hour?"

"Two merchants from Szechuen who have come to Shanghai in search of liberty," said my companion, holding up his hands in the manner described above.

Immediately the door was opened and I followed Nikola into the house. The passage was in darkness and terribly close. As soon as we had entered, the front gate was shut behind us, and we were told to walk straight forward. A moment later another door at the further end opened, and a bright light streamed forth. Our conductor signed to us to enter, and assuming an air of humility, and folding our hands in the prescribed fashion before us, we passed into a large apartment in which were seated possibly twenty men. Without addressing a word to one of them we crossed and took up our positions on a sort of divan at the further end. Pipes were handed to us, and for what must have been nearly five minutes we continued solemnly to puff out smoke, without a word being uttered in the room. If I were to say that I felt at my ease during this long silence it would hardly be the truth; but I flatter myself that, whatever my feelings may have been, I did not permit a sign of my embarrassment to escape me. Then an elderly Chinaman, who sat a little to our right, and who was, without doubt, the chief person present, turned to Nikola and questioned him as to his visit to Shanghai. Nikola answered slowly and gravely, after the Celestial fashion, deprecating any idea of personal advantage, and asserting that it was only to have the honour of saying he had been in Shanghai that he had come at all. When he had finished, the same question was addressed to me. I answered in similar terms, and then another silence fell upon us all. Indeed, it was not until we had been in the room nearly half an hour that any attempt at business was made. Then such a flow of gabble ensued that I could scarcely make head or tail of what I heard. Nikola was to the fore throughout. He invented plots for the overthrowing of dynasties, each of which had a peculiar merit of its own; he theoretically assassinated at least a dozen persons in high places, and, what was more, disposed of their bodies afterwards. To my thinking he out-heroded Herod in his zeal. One thing, however, was quite certain, before he had been an hour in the place he was at the head of affairs, and, had he so desired, could have obtained just what he wanted from those present. I did my best to second his efforts, but my co-operation was quite unnecessary. Three o'clock had passed before the meeting broke up. Then one by one the members left the room, until only Laohwan, the old man who had first addressed us, Nikola and myself remained in occupation.

Then little by little, with infinite tact, Nikola led the conversation round into the channel he wanted. How he had learnt that the old man knew anything at all of the matter was more than I could understand. But that he did know something, and that, with a little persuasion, he might be induced to give us the benefit of his knowledge, soon became evident.

"But these things are not for every one," he said, after a brief recital of the tales he had heard. "If my honourable friend will be guided by one who has had experience, he will not seek to penetrate further."

"The sea of knowledge is for all who desire to swim in it," answered Nikola, puffing solemnly at his pipe. "I have heard these things before, and I would convince myself of their truth. Can you help me to such inquiries? I ask in the name of the Light of Heaven."

As he spoke he took from a pocket under his upper coat the small stick he had obtained from Wetherell. The old man no sooner saw it than his whole demeanour changed; he knelt humbly at Nikola's feet and implored his pardon.

"If my lord had spoken before," he said tremblingly, "I would have answered truthfully. All that I have is my lord's, and I will withhold nothing from him."

"I want nothing," said Nikola, "save what has been arranged. That I must have at once."

"My lord shall be obeyed," said the old man.

"It is well," Nikola answered. "Let there be no delay, and permit no word to pass your lips. Send it to this address, so that I may receive it at once."

He handed the other a card and then rose to go; five minutes later we were back in our respective chairs being borne down the street again. When we reached the house from which we had started Nikola called me into the room where I had dressed.

"You have had an opportunity now of seeing the power of that stick," he said. "It was Laohwan who discovered that the man was a member of the society. All that talk of overthrowing the Manchu dynasty was simply balderdash, partly real, but in a greater measure meant to deceive. Now if all goes well the old fellow will open the first gate to us, and then we shall be able to go ahead. Let us change our clothes and get back to my own house. If I mistake not we shall have to be off up the coast before breakfast-time."

With that we set to work, and as soon as we were dressed in European habiliments, left the house and returned to the bungalow where I had first called upon Nikola. By this time day was breaking, and already a stir of life was discernible in the streets. Making our way into the house we proceeded direct to Nikola's study, where his servants had prepared a meal for us. We sat down to it, and were in the act of falling to work upon a cold pie, when a boy entered with the announcement that a Chinaman was in the hall and desired to speak with us. It was Laohwan.

"Well," said Nikola, "what message does the old man send?"

In reply Loahwan, who I soon found was not prodigal of speech, took from his sleeve a slip of paper on which were some words written in Chinese characters. Nikola glanced at them, and when he had mastered their purport handed it across the table to me. The message was as follows:

"In the house of Quong Sha, in the Street of a Hundred Tribulations, Tientsin."

That was all.

Nikola turned to Laohwan.

"At what time does the North China boat sail?" he asked.

"At half-past six," answered Laohwan promptly.

Nikola looked at his watch, thought for a moment, and then said:

"Go on ahead. Book your passage and get aboard as soon as you can; we will join her later. But remember: until we get to Tientsin you must act as if you have never set eyes on either of us before."

Laohwan bowed and left the room.

"At this point," said Nikola, pouring himself out a cup of black coffee, "the real adventure commences. It is a quarter to five now; we will take it easy for half an hour and then set off to the harbour and get aboard."

Accordingly, as soon as we had finished our meal, we seated ourselves in lounge chairs and lit cigars. For half an hour we discussed the events of the evening, speculated as to the future, and, exactly as the clock struck a quarter-past five, rose to our feet again. Nikola rang a bell and his principal boy entered.

"I am going away," said Nikola. "I don't know when I shall be back. It may be a week, it may be a year. In the meantime you will take care of this house; you will not let one thing be stolen; and if when I come back I find a window broken or as much as a pin missing I'll saddle you with ten million devils. Mr. McAndrew will pay your wages and look after you. If you want anything go to him. Do you understand?"

The boy nodded.

"That will do," said Nikola. "You can go."

As the servant left the room my curious friend gave a strange whistle. Next moment the black cat came trotting in, sprang on her master's knee and crawled up onto his shoulder. Nikola looked at me and smiled.

"He will not forget me if I am away five years," he said. "What wife would be so constant?"

I laughed; the idea of Nikola and matrimony somehow did not harmonize very well. He lifted the cat down and placed him on the table.

"Apollyon," said he, with the only touch of regret I saw him show throughout the trip, "we have to part for a year. Good-bye, old cat, good-bye."

Then having stroked the animal gently once or twice he turned briskly to me.

"Come along," he said; "let us be off. Time presses."

The cat sat on the table watching him and appearing to understand every word he uttered. Nikola stroked its fur for the last time, and then walked out of the room. I followed at his heels and together we passed into the compound. By this time the streets were crowded. A new day had begun in Shanghai, and we had no difficulty in obtaining 'rickshaws.

"The *Vectis Queen*," said Nikola, as soon as we were seated. The coolies immediately started off at a run, and in something under a quarter of an hour we had reached the wharf side of the Hwang-Pu River. The boat we were in search of lay well out in the stream, and for this reason it was necessary that we should charter a sampan to reach her.

Arriving on board we interviewed the purser, and, after we had paid our fares, were conducted to our cabins. The *Vectis Queen,* as all the East knows, is not a large steamer, and her accommodation is, well, to say the least of it, limited. But at this particular time of year there were not a great many people travelling, consequently we were not overcrowded. As soon as I had arranged my baggage, I left my cabin and went on deck. Small is the world! Hardly had I stepped out of the companion-ladder before I was accosted by a man with whom I had been well acquainted on the Australian coastal service, but whom I thought at the other end of the earth.

"Why, Wilfred Bruce!" he cried. "Who'd have thought of seeing you here!"

"Jim Downing!" I cried, not best pleased, as you may suppose, at seeing him. "How long have you been in China?"

"Getting on for a year," he answered, "I came up with one of our boats, had a row with the skipper, and left her in Hong-Kong. After that I joined this line. But though I don't think much of the Chinkies, I am fairly well satisfied. You're looking pretty well, old man; but it seems to me you've got precious sunburnt since I saw you last."

"It's the effect of too much rice," I said with a smile.

He laughed with the spontaneous gaiety of a man who is ready to be amused by anything, however simple, and then we walked up the deck together. As we turned to retrace our steps, Nikola emerged from the companion-hatch and joined us. I introduced Downing to him, and in five minutes you would

57

have supposed them friends of years' standing. Before they had been together a quarter of an hour Nikola had given him a prescription for prickly-heat, from which irritation Downing suffered considerably, and as soon as this proved successful, the young man's gratitude and admiration were boundless. By breakfast-time we were well down the river, and by midday Shanghai lay far behind us.

Throughout the voyage Nikola was in his best spirits; he joined in all the amusements, organized innumerable sports and games, and was indefatigable in his exertions to amuse. And while I am on this subject, let me say that there was one thing which struck me as being even more remarkable than anything else in the character of this extraordinary man, and that was his extreme fondness for children. There was one little boy in particular on board, a wee toddler scarcely four years old, with whom Nikola soon established himself on terms of intimacy; he would play with him for hours at a stretch, never tiring, and never for one moment allowing his attention to wander from the matter in hand. I must own that when I saw them amusing themselves together under the lee of one of the boats on the promenade deck, on the hatchways, or beneath the awning aft, I could scarcely believe my eyes. I had to ask myself if this man, whose entire interest seemed to be centred on paper boats, and pigs cut out of orange peel, could be the same Nikola from whom Wetherell, ex-Colonial Secretary of New South Wales, had fled in London as from a pestilence, and at the sight of whom Benwell, of the Chinese Revenue Service, had excused himself, and rushed out of the club in Shanghai. That, however, was just Nikola's character. If he were making a paper boat, cutting a pig out of orange peel, weaving a plot round a politician, or endeavouring to steal the secret of an all-powerful society, he would give the matter in hand his whole attention, make himself master of every detail, and never leave it till he had achieved his object, or had satisfied himself that it was useless for him to work at it any longer. In the latter case he would drop it without a second thought.

Throughout the voyage Laohwan, though we saw him repeatedly, did not for a moment allow it to be supposed that he knew us. He was located on the forward deck, and, as far as we could gather, spent his whole time playing *fan-tan* with half-a-dozen compatriots on the cover of the forehatch.

The voyage up the coast was not an exciting one, but at last, at sunset one evening, we reached Tientsin, which, as all the world knows, is a treaty port located at the confluence of the Yu-Ho, or Grand Canal, with the river Pei-Ho. As soon as we came alongside the jetty, we collected our baggage and went ashore. Here another thing struck me. Nikola seemed to be as well known in this place as he was in Shanghai, and as soon as we arrived on the Bund called 'rickshaws, and the coolies conveyed us, without asking a question, to the residence of a certain Mr. Williams in the European Concession.

This proved to be a house of modest size, built in the fashion usual in that part of the East. As we alighted from our 'rickshaws, a tall, elderly man, with a distinctly handsome cast of countenance, came into the verandah to welcome us. Seeing Nikola, he for a moment appeared to be overcome with surprise.

"Can it be possible that I see Dr. Nikola?" he cried.

"It is not only possible, but quite certain that you do," said Nikola, who signed to the coolie to lift his bag out, and then went up the steps. "It is two years since I had the pleasure of seeing you, Mr. Williams, and now I look at you you don't seem to have changed much since we taught Mah Feng that lesson in Seoul."

"You have not forgotten that business then, Dr. Nikola?"

"No more than Mah P'eng had when I saw him last in Singapore," my companion answered with a short laugh.

"And what can I do for you now?"

"I want you to let us tax your hospitality for a few hours," said Nikola. "This is my friend, Mr. Bruce, with whom I am engaged on an important piece of work."

"I am delighted to make your acquaintance, sir," said Mr. Williams, and having shaken hands with me he escorted us into the house.

Ten minutes later we were quite at home in his residence, and were waiting, myself impatiently, for a communication from Laohwan. And here I must pay another tribute to Nikola's powers of self-concentration. Anxious as the time was, peculiar as was our position, he did not waste a moment in idle conjecture, but taking from his travelling bag an abstruse work on chemistry, which was his invariable companion, settled himself down to a study of it; even when the messenger *did* come he did not stop at once, but continued the calculations upon which he was engaged until they were finished, when he directed Laohwan to inform him as to the progress he had made.

"Your arrival," said the latter, "is expected, and though I have not been to the place, I have learned that preparations are being made for your reception."

"In that case you had better purchase ponies and have the men in readiness, for in all probability we shall leave for Pekin to-morrow morning."

"At what time will your Excellency visit the house?" asked Laohwan.

"Some time between half-past ten and eleven this evening," answered Nikola; and thereupon our trusty retainer left us.

At seven o'clock our evening meal was served, After it was finished I smoked a pipe in the verandah while Nikola went into a neighbouring room for half an hour's earnest conversation with our host. When he returned he informed me that it was time for us to dress, and thereupon we went to our respective rooms and attired ourselves in our Chinese costumes. Having done this we let ourselves out by a side door and set off for the native city. It was fully half-past ten before we reached it, but for an infinity of reasons we preferred to allow those who were expecting us to wait rather than we should betray any appearance of hurry.

Any one who has had experience of Tientsin will bear me out when I say that of all the dirty and pestilential holes this earth of ours possesses, there are very few to equal it, and scarcely one that can surpass it. Narrow, irregular streets, but little wider than an average country lane in England, run in and out, and twist and twine in every conceivable direction. Overhead the second stories of the houses, decorated with sign-boards, streamers and flags, almost touch each other, so that even in the middle of the day a peculiar, dim, religious light prevails. At night, as may be supposed, it is pitch dark. And both by day and night it smells abominably.

Arriving at the end of the street to which we had been directed, we left our conveyances, and proceeded for the remainder of the distance on foot. Halfway down this particular thoroughfare—which was a little wider, and certainly a degree more respectable than its neighbours—we were met by Loahwan, who conducted us to the house of which we were in search.

In outward appearance it was not unlike its fellows, was one story high, had large overhanging eaves, a sort of trellis-shielded verandah, and a low, arched doorway. Upon this last our Chinese companion thumped with his fist, and at the third repetition the door was opened. Laohwan said something in a low voice to the janitor, who thereupon admitted us.

"There is but one sun," said the guardian of the gate humbly.

"But there be many stars," said Nikola; whereupon the man led us as far as the second door in the passage. Arriving at this he muttered a few words. It was instantly opened, and we stepped inside to find another man waiting for us, holding a queer-shaped lamp in his hand. Without questioning us he intimated that we should follow him, which we did, down a long passage, to bring up finally at a curtained archway. Drawing the curtain aside, he bade us pass through, and then redrew it after us.

On the other side of the arch we found ourselves in a large room, the floor, walls, and ceiling of which were made of some dark wood, probably teak. It was unfurnished save for a few scrolled banners suspended at regular intervals upon the walls, and a few cushions in a corner. When we entered it was untenanted, but we had not long to wait before our solitude was interrupted. I had turned to speak to Nikola, who was examining a banner on the left wall, when suddenly a quiet footfall behind me attracted my attention. I wheeled quickly round to find myself confronted by a Chinaman whose age could scarcely have been less than eighty years. His face was wrinkled like a sun-dried crab-apple, his hair was almost white, and he walked with a stick. One thing struck me as particularly curious about his appearance. Though the house in which we found ourselves was by no means a small one, though it showed every sign of care, and in places even betokened the possession of considerable wealth on the part of its owner, this old man, who was undoubtedly the principal personage in it, was clad in garments that evidenced the deepest poverty. When he reached Nikola, whom he seemed to consider, as indeed did every one else, the chief of our party, he bowed low before him, and after the invariable compliments had been exchanged, said:

"Your Excellency has been anxiously expected. All the arrangements for your progress onward have been made this week past."

"I was detained in Tsan-Chu," said Nikola. "Now tell me what has been done?"

"News has been sent on to Pekin," said the old man, "and the chief priest will await you in the Llamaserai. I can tell you no more."

"I am satisfied. And now let us know what has been said about my coming."

"It is said that they who have chosen have chosen wisely."

"That is good," said Nikola. "Now leave us; I am tired and would be alone. I shall remain the night in this house and go onwards at daybreak to-morrow morning. See that I am not disturbed."

The old man assured Nikola that his wishes should be respected, and having done so left the room. After he had gone Nikola drew me to the further end of the apartment and whispered hurriedly:

"I see it all now. Luck is playing into our hands. If I can only get hold of the two men I want to carry this business through, I'll have the society's secret or die in the attempt. Listen to me. When we arrived to-night I learnt from Williams, who knows almost as much of the under life of China as I do myself, that what I suspected has already taken place. In other words, after this long interval, there has been an election to fill the place of the man whom China Pete killed in the Llamaserai to obtain possession of that stick. The man chosen is the chief priest of the Llama temple of Hankow, a most religious and extraordinary person. He is expected in Pekin either this week or next. Misled by Laohwan, these people have mistaken me for him, and I mean that they shall continue in their error. If they find that we are hoodwinking them we are dead men that instant, but if they don't and we can keep this other man out of the way, we stand an excellent chance of getting from them all we want to know. It is a tremendous risk, but as it is an opportunity that might never come again, we must make the most of it. Now attend carefully to me. It would never do for me to leave this place to-night, but it is most imperative that I should communicate with Williams. I must write a letter to him, and you must take it. He must send two cablegrams first thing to-morrow morning."

So saying he drew from a pocket inside his sleeve a small notebook, and, what seemed strangely incongruous, a patent American fountain pen. Seating himself upon the floor he began to write. For nearly five minutes complete silence reigned in the room, then he tore two or three leaves from the book and handed them to me.

"Take these to Williams," he said. "He must find out where this other man is, without losing an instant, and communicate with the folk to whom I am cabling. Come what may they must catch him before he can get here, and then carry him out to sea. Once there he must not be allowed to land again until you and I are safely back in Shanghai."

"And who is Williams to cable to?"

"To two men in whom I have the greatest confidence. One is named Eastover, and the other Prendergast. He will send them this message."

He handed me another slip of paper.

"To Prendergast and Eastover, care Gregson, Hong-Kong—

"Come Tientsin next boat. Don't delay a moment. When you arrive call on Williams.

"Nikola."

Chapter 5

I Rescue A Young Lady

Having left the room in which Nikola had settled himself I found the same doorkeeper who had admitted us to the house, and who now preceded and ushered me into the street. Once there I discovered that the condition of the night had changed. When we had left Mr. Williams' residence it was bright starlight, now black clouds covered the face of the sky, and as I passed down the street, in the direction of the English Concession, a heavy peal of thunder rumbled overhead. It was nearly eleven o'clock, and, as I could not help thinking, a curious quiet lay upon the native city. There was an air of suppressed excitement about such Chinamen as I met that puzzled me, and when I came upon knots of them at street corners, the scraps of conversation I was able to overhear did not disabuse my mind of the notion that some disturbance was in active preparation. However, I had not time to pay much attention to them. I had to find Mr. Williams' house, give him the letter, and get back to Nikola with as little delay as possible.

At last I reached the Concession, passed the Consul's house, and finally arrived at the bungalow of which I was in search.

A bright light shone from one of the windows, and towards it I directed my steps. On reaching it I discovered the owner of the house seated at a large table, writing. I tapped softly upon the pane, whereupon he rose and came towards me. That he did not recognize me was evident from his reception of me.

"What do you want?" he asked in Chinese as he opened the window.

Bending a little forward, so as to reach his ear, I whispered the following sentence into it: "I should like to ask your honourable presence one simple question."

"This is not the time to ask questions, however simple," he replied; "you must come round in the morning."

"But the morning will be too late," I answered earnestly. "I tell you by the spirit of your ancestors that what I have to say must be said to-night."

"Then come in, and for mercy's sake say it," he replied a little testily, and beckoned me into the room. I did as he desired, and seated myself on the stool before him, covering my hands with my great sleeves in the orthodox fashion. Then, remembering the Chinese love of procrastination, I began to work the conversation in and out through various channels until I saw that his patience was well-nigh exhausted. Still, however, he did not recognize me. Then leaning towards him I said:

"Is your Excellency aware that your house has been watched since sundown?"

"By whom, and for what reason?" he inquired, looking, I thought, a little uncomfortable.

"By three men, and because of two strangers who arrived by the mail boat this afternoon."

"What strangers?" he inquired innocently. But I noticed that he looked at me rather more fixedly than before.

"The man whom we call 'The man with the Devil's eyes '—but whom you call Nikola—and his companion."

I gave Nikola's name as nearly as a Chinaman would be able to pronounce it, and then waited to see what he would say next. That he was disconcerted was plain enough, but that he did not wish to commit himself was also very evident. He endeavoured to temporize; but as this was not to my taste, I revealed my identity by saying in my natural voice and in English:

"It would seem that my disguise is a very good one, Mr. Williams."

He stared at me.

"Surely you are not Mr. Bruce?" he cried.

"I am," I answered; "and what's more, I am here on an important errand. I have brought you a letter from Nikola, which you must read and act upon at once."

As I spoke I produced from a pocket in my sleeve the letter Nikola had given me and handed it to him. He sat down again at the table and perused it carefully. When he had finished, he read it over again, then a third time. Having got it by heart he went across the room to a safe in the corner. This he unlocked, and having opened a drawer, carefully placed the slip of paper in it. Then he came back and took up his old seat again. I noticed that his forehead was contracted with thought, and that there was an expression of perplexity, and one might have almost said of doubt, about his mouth. At last he spoke.

"I know you are in Nikola's employment, Mr. Bruce," he said, "but are you aware of the contents of this letter?"

"Does it refer to the man who is expected in Pekin to take up the third stick in the society?"

"Yes," he answered slowly, stabbing at his blotting-pad with the point of a pen, "it does. It refers to him very vitally."

"And now you are revolving in your mind the advisability of what Nikola says about abducting him, I suppose?"

"Exactly. Can Nikola be aware, think you, that the man in question was chief priest of one of the biggest Hankow temples?"

"I have no doubt that he is. But you say 'was.' Has the man then resigned his appointment in order to embrace this new calling?"

"Certainly he has."

"Well, in that case it seems to me that the difficulty is considerably lessened."

"In one direction, perhaps; but then it is increased in another. If he is still a priest and we abduct him, then we fight the Government and the Church. On the other hand, if he is no longer a priest, and the slightest suspicion of what we are about to do leaks out, then we shall have to fight a society which is ten times as powerful as any government or priesthood in the world."

"You have Nikola's instructions, I suppose?"

"Yes; and I confess I would rather deal with the Government of China and the millions of the society than disobey him in one single particular. But let me tell you this, Mr. Bruce, if Nikola is pig-headed enough to continue his quest in the face of this awful uncertainty, I would not give a penny piece for either his life or that of the man who accompanies him. Consider for one moment what I mean. This society into whose secrets he is so anxious to penetrate—and how much better he will be when he has done so he alone knows—is without doubt the most powerful in the whole world. If rumour is to be believed, its list of members exceeds twenty millions. It has representatives in almost every town and village in the length and breadth of this great land, to say nothing of Malaysia, Australia and America; its rules are most exacting, and when you reflect for one moment that our friend is going to impersonate one of the three leaders of this gigantic force, with chances of detection menacing him at every turn, you will see for yourself what a foolhardy undertaking it is."

"I must own I agree with you, but still he is Nikola."

"Yes. In that you sum up everything. *He is NIKOLA.*"

"Then what answer am I to take back to him?"

"That I will proceed with the work at once. Stay. I will write it down, that there may be no possible mistake."

So saying he wrote for a moment, and when his letter was completed handed it to me.

I rose to go.

"And with regard to these telegrams?" I said.

"I will dispatch them myself the very moment the office is open," he answered. "I have given Nikola an assurance to that effect in my letter."

"We leave at daybreak for Pekin, so I will wish you good-bye now."

"You have no thought of turning back, I suppose?"

"Not the very slightest."

"You're a plucky man."

"I suppose I must be. But there is an old saying that just meets my case."

"And that is?"

"'Needs must when——'"

"Well, shall we say when Nikola——?"

"Yes. 'Needs must when Nikola drives.' Good-bye."

"Good-bye, and may good luck go with you."

I shook hands with him at the front door, and then descended the steps and set off on my return to the native city. As I left the street in which the bungalow stood a clock struck twelve. The clouds, which had been so heavy when I set out, had now drawn off the sky, and it was bright starlight once more.

As I entered the city proper my first impression was in confirmation of my original feeling that something out of the common was about to happen. Nor was I deceived. Hardly had I gone a hundred yards before a tumult of angry voices broke upon my ear. The sound increased in volume, and presently an excited mob poured into the street along which I was making my way. Had it been possible I would have turned into a by-path and so escaped them, but now this was impossible. They had hemmed me in on every side, and, whether I wished it or not, I was compelled to go with them.

For nearly half a mile they carried me on in this fashion, then, leaving the thoroughfare along which they had hitherto been passing, they turned sharply to the right hand and brought up before a moderate-sized house standing at a corner. Wondering what it all might mean, I accosted a youth by my side and questioned him. His answer was brief, but to the point:

"*Kueidzu!*" (devil), he cried, and picking up a stone hurled it through the nearest window.

The house, I soon discovered, was the residence of a missionary, who, I was relieved to hear, was absent from home. As I could see the mob was bent on wrecking his dwelling I left them to their work and proceeded on my way again. But though I did not know it, I had not done with adventure yet.

As I turned from the street, into another which ran at right angles to it, I heard a shrill cry for help. I immediately stopped and listened in order to discover whence it had proceeded. I had not long to wait, however, for almost at the same instant it rang out again. This time it undoubtedly came from a lane on my right. Without a second's thought I picked up my heels and ran across to it. At first I could see nothing; then at the further end I made out three figures, and towards them I hastened. When I got there I found that one was a girl, the second an old man, who was stretched upon the ground; both were English, but their assailant was an active young fellow of the coolie class. He was standing over the man's body menacing the girl with a knife. My sandals made no noise upon the stones, and as I came up on the dark side of the lane neither of the trio noticed my presence until I was close upon them. But swift as I was I was hardly quick enough, for just as I arrived the girl

68

threw herself upon the man, who at the same instant raised his arm and plunged his knife into her shoulder. It could not have penetrated very deep, however, before my fist was in his face. He rolled over like a ninepin, and for a moment lay on the ground without moving. But he did not remain there very long. Recovering his senses he sprang to his feet and bolted down the street, yelling "*Kueidzu! kueidzu!*" at the top of his voice, in the hope of bringing the mob to his assistance.

Before he was out of sight I was kneeling by the side of the girl upon the ground. She was unconscious. Her face was deadly pale, and I saw that her left shoulder was soaked with blood. From examining her I turned to the old man. He was a fine-looking old fellow, fairly well dressed, and boasting a venerable grey beard. He lay stretched out at full length, and one glance at his face was sufficient to tell me his fate. How it had been caused I could only imagine, but there was no doubt about the fact that he was dead. When I had convinced myself of this I returned to the girl. Her eyes were now open, and as I knelt beside her she asked in English what had happened.

"You have been wounded," I answered.

"And my father?"

There was nothing to be gained by deceiving her, so I said simply:

"I have sad news for you—I fear he is dead."

Upon hearing this she uttered a little cry, and for a moment seemed to lose consciousness again. I did not, however, wait to revive her, but went across to where her father lay, and picking the body up in my arms, carried it across the street to a dark corner. Having placed it there, I returned to the girl, and lifting her on to my shoulder ran down the street in the direction I had come. In the distance I could hear the noise of the mob, who were still engaged wrecking the murdered man's dwelling.

Arriving at the spot where I had stood when I first heard the cry for help, I picked up my old course and proceeded along it to my destination. In something less than ten minutes I had reached the house and knocked, in the way Laohwan had done, upon the door, which was immediately opened to me. I gave the password, and was admitted with my burden. If the custodian of the door thought anything, he did not give utterance to it, and permitted me to reach the second door unmolested.

Again I knocked, and once more the door was opened. But this time I was not to be allowed to pass unchallenged. Though I had given the password correctly, the door-keeper bade me wait while he scrutinized the burden in my arms.

"What have you here?" he asked.

"Have you the right to ask?" I said, assuming a haughty air. "His Excellency has sent for this foreign devil to question her. She has fainted with fright. Now stand aside, or there are those who will make you pay for stopping me."

He looked a trifle disconcerted, and after a moment's hesitation signed to me to pass. I took him at his word, and proceeded into the room where I had left my chief. That Nikola was eagerly expecting me I gathered from the pleasure my appearance seemed to give him.

"You are late," he cried, coming quickly across to me. "I have been expecting you this hour past. But what on earth have you got there?"

"A girl," I answered, "the daughter of a missionary, I believe. She has been wounded, and even now is unconscious. If I had not discovered her she would have been killed by the man who murdered her father."

"But what on earth made you bring her here?"

"What else could I do? Her father is dead, and I believe the mob has wrecked their house."

"Put her down," said Nikola, "and let me look at her."

I did as he bade me, and thereupon he set to work to examine her wound. With a deftness extraordinary, and a tenderness of which one would scarcely have believed him capable, he bathed the wound with water, which I procured from an adjoining room, then, having anointed it with some stuff from a small medicine chest he always carried about with him, he bound it up with a piece of Chinese cloth. Having finished he said:

"Lift her up while I try the effect of this upon her."

From the chest he took a small cut-glass bottle, shaped something like that used by European ladies for carrying smelling-salts, and having opened her mouth poured a few

70

drops of what it contained upon her tongue. Almost instantly she opened her eyes, looked about her, and seeing, as she supposed, two Chinamen bending over her, fell back with an expression of abject terror on her face. But Nikola, who was still kneeling beside her, reassured her, saying in English:

"You need have no fear. You are in safe hands. We will protect you, come what may."

His speech seemed to recall what had happened to her remembrance.

"Oh, my poor father!" she cried. "What have you done with him?"

"To save your life," I answered, "I was compelled to leave his body in the street where I had found it; but it is quite safe."

"I must go and get it," she said. And as she spoke she tried to rise, but Nikola put out his hand and stopped her.

"You must not move," he said. "Leave everything to me. I will take care that your father's body is found and protected."

"But I must go home."

"My poor girl," said Nikola tenderly, "you do not know everything. You have no home to go to. It was wrecked by the mob this evening."

"Oh dear! oh dear! Then what is to become of me? They have killed my father and wrecked our house! And we trusted them so."

Without discussing this point Nikola rose and left the room. Presently he returned, and again approached the girl.

"I have sent men to find your father's body," he said. "It will be conveyed to a safe place, and within half an hour the English Consul will be on the trail of his murderer. Now tell me how it all occurred."

"I will tell you what I can," she answered. "But it seems so little to have brought about so terrible a result. My father and I left our home this evening at half-past seven to hold a service in the little church our few converts have built for us. During the course of the service it struck me repeatedly that there was something wrong, and when we came out and saw the crowd that had collected at the door this impression was confirmed. Whether they intended to attack us or not I cannot say, but just as we were leaving a shout was raised, and instantly off the mob ran, I suppose in the direction of our house. I can see that now, though we did not suspect it then. Fearing to follow in the same direction, we passed down a side street, intending to proceed home by another route. But as we left the main thoroughfare and turned into the dark lane where you found us, a man rushed out upon my father, and with a thick stick, or a bar of iron, felled him to the ground. I endeavoured to protect him and to divert his attention to myself, whereupon he drew a knife and stabbed me in the shoulder. Then you came up and drove him off."

As she said this she placed her hand upon my arm.

"I cannot tell you how grateful I am to you," she said.

"It was a very small service," I answered, feeling a little confused by her action. "I only wished I had arrived upon the scene earlier."

"Whatever am I to do?"

"Have you any friends in Tientsin?" inquired Nikola. "Any one to whom you can go?"

"No, we know no one at all," the girl replied. "But I have a sister in Pekin, the wife of a missionary there. Could you help me to get so far?"

"Though I cannot take you myself," said Nikola, "if you like I will put you in the way of getting there. In the meantime you must not remain in this house. Do not be alarmed, however; I will see that you are properly taken care of."

Again he left the room, and while he was gone I looked more closely at the girl whom I had rescued. Her age might have been anything from twenty to twenty-three, her face was a perfect oval in shape, her skin was the most delicate I had ever seen, her mouth was small, and her eyes and hair were a beautiful shade of brown. But it was her sweet expression which was the chief charm of her face, and this was destined to haunt me for many a long day to come.

I don't think I can be said to be a ladies' man (somehow or another I have never been thrown much into feminine society), but I must confess when I looked into this girl's sweet face, a thrill, such as I had never experienced before, passed over me.

"How can I ever thank you for your goodness?" she asked simply.

"By bearing your terrible trouble bravely," I answered. "And now, will you consider me impertinent if I ask your name?"

"Why should I? My name is Medwin—Gladys Mary Medwin. And yours?"

"It ought to be Mah Poo in this dress, oughtn't it? In reality it is Wilfred Bruce."

"But if you are an Englishman why are you disguised in this fashion?"

"That, I am sorry to say, I cannot tell you," I answered. "Do you know, Miss Medwin, it is just possible that you may be the last Englishwoman I shall ever speak to in my life?"

"What do you mean?" she asked.

"Again I can only say that I cannot tell you. But I may say this much, that I am going away in a few hours' time to undertake something which, more probably than not, will cost me my life. I don't know why I should say this to you, but one cannot be prosaic at such moments as these. Besides, though our acquaintance is only an hour or so old, I seem to have known you for years. You say I have done you a service; will you do one for me?"

"What can I do?" she asked, placing her little hand upon my arm.

"This ring," I said, at the same time drawing a plain gold circlet from my finger, "was my poor mother's last gift to me. I dare not take it with me where I am going. Would it be too much to ask you to keep it for me? In the event of my not returning, you might promise me to wear it as a little memento of the service you say I have done you to-night. It would be pleasant to think that I have one woman friend in the world."

As I spoke I raised the hand that lay upon my arm, and, holding it in mine, placed the ring upon her finger.

"I will keep it for you with pleasure," she said. "But is this work upon which you are embarking really so dangerous?"

"More so than you can imagine," I replied. "But be sure of this, Miss Medwin, if I do come out of it alive, I will find you out and claim that ring."

"I will remember," she answered, and just as she had finished speaking Nikola re-entered the room.

"My dear young lady," he said hurriedly, "I have made arrangements for your safe conduct to the house of a personal friend, who will do all he can for you while you remain in Tientsin. Then as soon as you can leave this place he will have you escorted carefully to your sister in Pekin. Now I think you had better be going. A conveyance is at the door, and my friend will be waiting to receive you. Mr. Bruce, will you conduct Miss Medwin to the street?"

"You are very good to me."

"Not at all. You will amply compensate me if you will grant me one favour in return."

"How can I serve you?"

"By never referring in any way to the fact of your having met us. When I tell you that our lives will in a great measure depend upon your reticence, I feel sure you will comply with my request."

"Not a word shall escape my lips."

Nikola bowed, and then almost abruptly turned on his heel and walked away. Seeing that his action was meant as a signal that she should depart, I led the way down the passage into the street, where a chair was in waiting. Having placed her in it, I bade her good-bye in a whisper.

"Good-bye," I said. "If ever I return alive I will inquire for you at the house to which you are now going,"

"Good-bye, and may God protect you!"

She took my hand in hers, and next moment I felt something placed in the palm. Then I withdrew it; the coolies took up the poles, and presently the equipage was moving down the street.

I waited until it was out of sight, and then went back into the house, where I found Nikola pacing up and down the room, his hands behind his back and his head bowed low upon his breast. He looked up at me, and, without referring to what had happened, said quickly;

"The ponies will be at the door in an hour's time. If you want any rest you had better take it now. I am going to have an interview with the old man we saw to-night. I want to try and worm some more information for our guidance out of him. Don't leave this room until my return, and, above all, remember in your future dealings with me that I am a chief priest, and **as** such am entitled to the deepest reverence. Always bear in mind the fact that one little mistake may upset all our plans, and may land both our heads on the top of the nearest city gate."

"I will remember," I said. And he thereupon left the room.

When he had gone I put my hand into my pocket and drew out the little keepsake Miss Medwin had given me. It proved to be a small but curiously chased locket, but, to my sorrow, contained no photograph. She had evidently worn it round her neck, for a small piece of faded ribbon was still attached to it. I looked at it for a moment, and then slipped the ribbon round my own neck, for so only could I hope to prevent its being stolen from me. Then I laid myself down upon a mat in a corner, and in less time than it takes to tell fell fast asleep. When I woke it was to find Nikola shaking me by the shoulder.

"Time's up," he said. "The ponies are at the door, and we must be off."

I had hardly collected my faculties and scrambled to my feet before the old man whom I had seen on the previous evening entered the room, bringing with him a meal, consisting principally of rice and small coarse cakes made of maize. We fell to work upon them, and soon had them finished, washing them down with cups of excellent tea.

Our meal at an end, Nikola led the old man aside and said something to him in an undertone, emphasizing his remarks with solemn gestures. Then, with the whole retinue of the house at our heels to do us honour, we proceeded into the courtyard, where Laohwan was in waiting with five ponies. Two were laden with baggage, upon one of the others Nikola seated himself, I appropriated the second, Laohwan taking the third. Then, amid the respectful greeting of the household, the gates were opened, and we rode into the street. We had now embarked upon another stage of our adventures.

Chapter 6

On The Road To Pekin

As we left the last house of the native city of Tientsin behind us the sun was in the act of rising. Whatever the others may have felt I cannot say, but this I know, that there was at least one person in the party who was heartily glad to have said good-bye to the town. Though we had only been in it a short time we had passed through such a series of excitements during that brief period as would have served to disgust even such a glutton as Don Quixote himself with an adventurous life.

For the first two or three miles our route lay over a dry mud plain, where the dust, which seemed to be mainly composed of small pebbles, was driven about our ears like hail by the dawn wind. We rode in silence. Nikola, by virtue of his pretended rank, was some yards ahead, I followed next; Laohwan came behind me, and the baggage ponies and the Mafoos (or native grooms) behind him again. I don't know what Nikola was thinking about, but I'm not ashamed to confess that my own thoughts reverted continually to the girl whom I had been permitted the opportunity of rescuing on the previous evening. Her pale sweet face never left me, but monopolized my thoughts to the exclusion of everything else. Though I tried again and again to bring my mind to bear upon the enterprise on which we were embarking, it was of no use; on each occasion I came back to the consideration of a pair of dark eyes and a wealth of nut-brown hair. That I should ever meet Miss Medwin again seemed most unlikely; that I wanted to I will not deny; and while I am about it I will even go so far as to confess that, not once but several times, I found myself wishing, for the self-same reason, that I had thought twice before accepting Nikola's offer. One moment's reflection, however, was sufficient to show me that had I not fallen in with Nikola I should in all probability not only have never known her at all, but, what was more to the point, I should most likely have been in a position where love-making would not only have been foolish, but indeed quite out of the question.

When we had proceeded something like five miles Nikola turned in his saddle and beckoned me to his side.

"By this time," he said, "Prendergast and Eastover will have received the telegrams I requested Williams to dispatch to them. They will not lose a moment in getting on their way, and by the middle of next week they should have the priest of Hankow in their hands. It will take another three days for them to inform us of the fact, which will mean that we shall have to wait at least ten days in Pekin before presenting ourselves at the Llamaserai. This being so, we will put up at a house which has been recommended to me in the Tartar city. I shall let it be understood there that I am anxious to undertake a week's prayer and fasting in order to fit myself for the responsibilities I am about to take upon me, and that during that time I can see no one. By the end of the tenth day, I should have heard from Prendergast and know enough to penetrate into the very midst of the monks. After that it should be all plain sailing."

"But do you think your men will be able to abduct this well-known priest without incurring suspicion?"

"They will have to," answered Nikola. "If they don't we shall have to pay the penalty. But there, you need have no sort of fear. I have the most perfect faith in the men. They have been well tried, and I am sure of this, if I were to tell either of them to do anything, however dangerous the task might be, they would not think twice before obeying me. By the way, Bruce, I don't know that you are looking altogether well."

"I don't feel quite the thing," I answered; "my head aches consumedly, but I don't doubt it will soon pass off."

"Well, let us push on. We must reach the rest-house to-night, and to do that we have got a forty-mile ride ahead of us."

It is a well-known fact that though Chinese ponies do not present very picturesque outward appearances, there are few animals living that can equal them in pluck and endurance. Our whole cavalcade, harness and pack-saddles included, might have been purchased for a twenty-pound note; but I very much doubt if the most costly animals to be seen in Rotten

Row, on an afternoon in the season, could have carried us half so well as those shaggy little beasts, which stood but little more than thirteen hands.

In spite of the fact that we camped for a couple of hours in the middle of the day, we were at the rest-house, half-way to Pekin, before sundown. And a wretched place it proved—a veritable Chinese inn, with small bare rooms, quite unfurnished, and surrounded by a number of equally inhospitable stables.

As soon as we arrived we dismounted and entered the building, on the threshold of which the boorish Chinese landlord received us. His personality was in keeping with his house; but observing that we were strangers of importance he condescended to depart so far from his usual custom as to show us at least the outward signs of civility. So we chose our rooms and ordered a meal to be instantly prepared. Our blankets were unpacked and spread upon the floor of our bedrooms, and almost as soon *as* this was done the meal was announced as ready.

It consisted, we discovered, of half a dozen almost raw eggs, two tough fowls, and a curiously cooked mess of pork. The latter dish, as every one knows who has had anything to do with the Celestial Empire, is one of the staple diets of all but Mohammedan Chinamen.

Swarms of beggars, loathsome to a degree, infested the place, begging and whining for any trifle, however insignificant. They crawled about the courtyards and verandahs, and at last became so emboldened by success that they ventured to penetrate our rooms. This was too much of a good thing, and I saw that Nikola thought so too.

When one beggar, more impertinent than the rest, presented himself before us, after having been warned repeatedly, Nikola called Laohwan to him and bade him take the fellow outside and, with the assistance of two coolies, treat him to a supper of bamboo. Any one who has seen this peculiar punishment will never forget it; and at last the man's cries for mercy became so appalling as to warrant my proceeding to the courtyard and bidding them let him go.

After I returned to my room, which adjoined that occupied by Nikola, we sat talking for nearly an hour, and then retired to rest.

But though I disrobed myself of my Chinese garments, and stretched myself out upon the blankets, sleep would not visit my eyelids. Possibly I was a little feverish; at any rate I began to imagine all sorts of horrible things. Strange thoughts crowded upon my brain, and the most uncanny sounds spoke from the silence of the night. Little noises from afar concentrated themselves until they seemed to fill my room. A footfall in the street would echo against the wall with a mysterious distinctness, and the sound of a dog barking in a neighbouring compound was intensified till it might have been the barking of a dozen. So completely did this nervousness possess me that I soon found myself discovering a danger in even the creaking of the boards in an adjoining room, and the chirrup of an insect in the roof.

How long I remained in this state I cannot say. But at last I could bear it no longer. I rose therefore from my bed and was about to pace the room, in the hope of tiring myself into sleeping, when the sound of a stealthy footstep in the corridor outside caught my ears. I stood rooted to the spot, trying to listen, with every pulse in my body pumping like a piston rod. Again it sounded, but this time it was nearer my door. There was a distinct difference, however; it was no longer a human step, as we are accustomed to hear it, but an equalized and heavy shuffling sound that for a moment rather puzzled me. But my mystification was of scarcely an instant's duration. I had heard that sound before in the Manillas the same night that a man in my hotel was murdered. One second's reflection told me that it was made by some one proceeding along the passage upon his hands and knees. But why was he doing it? Then I remembered that the wall on the other side of the corridor was only a foot or two high. The intruder, whoever he might be, evidently did not wish to be seen by the occupants of the rooms across the square. I drew back into a corner, took a long hunting-knife that I always carried with me, from beneath my pillow, and awaited the turn of events. Still the sound continued; but by this time it had passed my door, and as soon as I realized this, I crept towards the passage and looked out.

From where I stood I was permitted a view of the narrow corridor, but it was empty. Instinct told me that the man had entered the room next to mine. Since I had first heard him he would not have had time to get any further. The adjoining apartment was Nikola's, and after the fatigue of the day it was ten chances to one he would be asleep. That the fellow's mission was an evil one it did not require much penetration to perceive. A man does not crawl about lonely corridors, when other men are asleep, on hands and knees, for any good purpose. Therefore, if I wished to save my employer's life, I knew I must be quick about it.

A second later I had left my own room and was hastening up the passage after him. Reaching the doorway I stood irresolute, trying to discover by listening whereabouts in the room the man might be. It was not long before I heard a heavy grunt, followed by a muttered ejaculation. Then I rushed into the room, and across to where I knew Nikola had placed his bed. As I did so I came in contact with a naked body, and next moment we were both rolling and tumbling upon the floor.

It was a unique experience that fight in the dark. Over and over the man and I rolled, clinging to each other and putting forth every possible exertion to secure a victory. Then I heard Nikola spring to his feet, and run towards the door. In response to his cry there was an immediate hubbub in the building, but before lights could reach us I had got the upper hand and was seated across my foe.

Laohwan was the first to put in an appearance, and he brought a torch. Nikola took it from him and came across to us. Signing me to get off the man whom I was holding, toe bent down and looked at him.

"Ho, ho!" he said quietly. "This is not burglary then, but vengeance. So, you rogue, you wanted to repay me for the beating you got to-night, did you? It seems I have had a narrow escape."

It was as he said. The man whom I had caught was none other than the beggar whose persistence had earned him a beating earlier in the evening.

"What will your Excellency be pleased to do with him?" asked Laohwan.

Nikola saw his opportunity. He told the man to stand up. Then looking him straight in the eyes for perhaps a minute, he said quietly:

"Open your mouth."

The man did as he was ordered.

"It is impossible for you to shut it again," said Nikola. "Try."

The poor wretch tried and tried in vain. His jaws were as securely fastened as if they had been screwed top and bottom. He struggled with them, he tried to press them together, but in vain; they were firmly fixed and defied him. In his terror he ran about the room, perspiration streaming from his face, and all the time uttering strange cries.

"Come here!" said Nikola. "Stand before me. Now shut your mouth."

Instantly the man closed his mouth.

"Shut your eyes."

The man did as he was ordered.

"You are blind and dumb; you cannot open either your eyes or your mouth."

The man tried, but with the same result as before. His mouth and eyes were firmly sealed. This time his terror was greater than any words could express, and he fell at Nikola's feet imploring him in inarticulate grunts to spare him. The crowd who had clustered at the door stood watching this strange scene open-mouthed.

"Get up!" said Nikola to the miserable wretch at his feet. "Open your mouth and eyes. You would have murdered me, but I have spared you. Try again what you have attempted to-night, and both sight and speech will be instantly taken from you and never again restored. Now go!"

The man did not wait to be bidden twice, but fled as if for his life, parting the crowd at the doorway just as the bows of a steamer turn away the water on either side.

When only Laohwan remained, Nikola called him up.

"Are you aware," he said, "that but for my friend's vigilance here I should now be a dead man? You sleep at the end of the passage, and it was your duty to have taken care that nobody passed you. But you failed in your trust. Now what is your punishment to be?"

In answer the man knelt humbly at his master's feet.

"Answer my question! What is your punishment to be?" the same remorseless voice repeated. "Am I never to place trust in you again?"

"By the graves of my ancestors I swear that I did not know that the man had passed me."

"That is no answer," said Nikola. "You have failed in your duty, and that is a thing, as you know, I never forgive. But as you have been faithful in all else, I will not be too hard upon you. In an hour's time you will saddle your horse and go back to Tientsin, where you will seek out Mr. Williams and tell him that you are unsatisfactory, and that I have sent you back. You will remain with him till I communicate with you again. Fail to see him or to tell him what I have said, and you will be dead in two days. Do you understand me?"

Once more the man bowed low.

"Then go!"

Without a word the fellow rose to his feet and went towards the door. In my own heart I felt sorry for him, and when he had left, I said as much to Nikola, at the same time inquiring if he thought it prudent to make an enemy of a man who held our lives in his hand.

"My friend," he answered, "there is a Hindu proverb which says, 'A servant who cannot be trusted is as a broken lock upon the gateway of your house.' As to what you say about prudence, you need have no fear. I have had many dealings with Laohwan, and he knows me. He would rather die the death of a Thousand Cuts than betray me. But while I am blaming him I am forgetting to do justice to you. One thing is very certain, but for your intervention I should not be talking to you now. I owe you my life. I can only ask you to believe that, if ever the chance occurs, you will not find me ungrateful."

"It was fortunate," I said, "that I heard him pass along the passage, otherwise we might both have perished."

"It was strange, after all the exertions of the day, that you should have been awake. I was sleeping like a top. But let me look at you. Good heavens, man! I told you this morning you were looking ill. Give me your wrist."

He felt my pulse, then stared anxiously into my face. After this he took a small bottle from a travelling medicine-chest, poured a few drops of what it contained into a glass, filled it up from a Chinese water-bottle near by, and then bade me drink it. Having done so I was sent back to bed, and within five minutes of arriving there was wrapped in a dreamless sleep.

When I woke it was broad daylight and nearly six o'clock. I felt considerably better than when I had gone to bed the previous night, but still I was by no means well. What was the matter with me, however, I could not tell.

At seven o'clock an equivalent for breakfast was served to us, and at half-past the ponies were saddled and we proceeded on our journey. As we left the inn I looked about to see if I could discover any signs of poor Loahwan, but as he was not there I could only suppose he had accepted Nikola's decision as final and had gone back to Tientsin.

As usual Nikola rode on ahead, and it was not difficult to see that the story of his treatment of his would-be murderer had leaked out. The awe with which he was regarded by the people with whom we came in contact was most amusing to witness. And you may be sure he fully acted up to the character which had been given him.

After halting as usual at midday we proceeded on our way until four o'clock, when a pleasurable sensation was in store for us. Rising above the monotonous level of the plain were the walls of the great city of Pekin. They seemed to stretch away as far as the eye could reach. As we approached them they grew more imposing, and presently an enormous tower, built in the usual style of Chinese architecture, and pierced with innumerable loop-holes for cannon, appeared in sight. It was not until we were within a couple of hundred yards of it, however, that we discovered that these loop-holes were only counterfeit, and that the whole tower was little more than a sham.

We entered the city by a gateway that would have been considered insignificant in a third-rate Afghan village, and, having paid the tolls demanded of us, wondered in which direction we had best proceed, in order to find the lodgings to which our friend in Tientsin had directed us.

Having pressed a smart-looking youth into our service as guide, we were conducted by a series of tortuous thoroughfares to a house in a mean quarter of the city. By the time we reached it it was quite dark, and it was only after much waiting and repeated knockings upon the door that we contrived to make those within aware of our presence. At last, however, the door opened and an enormously stout Chinaman stood before us.

"What do you want?" he asked of Nikola, who was nearest to him.

"That which only peace can give," said Nikola.

The man bowed low.

"Your Excellency has been long expected," he said.

"If you will be honourably pleased to step inside, all that my house contains is yours."

We followed him through the dwelling into a room at the rear. Then Nikola bade him call in the chief Mafoo, and when he appeared, discharged his account and bade him be gone."

"We are now in Pekin," said Nikola to me as soon as we were alone, "and it behooves us to play our cards with the utmost care. Remember, as I have so often told you, I am a man of extreme sanctity, and I shall guide my life and actions accordingly. There is, as you see, a room leading out of this. In it I shall take up my abode. You will occupy this one. It must be your business to undertake that no one sees me. And you must allow it to be understood that I spend my time almost exclusively in study and upon my devotions. Every night when darkness falls I shall go out and endeavour to collect the information of which we stand in need. You will have charge of the purse and must arrange our commissariat."

Half an hour later our evening meal was served, and when we had eaten it, being tired, we went straight to bed. But I was not destined to prove of much assistance to my friend, for next morning when I woke my old sickness had returned upon me, my skin was dry and cracked, and my head ached to distraction. I could eat no breakfast, and I could see that Nikola was growing more and more concerned about my condition.

After breakfast I went for a walk. But I could not rid myself of the heaviness which had seized me, so returned to the house feeling more dead than alive. During the afternoon I lay down upon my bed, and in a few minutes lost consciousness altogether.

Chapter 7

A Serious Time

It was broad daylight when I recovered consciousness, the sunshine was streaming into my room, and birds were twittering in the trees outside. But though I sat up and looked about me I could make neither head nor tail of my position; there was evidently something wrong about it. When I had fallen asleep, as I thought, my couch had been spread upon the floor, and was composed of Chinese materials. Now I lay upon an ordinary English bedstead, boasting a spring mattress, sheets, blankets, and even a counterpane. Moreover, the room itself was different. There was a carpet upon the floor, and several pretty pictures hung upon the walls. I felt certain they had not been there when I was introduced to the apartment. Being, however, too weak to examine these wonders for very long, I laid myself down upon my pillow again and closed my eyes. In a few moments I was once more asleep and did not wake until towards evening.

When I did it was to discover some one sitting by the window reading. At first I looked at her—for it was a woman—without very much interest. She seemed part of a dream from which I should presently wake to find myself back again in the Chinese house with Nikola. But I was to be disabused of this notion very speedily.

After a while the lady in the chair put down her book, rose, and came across to look at me. *Then it was that I realized a most astounding fact; she was none other than Miss Medwin, the girl I had rescued in Tientsin!* She touched my hand with her soft fingers, to see if I were feverish, I suppose, and then poured into a medicine-glass, which stood upon a table by my side, some doctor's physic. When she put it to my lips I drank it without protest and looked up at her.

"Don't leave me, Miss Medwin," I said, half expecting that, now I was awake, she would gradually fade away and disappear from my sight altogether.

"I am not going to leave you," she answered; "but I am indeed rejoiced to see that you recognise me again."

"What is the matter with me, and where am I?" I asked.

"You have been very ill," she answered, "but you are much better now. You are in my brother-in-law's house in Pekin."

I was completely mystified.

"In your brother-in-law's house," I repeated. "But how on earth did I get here? How long have I been here? and where is Nikola?"

"You have been here twelve days to-morrow," she answered; "you were taken ill in the city, and as you required careful nursing, your friend, Dr. Nikola, had you conveyed here. Where he is now I cannot tell you; we have only seen him once. For my own part I believe he has gone into the country, but in which direction, and when he will be back, I am afraid I have no idea. Now you have talked quite enough, you must try and go to sleep again."

I was too weak to disobey her, so I closed my eyes, and in a few minutes was in the land of Nod, once more.

Next day I was so much stronger that I was able to sit up and partake of more nourishing food, and, what was still more to my taste, I was able to have a longer conversation with my nurse. This did me more good than any doctor's physic, and at the end of half an hour I was a different man. The poor girl was still grieving for her father, and I noticed that the slightest reference to Tientsin flooded her eyes with tears. From what I gathered later the Consul had acted promptly and energetically, with the result that the ringleaders of the mob which had wrecked the house had been severely punished, while the man who had gone further and murdered the unfortunate missionary himself had paid the penalty of his crime with his life.

Miss Medwin spoke in heartfelt terms of the part I had played in the tragic affair, and it was easy to see that she was also most grateful to Nikola for the way in which he had behaved towards her. Acting on his employer's instructions, Williams had taken her in and had at once communicated with the Consul. Then when Mr. Medwin had been buried in the English

86

cemetery and the legal business connected with his murder was completed, trustworthy servants had been obtained, and she had journeyed to Pekin in the greatest comfort.

During the morning following she brought me some beef-tea, and, while I was drinking it, sat down beside my bed.

"I think you might get up for a little while this afternoon, Mr. Bruce," she said; "you seem so much stronger."

"I should like to," I answered. "I must do everything in my power to regain my strength. My illness has been a most unfortunate one, and I expect Nikola will be very impatient."

At this she looked a little mortified, I thought, and an instant later I saw what a stupid thing I had said.

"I am afraid you will think me ungrateful," I hastened to remark; "but believe me I was looking at it from a very different standpoint. I feel more gratitude to you than I can ever express. When I said my illness was unfortunate, I meant that at such a critical period of our affairs my being incapacitated from work was most inconvenient. You do not think that I am not properly sensible of your kindness, do you?"

As I spoke I assumed possession of her hand, which was hanging down beside her chair. She blushed a little and lowered her eyes.

"I am very glad we were able to take you in," she answered. "I assure you my brother and sister were most anxious to do so, when they heard what a service you had rendered me. But, Mr. Bruce, I want to say something to you. You talk of this critical position in your affairs. You told me in Tientsin that if you continued the work upon which you were embarking you 'might never come out of it alive.' Is it quite certain that you *must* go on with it—that you *must* risk your life in this way?"

"I regret to say it is. I have given my word and I cannot draw back. If you only knew how hard it is for me to say this I don't think you would try to tempt me."

"But it seems to me so wicked to waste your life in this fashion."

"I have always wasted my life," I answered, rather bitterly. "Miss Medwin, you don't know what a derelict I am. I wonder if you would think any the worse of me if I told you that when I took up this matter upon which I am now engaged I was in abject destitution, and mainly through my own folly? I am afraid I am no good for anything but getting into scrapes and wriggling my way out of them again."

"I expect you hardly do yourself justice," she answered. "I cannot believe that you are as unfortunate as you say."

As she spoke there was a knock at the door, and in response to my call "come in," a tall handsome man entered the room. He bore the unmistakable impress of a missionary, and might have been anything from thirty to forty years of age.

"Well, Mr. Bruce," he said cheerily, as he came over to the bed and held out his hand, "I am glad to hear from my sister that you are progressing so nicely. I should have come in to see you, but I have been away from home. You have had a sharp touch of fever, and, if you will allow me to say so, I think you are a lucky man to have got over it so satisfactorily."

"I have to express my thanks to you," I said, "for taking me into your house; but for your care I cannot imagine what would have become of me."

"Oh, you mustn't say anything about that," answered Mr. Benfleet, for such was his name. "We English are only a small community in Pekin, and it would be indeed a sorry thing if we did not embrace chances of helping each other whenever they occur."

As he said this I put my hand up to my head. Immediately I was confronted with a curious discovery. When I was taken ill I was dressed as a Chinaman, wore a pigtail, and had my skin stained a sort of pale mahogany. What could my kind friends have thought of my disguise?

It was not until later that I discovered that I had been brought to the house in complete European attire, and that when Nikola had called upon Mr. and Mrs. Benfleet to ask them to take me in he had done so clad in orthodox morning dress and wearing a solar topee upon his head.

"Gladys tells me you are going to get up this afternoon," said Mr. Benfleet. "I expect it will do you good. If I can be of any service to you in your dressing I hope you will command me."

I thanked him, and then, excusing himself on the plea that his presence was required at the mission-house, he bade me good-bye and left the room.

I was about to resume my conversation with Miss Medwin, but she stopped me.

"You must not talk any more," she said with a pretty air of authority. "I am going to read to you for half an hour, and then I shall leave you to yourself till it is time for tiffin. After that I will place your things ready for you, and you must get up."

She procured a book, and seating herself by the window, opened it and began to read. Her voice was soft and musical, and she interpreted the author's meaning with considerable ability. I am afraid, however, I took but small interest in the story; I was far too deeply engaged watching the expressions chasing each other across her face, noting the delicate shapeliness and whiteness of the hands that held the book, and the exquisite symmetry of the little feet and ankles that peeped beneath her dress. I think she must have suspected something of the sort, for she suddenly looked up in the middle of a passage which otherwise would have monopolized her whole attention. Her heightened colour and the quick way in which the feet slipped back beneath their covering confirmed this notion. She continued her reading, it is true, but there was not the same evenness of tone as before, and once or twice I noticed that the words were rather slurred over, as if the reader were trying to think of two things at one and the same time. Presently she shut the book with a little snap and rose to her feet.

"I think I must go now and see if I can help my sister in her work," she said hurriedly.

"Thank you so much for reading to me," I answered. "I have enjoyed it very much."

Whether she believed what I said or not I could not tell, but she smiled and looked a little conscious, as if she thought there might possibly be another meaning underlying my remark. After that I was left to myself for nearly an hour. During that time I surrendered myself to my own thoughts. Some were pleasant, others were not; but there was one conclusion to which I inevitably, however much I might digress, returned. That conclusion was that of all the girls I had ever met, Miss Gladys Medwin was by far the most adorable. She seemed to possess all the graces and virtues with which women are endowed, and to have the faculty of presenting them to the best advantage. I could not help seeing that my period of convalescence was likely to prove a very pleasant one, and you will not blame me, I suspect, if I registered a vow to make the most of it. How long I should be allowed to remain with them it was impossible for me to say. Nikola, my Old Man of the Sea, might put in an appearance at any moment, and then I should be compelled to bid my friends good-bye in order to plunge once more into his mysterious affairs.

When tiffin was finished I dressed myself in the garments which had been put out for me, and as soon as my toilet was completed took Mr. Benfleet's arm and proceeded to a terrace in the garden at the back of the house. Here chairs had been placed for us, and we sat down. I looked about me, half expecting to find Miss Medwin waiting for us, but she did not put in an appearance for some considerable time. When she did, she expressed herself as pleased to see me about again, and then went across to where a little Chinese dog was lying in the sunshine at the foot of a big stone figure. Whether she was always as fond of the little cur I cannot say, but the way she petted and caressed it on this particular occasion would have driven most men mad with jealousy. I don't know that I am in any way a harsh man with animals, but I am afraid if I had been alone and that dog had come anywhere near me I should have been tempted to take a stick to him, and to have treated him to one of the finest beatings he had ever enjoyed in his canine existence.

Presently she looked up, and, seeing that I was watching her, returned to where we sat, uttered a few commonplaces, more than half of which were addressed to her brother-in-law, and finally made an excuse and returned to the house. To say that I was disappointed would scarcely be the truth; to describe myself as woefully chagrined would perhaps be nearer the mark. Had I offended her, or was this the way of women? I had read in novels that it was their custom, if they thought they had been a little too prodigal of their favours whilst a man was in trouble, to become cold and almost distant to him when he was himself again. If this were so, then her action on this particular occasion was only in the ordinary course of things, and must be taken as such. That I was in love I will not attempt to deny; it was, however; the first time I had experienced the fatal passion, and, like measles caught in later life, it was doubly severe. For this reason the treatment to which I had just been subjected was not, as may be expected, of a kind calculated to make my feelings easier.

Whether Mr. Benfleet thought anything I cannot say, he certainly said nothing to me upon the subject. If, however, my manner, after Miss Medwin's departure did not strike him as peculiar, he could not have been the clear-headed man of the world his Pekin friends believed him. All I know is that when I returned to the house, I was about as irritable a piece of man-flesh as could have been found in that part of Asia.

But within the hour I was to be treated to another example of the strange contrariness of the feminine mind. No sooner had I arrived in the house than everything was changed. It was hoped that I had not caught a fresh cold; the most comfortable chair was set apart for my use, and an unnecessary footstool was procured and placed at my feet. Altogether I was the recipient of as many attentions and as much insinuated sympathy as I had been subjected to coldness before. I did not know what to make of it; however, under its influence, in less than half an hour I had completely thawed, and my previous ill-temper was forgotten for good and all.

Next day I was so much stronger that I was able to spend the greater part of my time in the garden. On this occasion, both Mr. and Mrs. Benfleet being otherwise engaged, Miss Medwin was good enough to permit me a considerable amount of her company. You may be sure I made the most of it, and we whiled the time away chatting pleasantly on various subjects.

At tiffin, to which I sat up for the first time, it was proposed that during the afternoon we should endeavour to get as far as the Great Wall, a matter of a quarter of a mile's walk. Accordingly, as soon as the meal was over, we set off. The narrow streets were crowded with coolies, springless private carts, sedan chairs, ponies but little bigger than St. Bernard dogs, and camels, some laden with coal from the Western Hills, and others bearing brick-tea from Pekin away up into the far north. Beggars in all degrees of loathsomeness, carrying the scars of almost every known ailment upon their bodies, and in nine cases out of ten not only able but desirous of presenting us with a replica of the disease, swarmed round us, and pushed and jostled us as we walked. Add to this the fact that at least once in every few yards we were assailed with scornful cries and expressions that would bring a blush to the cheek of the most blasphemous coalheaver in existence, accompanied by gestures which made my hands itch to be upon the faces of those who practised them. Mix up with all this the sights and smells of the foulest Eastern city you can imagine, add to it the knowledge that you are despised and hated by the most despicable race under the sun, fill up whatever room is left with the dust that lies on a calm day six inches deep upon the streets, and in a storm—and storms occur on an average at least three times a week—covers one from head to foot with a coating of the vilest impurity, you will have derived but the smallest impression of what it means to take a walk in the Streets of Pekin. To the Englishman who has never travelled in China this denunciation may appear a little extravagant. My regret, however, is that personally I do not consider it strong enough.

Not once but a hundred times I found good reason to regret having brought Miss Medwin out. But, thank goodness, we reached the Wall at last.

Having once arrived there, we seated ourselves on a bastion, and looked down upon the city. It was an extraordinary view we had presented to us. From the Wall we could see the Chien-Men, or Great Gate; to the north lay the Tartar city. Just below us was a comparatively small temple, round which a multitude of foot-passengers, merchants, coolies, carts, camels, ponies, private citizens, beggars, and hawkers, pushed and struggled. Over our heads rose the two great towers, which form part of the Wall itself, while to right and left, almost as far as the eye could reach, and seeming to overlap each other in endless confusion, were the roofs of the city, covered, in almost every instance, with a quantity of decaying brown grass, and in many cases having small trees and shrubs growing out of the interstices of the stones themselves. Away in the distance we could see the red wall of the "Forbidden City," in other words, the Imperial Palace; on another side was the Great Bell Tower, with the Great Drum Tower near it, and farther still the roofs of the Llamaserai. The latter, as you will suppose, had a particular attraction for me, and once having seen them, I could hardly withdraw my eyes.

When we had examined the view and were beginning to contemplate making our way home again, I turned to my companion and spoke the thoughts which were in my mind.

"I suppose, now that I am well again, I shall soon have to be leaving you," I began. "It cannot surely be very long before I hear from Nikola."

She was quiet for a moment, and then said:

"You mustn't be angry with me, Mr. Bruce, if I tell you that I do not altogether like your friend. He frightens me."

"Why on earth should he?" I asked, as if it were a most unusual effect for Nikola to produce. Somehow I did not care to tell her that her opinion was shared by almost as many people as knew him.

"I don't know why I fear him," she answered, "unless it is because he is so different from any other man I have ever met. Don't laugh at me if I tell you that I always think his eyes are like those of a snake, so cold and passionless, yet seeming to look you through and through, and hold you fascinated until he withdraws them again. I never saw such eyes in my life before, and I hope I never may again."

"And yet he was very kind to you."

"I can't forget that," she answered, "and it makes me seem so ungrateful; but one cannot help one's likes and dislikes, can one?"

Here I came a little closer to her.

"I hope, Miss Medwin, you have not conceived such a violent antipathy to me?" I said.

She began to pick at the mud between the great stones on which we were sitting.

"No, I don't think I have," she answered softly, seeming to find a source of interest in the movements of a tiny beetle which had come out of a hole, and was now making its way towards us.

"I am glad of that," I replied; "I should like you to think well of me."

"I am sure I do," she answered. "Think how much I owe to you. Oh, that dreadful night! I shall never be able to drive the horror of it out of my mind. Have you forgotten it?"

I saw that she was fencing with me and endeavouring to divert the conversation to a side issue. This I was not going to permit. I looked into her face, but she turned away and stared at a cloud of dun-coloured dust that was rising on the plain behind.

"Miss Medwin," I said, "I suppose into the life of every man there must, sooner or later, come one woman who will be all the world to him. Gladys, can you guess what I am going to say?"

Once more she did not answer; but the unfortunate beetle, who had crawled unnoticed within reach of her foot, received his death-blow. And yet at ordinary times she was one of the kindest and most gentle of her sex. This significant little action showed me more than any words could have done how perturbed her feelings were.

"I was going to say," I continued, "that at last a woman—the one woman, of all others—has come into *my* life. Are you glad to hear it?"

"How can I be if I do not know her?" she protested feebly.

"If *you* do not," I said, "then nobody else does. Gladys, *you* are that woman. I know I have no right to tell you this, seeing what my present position is, but God knows I cannot help it. You are dearer to me than all the world; I have loved you since I first saw you. Can you love me a little in return? Speak your mind freely, tell me exactly what is in your heart, and, come what may, I will abide by your decision."

She was trembling violently, but not a word passed her lips. Her face was very pale, and she seemed to find a difficulty in breathing, but at any cost I was going to press her for an answer. I took her hand.

"What have you to say to me, Gladys?"

"What *can* I say?"

"Say that you love me," I answered.

"I love you," she answered, so softly that I could scarcely hear the words.

And then, in the face of all Pekin, I kissed her on the lips.

Once in most men's lives—and for that reason I suppose in most women's also—there comes a certain five minutes when they understand exactly what unalloyed happiness means—a five minutes in their little spans of existence when the air seems to ring with joy-bells, when time stands still, and there is no such thing as care. That was how I felt at the moment of which I am writing. I loved and *was* loved; but almost before I had time to realize my happiness a knowledge of my real position sprang up before my eyes, and I was cast down into the depths again. What right had I, I asked myself, to tell a girl that I loved her, when it was almost beyond the bounds of possibility that I could ever make her my wife? None at all. I had done a cruel thing, and now I must go forward into the jaws of death, leaving behind me all that could make life worth living, and with the knowledge that I had brought pain into the one life of all others I desired to be free from it. True, I did not doubt but that if I appealed to Nikola he would let me off my bargain, but would that be fair when I had given my word that I would go on with him? No, there was nothing for it but for me to carry out my promise and trust to Fate to bring me safely back again to the woman I loved.

The afternoon was fast slipping by, and it was time for us to be thinking about getting home. I was disposed to hurry, for I had no desire to take a lady through the streets of Pekin after dusk. They, the streets, were bad enough in the daytime, at night they were ten times worse. We accordingly descended from the Wall, and in about ten minutes had reached the Benfleets' bungalow once more.

By the time we entered the house I had arrived at a determination. As an honourable man there were only two courses open to me: one was to tell Mr. Benfleet the state of my affections, the other to let Gladys firmly understand that, until I returned—if return I did—from the business for which I had been engaged, I should not consider her bound to me in any shape or form. Accordingly, as soon as the evening meal was finished, I asked the missionary if he could permit me five minutes' conversation alone. He readily granted my request, but not, I thought, without a little cloud upon his face. We passed into his study, which was at the other end of the building, and when we got there he bade me take a seat, saying as he did so:

"Well, Mr. Bruce, what is it you have to say to me?"

Now I don't think I am a particularly nervous man, but I will confess to not feeling at my ease in this particular situation. I cast about me for a way to begin my explanation, but for the life of me I could find none that suited me.

"Mr. Benfleet," I said at last in desperation, "you will probably be able to agree with me when I assert that you know very little about me."

"I think I can meet you there," said the clergyman with a smile. "If I am to be plain with you, I will admit that I know *very* little about you."

"I could wish that you knew more."

"For what reason?"

"To be frank, for a very vital one. You will understand when I tell you that I proposed to your sister-in-law, Miss Medwin, this afternoon."

"I must confess I thought you would." he said. "There have been signs and wonders in the land, and though Mrs. Benfleet and I live in Pekin, we are still able to realize what the result is likely to be when a man is as attentive to a girl as you have been to my sister-in-law of late."

"I trust you do not disapprove?"

"Am I to say what I think?"

"By all means. I want you to be perfectly candid."

"Then I am afraid I must say that I *do* disapprove."

"You have, of course, a substantial reason?"

"I don't deny it is one that time and better acquaintance might possibly remove. But first let us consider the light in which you stand to us. Until a fortnight or so ago, neither I, my wife, nor Miss Medwin were aware that there was such a person in the world. But you were ill, and we took you in, knowing nothing, remember, as to your antecedents. You will agree with me, I think, that an English gentleman who figures in Chinese costume, and does not furnish a reason for it, and who perambulates China with a man who is very generally feared, is not the sort of person one would go out of one's way to accept for the husband of a sister one loves. But I am not a bigoted man, and I know that very often when a man has been a bit wild a good woman will do him more good than ever the Archbishop of Canterbury and all his clergy could effect. If you love her you will set yourself to win her, and, in sporting parlance, this is a race that will have to be won by waiting. If you think Gladys is worth working and waiting for, you will do both, and because I like what I have seen of you I will give you every opportunity in my power of achieving your end. If you don't want to work or to wait for her, then you will probably sheer off after this conversation, in which case we shall be well rid of you. And vice versa. One thing, however, I think would be prudent, and that is that you should leave my house to-morrow morning."

For the whole of the time that I was absent with Nikola we would not communicate in any way. By this means we should be able to find out the true state of our own minds, and whether our passion was likely to prove lasting or not.

"But oh! how I wish that I knew what you are going to do," said Gladys, when we had discussed the matter in all its bearings save one.

"I am afraid that is a thing I cannot tell even you," I answered. "I am hemmed in on every side by promises. You must trust me, Gladys."

"It isn't that I don't trust you," she said, with almost a sob in her voice. "I am thinking of the dangers you will run, and of the long time that will elapse before I shall hear of you or see you again."

"I'm afraid that cannot be helped," I said. "If I had only met you before I embarked on this wild-goose chase things might have been arranged differently, but now I have made my bed and must lie upon it."

"As I said this afternoon, I am so afraid of Nikola."

"But you needn't be. I get on very well with him, and as long as I play fair by him he will play fair by me. You might tremble for my safety if we were enemies, but so long as we remain friends I assure you you need have no fear."

"And you are to leave us to-morrow morning?"

"Yes, darling, I *must* go! As we are placed towards each other, more than friends, and yet in the eyes of the world, less than lovers, it would hardly do for me to remain here. Besides, I expect Nikola will be requiring my services. And now, before I forget it, I want you to give me the ring I gave you in Tientsin."

She left the room to return with it in a few moments. I took it from her and, raising her hand, placed it upon her finger, kissing her as I did so.

"I will wear it always," she said; as she spoke, Mrs. Benfleet entered the room. A moment later I caught the sound of a sharp, firm footstep in the passage that was unpleasantly familiar to me. Then Nikola entered and stood before us.

Chapter 8

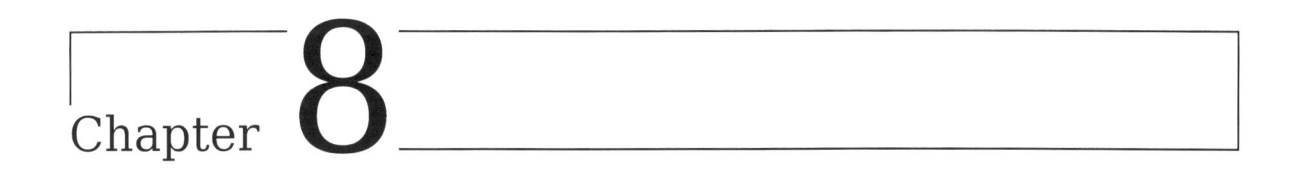

How Prendergast Succeeded

To say that I was surprised at Nikola's sudden entry into the Benfleets' drawing-room would be to put too tame a construction upon my feelings. Why it should have been so I cannot say, but Nikola's appearance invariably seemed to cause me astonishment. And curiously enough I was not alone in this feeling; for more than one person of my acquaintance has since owned to having experienced the same sensation. What it was about the man that produced it, it would be difficult to say. At any rate this much is certain, it would be impossible for Nikola to say or do a common-place thing. When he addressed you, you instinctively felt that you must answer him plainly and straightforwardly, or not at all; an evasive reply was not suited to the man. It occurred to you, almost unconsciously, that he was entitled to your best service, and it is certain that whether he was worthy or not he invariably got it. I have seen Nikola take in hand one of the keenest and, at the same time, most obstinate men in China, ask of him a favour which it would have been madness to expect the fellow to grant, talk to Kirn in his own quiet but commanding fashion, and in less than ten minutes have the matter settled and the request granted.

One other point struck me as remarkable in this curious individual's character, and that was that he always seemed to know, before you spoke, exactly what sort of answer you were going to return to his question, and as often as not he would anticipate your reply. In my own case I soon began to feel that I might spare myself the trouble of answering at all.

Having entered the room, he crossed to where Gladys was sitting and, bowing as he took her hand, wished her good-evening. Then turning to me, and accompanying his remark with one of his indescribable smiles, he said—

"My dear Bruce, I am rejoiced to see you looking so well. I had expected to find a skeleton, and to my delight I am confronted with a man. How soon do you think you will be fit to travel again?"

"I am ready as soon as you are," I answered, but not without a sinking in my heart as I looked across to Gladys and realized that the moment had indeed come for parting.

"I am indeed glad to hear it," he answered, "for time presses. Do you think you can accompany me in a few minutes? You can?—that's right. Now, if he will permit me, I should like to have a little talk with Mr. Benfleet, and then we must be off."

He went out of the room, accompanied by our hostess, and for ten minutes or so Gladys and I were left alone.

I will give you no description of what happened during that last interview. Such a parting is far too sacred to be described. It is enough to say that when it was over I joined Nikola in the verandah and we left the house together. With the shutting of the front door behind us all the happiness of my life seemed to slip away from me. For nearly five minutes I walked by my companion's side in silence, wondering whether I should ever again see those to whom I had just said good-bye. Nikola must have had some notion of what was passing in my mind, for he turned to me and said confidentially—

"Cheer up, Bruce! we shall be back again before you know where you are, and remember you will then be a comparatively rich man. Miss Medwin is a girl worth waiting for, and if you will allow me to do so, I will offer you my congratulations."

"How do you know anything about it?" I asked in surprise.

"Haven't I just seen Mr. Benfleet?" he answered.

"But surely he didn't tell you?"

"It was exactly what I went in to see him about," said Nikola. "You are my friend, and I owe you a good turn; for that reason, I wanted to try and make things as smooth for you as I could. To tell the truth, I am glad this has happened; it will make you so much the more careful. There's nothing like love—though I am not a believer in it as a general rule—for making a man mindful of his actions."

"It is very good of you to take so much trouble about my affairs," I said warmly.

"Not at all," he answered. "There can be no question of trouble between two men situated as we are. But now let us march along as quickly as we can. I have a lot to talk to you about, and we have many preparations to make before to-morrow morning."

"But where are we going? This is not the way back to the house in which I was taken ill."

"Of course not," said Nikola. "We're going to another place—the property of an Englishman of my acquaintance. There we shall change into our Chinese dresses again."

"This, then, will probably be our last walk in European costume?"

"For many months at any rate."

After this we again walked some time without speaking, Nikola revolving in his mind his interminable intrigues, I suppose; I thinking of the girl I had left behind me. At last, however, we reached the house to which we had been directing our steps, and, on knocking upon the door, were at once admitted. It was a tiny place, situated in a side street leading out of a busy thoroughfare. The owner was an Englishman, whose business often necessitated his taking long journeys into the interior; he was a bachelor, and, as I gathered from Nikola, by no means particular as to his associates, nor, I believe, did he bear any too good a reputation in Pekin. Before I had been five minutes in his company I had summed the man up exactly, though I could not for the life of me understand why Nikola had chosen him. That he was afraid of Nikola was self-evident, and that Nikola intended he should be was equally certain. To cover his nervousness the fellow, whose name was Edgehill, affected a jocular familiarity which intensified rather than concealed what he was so anxious to hide.

"You're not looking quite up to the mark, Mr. Bruce," he said, when I was introduced to him; then, with a leer, he imitated a man pulling a cork and continued—

"Eyes bright, hands shaky—the old thing. I suppose?"

"I have been down with fever," I answered.

"Too much Pekin air," he replied. "This beastly country would make an Egyptian mummy turn up his toes. But never fear, keep your pecker up, and you'll pull through yet."

I thanked him for this assurance, and then turned to Nikola, who had seated himself in a long cane chair, and, with his finger-tips pressed together, was staring hard at him. Something seemed to have ruffled his feathers. When he spoke it was distinctly and very deliberately, as if he desired that every word he uttered should be accepted by the person to whom it was addressed at its full value.

"And so, Mr. Edgehill, after my repeated warnings you have informed your Chinese friends that you have a visitor?"

The man stepped back as if he had received a blow, his face flushed crimson and immediately afterwards became deathly pale. He put out his hand to the wall behind him as if for support; I also noticed that he drew such deep breaths that the glasses on the sideboard beside him rattled against each other.

"Your two Chinese friends," said Nikola slowly and distinctly, "must have placed a peculiar value upon the information with which you were able to furnish them if they were willing to pay so high a price for it."

The man tried to speak, but without success. All his bounce had departed; now he was only a poor trembling coward who could not withdraw his eyes from that calm but cruel face that seemed to be looking into his very heart.

Then Nikola's manner changed, and he sprang to his feet with sudden energy.

"You dog!" he cried, and the intensity of his tone cut like a knife. "You pitiful hound! So you thought you could play Judas with me, did you? How little you know Dr. Nikola after all. Now listen, and remember every word I say to you, for I shall only speak once. To-night, at my dictation, you will write a letter to your Chinese friends, and to-morrow morning at six o'clock you will saddle your horse and set off for Tientsin. Arriving there you will go to Mr. Williams, whose address you know, and will tell him that I have sent you. You will say that you are to remain in his house, as his prisoner, for one calendar month; and if you dare to communicate with one single person concerning me or my affairs during that or any other time, I'll have your throat cut within half an hour of your doing so. Can it be possible that you think so little of me as to dare to pit your wits against mine? You fool! When you get out of my sight go down on your knees, and thank Providence that I haven't killed you

102

at once for your presumption. Do you remember Hanotat? You do? Well, then, take care my friend that I do not treat you as I did him. Like you he thought himself clever, but eventually he preferred to blow his brains out rather than fight me further. You have been warned, remember. Now go and prepare for your journey. I will communicate with Williams myself. If you are not in his house by breakfast time on Thursday morning it will save you expense, for you will never have the appetite for another meal."

Not a word did the man utter in reply, but left the room directly he was ordered, looking like a ghost.

When he had gone I turned to Nikola, for my astonishment exceeded all bounds, and said—

"How on earth did you know that he had given any information about us?"

In reply Nikola stooped and picked up from the floor two small stubs. On examination they proved to be the remains of two Chinese cigarettes. He then went across the room to a small curtained shelf, from which he produced a brandy bottle. Three glasses, all of which had been used, stood by the bottle, which was quite empty. Having pointed out these things to me he went back to his chair and sat down.

"Edgehill," he explained, "doesn't drink brandy, except when he has company; even then he takes very little. Before I left the house this evening to fetch you I took the precaution to look behind the curtain. That bottle was then more than three parts full, and I am quite certain that there were no ends of Chinese cigarettes upon the floor, because I looked about. Before that I had noticed that two men were watching the house from across the way. As I went down the street I picked up the end of a cigarette one of them had been smoking. There it is; you can compare them if you like. The man's manner when he let us in added another link to the chain of evidence, and his face, when I asked him the first question, told me the rest. Of course it was all guess-work; but I have not learned to read faces for nothing. At any rate you saw for yourself how true my accusation proved."

"But what do you think the man can have told them?" I asked. "And who could the people have been who questioned him?"

"He can't have told them very much," Nikola replied, "because there wasn't much to tell; but who the men could have been I am quite unable even to conjecture. I distrust them on principle, that's all."

"But why did you send him to Williams?"

"To keep him out of the way of further mischief until we have had a fair start; also because I wanted to teach him a lesson. I may have occasion to use him at some future date, and a little bit of discipline of this sort will do him no harm. But now let us change the subject. I have something else I want to talk to you about. First see that there is no one at the door, and then bring your chair nearer to mine."

I tip-toed over to the door. After I had reached it I waited for a moment and then opened it suddenly. There was no one outside, so I came back again and drew my chair nearer to Nikola. He had taken a letter from his pocket, and was evidently preparing to read it to me. Before he did so, however, he said in a low voice—

"This communication is from Prendergast. It was brought to me by special messenger at midday to-day. If you will give me your attention I will read it to you. It is dated from Tientsin, and runs as follows:—

"'To **dr.** Nikola, pekin.

"'Dear sir—I have to inform you that on Thursday week last I received a telegram from Mr. Williams of this place bidding me come to him at once in order to negotiate some important business on your behalf. I had hardly received your wire before Mr. Eastover called upon me to say that he was also in receipt of a telegram to the same effect. Understanding that no time must be lost, within two hours of receiving the messages, we were on board the steamer *James Monaghan, en route* for Tientsin.

"'That place we reached in due course, and immediately reported our arrival to your agent, Mr. Williams, from whom we learned the nature of the work upon which we were to be employed. Its danger was quite apparent to us, and at first, I must confess, the difficulties that surrounded it struck me as insurmountable. The Chief Priest of the Hankow Temple is a well-known personage, and very popular. His private life may almost be said to be nil. He never moves out unless he has a troop of people about him, while to attempt to get at him in his own town would only be to bring a mob of howling devils round our ears and ruin the whole enterprise beyond redemption. I immediately placed myself in communication with Chung-Yein, who fortunately was in Hankow at the time. It was through his agency we discovered that the priest—who, as you know, has resigned his office in the temple—was in the act of setting out upon a long journey.

"'As soon as I learned this I instructed Chung-Yein to endeavour to elicit the route. He did so, and informed me that the man proposed travelling by way of Hang-Chu and Fon-Ching to Tsan-Chu, thence up the Grand Canal by way of Tsing-Hai to Tientsin, whence it was said he was going to make his way on to Pekin. I examined a chart of the country very carefully, and also conferred with Mr. Williams and Mr. Eastover, who both agreed with me that any action which might be necessary should be contrived and carried out at Tsan-Chu, which, as you know, is a town a little below the point where the canal, running to Nans-Shing, joins the Yun-Liang-Ho river.

"'This settled, the next thing to be done was to endeavour to discover how the abduction of the priest could be effected. To suit your purposes we saw that it must be arranged in such a fashion that no scandal could possibly ensue. He would have to be abducted in such a manner that his followers would suppose he had left them of his own accord. But how to do this was a problem very difficult to work out. The man is old and exceedingly suspicious. He has a reputation for trusting nobody, and he invariably acts up to it. Unless, therefore, we could invent some really plausible excuse he would be almost impossible to catch, and foreseeing this I again called in Chung-Yein to my assistance. At any cost, I told him, he must manage to get into the priest's service, and once there to begin to ingratiate himself with his master to the very best of his ability. The time was so short that we dared not wait to cultivate an opportunity, but had to work in our chances, as they rose, to suit ourselves.

"'At great risk Chung-Yein managed to get himself appointed a member of the priest's travelling party. Once this was done his peculiar abilities soon brought him under his master's notice, and that end having been achieved the rest was easy.

"'Within three days of his arrival the household was broken up, and the priest, with a numerous retinue, commenced his journey. By the time they had travelled a hundred miles Chung-Yein was on very familiar terms with him; he discovered many means of adding to the priest's comfort, and during the march he was so assiduous in his attentions that his master began to place more and more trust in him. When they reached Fon-Ching he was advanced to the post of secretary, and then the plot which I had arranged was ready to be put into execution.

"'Little by little Chung-Yein dropped into his master's willing ears the news of a fortune which he assured him might be obtained with very little risk. The avaricious old man swallowed the bait only too readily, and when he had digested the letters which the astute Chung read him from time to time, and which were supposed to have been written by his cousin Quong-Ta, from Tsan-Chu, he was as good as caught.

"'After eight days of continuous travelling the company arrived at the entrance to the canal. Eastover and I had left Tientsin by this time, and had travelled post haste down to meet them. Once they were fairly installed at the principal inn Chung-Yein came to see me. He had arranged everything most carefully, it appeared, even to the extent of having it circulated among his fellow-servants that after leaving Tsan-Chu the high priest intended dispensing with their services and going on alone. It now only remained for us to arrange a meeting with him, and to have some means prepared whereby we might convey him across country, over the forty odd miles that separated Tsan-Chu from Chi-Kau-Ho, to where a junk was already waiting to receive him. While Eastover undertook the arrangement of this part of the business I drew up the plan which was to give us possession of the priest's person.

"'Chung-Yein was to represent to him that he was the unhappy possessor of a cousin who was a noted robber. By virtue of his evil habits he had accumulated great riches, but finding himself now likely to come within reach of the finger-tips of the law he was most anxious to purchase a friend who would stand by him in case of evil happening.

"'The greedy old priest, intending to ask a large share of the plunder for the favour accorded, consented to bestow his patronage upon the youth, and when he was brought to understand that his share of the transaction would amount to something like six thousand taels, his anxiety to obtain possession of the coin became more and more intense. He discussed the matter with Chung-Yein times out of number, and finally it was decided that that night they should proceed together to a certain house in the village, where he should interview the culprit and also receive his share of the gains.

"'As soon as I was made conversant with what had been arranged I pushed forward my plans, arranged with one of my own men to impersonate the cousin, and by the time dusk had fallen had everything in readiness. Relays of ponies were stationed at intervals along the road to the coast, and the skipper of the junk only waited to have his passenger aboard to weigh anchor and be off.

"'At eight o'clock, almost to the minute, the priest, disguised, and accompanied by Chung-Yein, appeared at the door.

"'They were admitted by the counterfeit cousin, who conducted them forthwith to the back of the house. Once in the room, negotiations were commenced, and the priest lost no time in severely reprimanding the young man for the evil life he had hitherto been leading. Then, that he might the better be able to understand what a nefarious career it had been, he demanded a glimpse of the profits that had accrued from it. They included a bag of dollars, a good selection of gold leaf, a quantity of English money, and a small bag of precious stones. All of these things had been prepared at considerable cost for his inspection.

"'His old eyes twinkled greedily as they fell upon this goodly store, and his enthusiasm rose as each successive bag was opened. When at last the contents of the bag of stones were spread out before him he forgot his priestly sanctity altogether in his delight and stooped to examine them. As he did so Chung-Yein sprang forward, and threw a noose over his head, a chloroformed sponge was clapped against his nose, while the spurious cousin pulled his heels from under him and threw him on his back upon the floor.

"'The anaesthetic did its work well, and in a short time the old gentleman was in our power. Half an hour later he was safely tied up in a chair, and was being deported as fast as his bearers could conduct him to Chi-Kau-Ho.

"'In the meantime Chung-Yein had returned to the inn, where he paid off the retinue and informed them that their master had received a sudden summons and had started up the canal for Tientsin alone. Then Eastover and myself mounted our ponies and followed the worthy priest to the sea.

"'Chi-Kau-Ho, which, as you know, is a place of abject poverty, and is only visited by junks bringing millet from Tientsin to exchange for fish, was the very place for our purpose. Fortunately it was high tide, and for that reason we were able to get our burden on board the junk without very much difficulty. At other times it is impossible for a boat drawing any depth of water at all to come within seven miles of the village. The bar, as doubtless you are aware, renders this impossible.

"'As soon as we had handed over the man to the skipper we returned to the shore. An hour later the vessel set sail, and by the time you receive this letter the Chief Priest of Hankow will in all probability be somewhere among the pirates of Along Bay. As his captors on board the junk have no respect for his creed, and he has no money upon his person to bribe them to set him ashore again, I think he will find it difficult to get back to the mainland. But to prevent anything of the sort occurring I have told the owner of the junk that if, on the 21st day of August, six months ahead, he conveys him to Michel Dugenne, who by that time will be in Formosa, he will receive £100 English in exchange for his person. I think this will suit your purpose.

"'As to our own movements, they were as follows.

"'Leaving Chi-Kau-Ho we chartered a junk and proceeded up the coast to Pea-Tang-Ho, thence making our way on pony back to Tientsin, at which place we arrived two days since. Chung-Yein I have rewarded with 2,000 dollars, and he is now on his way, as fast as he can travel, to Hong-Kong. He intends, I believe, to make for Singapore, where he will reside till all chance of trouble has blown over. I have taken the precaution to register his address in case we should require his services again. Should you desire to see either Mr. Eastover or myself, we will remain in Tientsin for a fortnight longer. After that Eastover purposes crossing to Japan, while I return to Hong-Kong, where I can always be heard of at the old address.

"'Trusting that the manner in which we have conducted this dangerous affair will be to your satisfaction, I have the honour to subscribe myself, your obedient servant,

"'William Prendergast.'

"Now," said Nikola as he folded up this precious document, "the coast is clear, and for the future I intend to be the Chief Priest of Hankow. During the time you have been ill I have been making a number of important inquiries, and I think I know pretty well the kind of course I shall have to steer. To-morrow morning I intend that we shall enter the Llamaserai, where it will be imperative that we have all our wits about us. A change *in* our dress will also be necessary, particularly in mine. The priest is an old man, and I must resemble him as nearly as possible."

"It will be a difficult character to support for so long. Do you think you are capable of it?"

He looked at me with one of his peculiar smiles.

"There was a time in my life," he said, "when I used to be a little uncertain as to my powers; since then I have taught myself to believe that if a man makes up his mind there is nothing in this world he cannot do. Yes, I shall manage it. You need have no fear on that score."

"I have no fear," I answered truthfully. "I have the most implicit faith in you."

"I am glad to hear it," said Nikola, "for you will want it all. Now let us retire to rest. At five o'clock we must begin to dress; at six I have to see that Edgehill starts for Tientsin."

Without more ado we procured blankets and stretched ourselves upon the floor. In less than five minutes I was asleep, dreaming that I was helping the priest of Hankow to abduct Nikola from the Llamaserai, where he had gone to deposit the stick that Wetherell had given him.

When I woke, it was to hear horse-hoofs clattering out of the yard. It was broad daylight, and on looking about me I discovered that Nikola was not in the room. Presently he entered.

"Edgehill has departed," he said, with a queer expression upon his face. "I have just seen him off. Somehow I think it will be a long day before he will attempt to play tricks with Dr. Nikola again."

Chapter 9

The Llamaserai

"Come," said Nikola, when the last sounds of Edgehill's departure had died away; "there is no time to lose; let us dress."

I followed him into an adjoining room, which, though somewhat larger than that in which we had hitherto sat, was even more poorly furnished. Here a number of dresses lay about on chairs, and from these Nikola chose two.

"The first thing to be considered," he said, as he seated himself on a chair and looked at me, "is that we have to change the form of our disguises in almost every particular. I have been thinking the matter most carefully out, and, as I said just now, we are going to be entirely different men. I shall be the Priest of Hankow, you will be his secretary. Here are your things; I should advise you to dress as quickly as you possibly can."

I took him at his word, and appropriating the garments he assigned to me, returned with them to the front room. At the end of a quarter of an hour I was no longer an Englishman. My dress was of the richest silk, figured and embroidered in every conceivable fashion, my shoulders were enclosed in a grey cloak of the finest texture, my pigtail was of extraordinary length and thickness, while my sandals and hat were of the most fashionable make. If my rank had been estimated by the gorgeousness of my attire and the value of the material, I might have been a Taotai of a small province, or secretary to some metropolitan dignitary. When I had dressed myself I sat down and waited for Nikola to make his appearance.

A short while later a tall gaunt Chinaman, certainly fifty years of age, upon the chin of whose weather-beaten countenance an ill-trimmed beard was beginning to show itself, came into the room, accompanied by a smaller man much bent with age. I was resolved not to be hoodwinked this time, so I said in

Chinese to the man who entered first, and who I estimated was nearer Nikola's size:

"You've not been long in getting ready."

"It would be folly to be slow," he answered; "we have much to do," and then without another word led the way down the passage towards the rear of the house. Arriving at the yard we discovered a perfect cavalcade drawn up. There were several led ponies, half a dozen mounted men, and about twice that number of hangers on.

"One word," I said, drawing Nikola, as I thought, on one side. "What part am I to play in this pageant?"

"Is there not some little mistake?" the man said. "For whom do you take me?"

"For my master," I answered.

"Then I'm afraid you have chosen the wrong man," he returned. "If you want Dr. Nikola, there he is mounting that pony yonder."

I could hardly believe my eyes. The second man resembled Nikola in no possible particular. He was old, thin, and nearly bent double. His face was wrinkled into a hundred lines, and his eyes were much sunken, as also were his cheeks. If this were Nikola he might have gone through the whole length and breadth of China without any fear of his identity being for one moment questioned. I went across to him, and, scarcely believing what I had been told, addressed him as follows:

"If you are Nikola," I said—"and I can hardly credit it—I want you to give me my instructions."

"You don't recognize me then?" he whispered. "I'm glad of that; I wanted to try you. I thought to myself, if he does not find me out it is scarcely likely that any one else will. Your own disguise is most excellent; I congratulate you upon it. With regard to your position, you are of course supposed to be my secretary. But I will give you a few points as we proceed. Now let us be starting."

"But first, who is the man whom I mistook for you?"

"He is a fellow for whom I sent to Tientsin while you were ill; and as I have taken some trouble to ensure his fidelity you need have no fear of his betraying us. He will only accompany us as far as the Llamaserai, and then, having posed as chief of my retinue, he will leave us and return to the coast. Now mount your animal and let us start."

I went back to my pony, and when I was in the saddle we filed slowly out of the gateway, down the crowded street and through the gates towards the Yung-Ho-Kung, or the great Llama temple. This enormous building, which has the reputation of being one of the most inaccessible places in China to Europeans, is located on the outskirts of the city, nearly five miles from the quarter in which Edgehill's house was situated.

Remembering its sinister reputation, you may imagine my sensations as we rode up to the first great gate. I could not help wondering what the Fates had in store for us inside. For all I knew to the contrary I might be destined never to see the world outside the walls again. It was not a cheering thought, and I tried to divert my attention from it by looking about me.

Strangely enough the first two gates were by no means hard to pass, but at the third the real difficulty began.

It was shut in our faces, and though we knew our coming had been observed by those inside, not a sign of any living soul presented itself. An awe-inspiring silence reigned in the great building, and for some time our servants hammered upon the door in vain. Then a shaven head appeared at a small grille and inquired our business.

Whether the answer he received was satisfactory or not I could not say, but seeing that it did not unbar the gate, Nikola rode forward and, leaning over in his saddle, said something in a low voice. The effect was magical: the doors flew open instantly. Then a man came forward and assisted Nikola to alight. He signed to me to do the same, and I accordingly dismounted beside him. As I did so a servant approached him and, greeting him with the utmost reverence, never daring to raise his eyes to his face, said something which I could not hear. When he had got through with it Nikola turned to me, and bade me pay off the men. I did so, and they immediately returned to the city by the way they had come. Then turning to the monk who was still waiting, Nikola said, pointing to me:

"This is my secretary. He is necessary to my well-being, so I beg that he may be allowed to enter with me." The monk nodded, and then the gate being opened wide we passed through it. Once inside we ascended, by means of a long flight of stone steps, to a courtyard, round which were a number of small stone rooms not unlike cells. In the centre stood an enormous wooden statue of Buddha which riveted the attention at once; the figure was at least seventy feet high, was covered with all sorts of beautiful ornamentation, and held an enormous flower resembling a lotus in either hand. On its head was a gold crown, and in each section of the latter I could discern a smaller image, reproducing the large one in every particular.

Above the cells, just described, were a series of long galleries, which were reached by stairs from the courtyard, and above them again rose roof after roof and tower after tower. From this terrace, if one may so call it, we passed on to another, the approach to which was guarded by two magnificent bronze lions. Making our way through many temples, each decorated with Chinese hangings, to say nothing of ornaments in gold, silver, ivory, bronze and enamel, we came at last to one where we were requested to wait while our guide, who was evidently a person in authority, went off in search of the High Priest.

For nearly twenty minutes we remained alone together. The place was eerie in the extreme. The wind, entering by the windows on either side, rustled the long silken hangings; there was an intolerable odour of joss-sticks; and, as if this were not enough, we had the pleasure of knowing that we were only impostors, dependent upon our wits for our lives. If but one suspicion entered the minds of those we were deceiving, we might consider ourselves as good as dead men. In such an enormous building, unvisited by foreigners, and owning hardly any allegiance—if indeed such a feeble reed could help us—to the Emperor of China, the news of our death would excite no concern, and we would be as completely lost as the bubble which rises majestically from a child's pipe, only to burst unnoticed in mid-air.

As I watched the morning light playing among the hangings and listened to the booming of a gong which came to us from some distant part of the building, I could not help thinking of the sweet girl to whom I had plighted my troth, and who at that very moment might also be thinking of me and wondering how I fared. That I did not deserve such consideration on her part was only too certain, for surely never in the history of the world had a man embarked upon a more foolish undertaking. Columbus in his lonely little ship ploughing its way across the unknown ocean in search of a continent, the existence of which at times *he* must almost have doubted himself, was not one whit less desperate than we were at that moment. Franklin amid the ice, unconscious whether another week might not find his vessel ground to powder between the ice floes, and himself floating in the icy water, was not one tittle nearer death than we were while we waited for an audience with the father abbot of this most awesome monastery.

At the end of the twenty minutes my ears—which of late had been preternaturally sharp—detected the pattering of sandalled feet upon the stone staircase at the further end of the room. Next moment three figures appeared, two of whom were leading a third between them. The supporters were men in the prime of life. The third must have been at least eighty years of age. One glance was sufficient to show me that he was not a pure Mongol, but had probably Thibetan blood in his veins. Both he and his monks were attired in the usual coarse dress of the Buddhist priests, their heads being as destitute of hair as a billiard ball.

Having brought the old fellow down to the bottom of the stairs, the young men left him there, and returned up the steps again. Then it was that we made the discovery that, besides being old and infirm, the High Priest of the Llamaserai was nearly blind. He stood perfectly still for a moment after he had entered, a queer trembling figure, dressed in dingy yellow. Finally, with hands outstretched, he came towards where we stood.

"I beg you to tell me," he said, "who you are, and how it comes about that you thus crave our hospitality?"

He put the question in a high tremulous voice, more like a woman's than a man's.

"I am the Priest of the Temple of Hankow," said Nikola gravely. "And I am here for reasons that are best known to those who called me."

"If it is as you say, how shall I know you?"

"Is the moon no longer aware that there are little stars?" asked Nikola, speaking with a perfection of accent that no Chinaman living could have excelled.

"Yea, but the dawn makes all equal," replied the old man. "But if you be he whom we have expected these last three weeks, there are other means whereby you can assure us of the truth of what you say."

Nikola slipped his right hand inside his long outer jacket and drew from his pocket the tiny stick he had obtained from Wetherell, and handed it to the old man. No sooner had he received it, and run his fingers over the quaint Chinese characters engraved upon it, than the old fellow's demeanour changed entirely. Dropping upon his knees he kissed the hem of Nikola's dress.

"It is sufficient. I am satisfied that my lord is one of the Masters of Life and Death. If my lord will be pleased to follow his servant, accommodation shall be found for him."

As he spoke he fumbled his way towards the staircase by which he had entered the room. Nikola signed to me to follow, and in single file we made our way to the room above. As we went I could not help noticing the solidity of the building. The place might have withstood a siege with the greatest ease, for the walls were in many cases two feet, and in not a few nearly three feet thick.

The stairs conducted us to a long passage, on either side of which were small rooms or cubicles. Leaving these behind us, we approached another flight of steps which led to the highest floor of the building. At the end of a long corridor was a small ante-chamber hung round with dark coloured silks, just as we had seen hi the great hall below. From this we entered another nearly twice the size, which was lighted with three narrow windows. From one of these, I afterwards discovered, a good view of the city of Pekin was obtainable.

As soon as we were safely inside, the High Priest assured us, in a quavering voice, that everything we might find in his humble dwelling was at our disposal, and that we might consider his rooms our home during our stay in the monastery. Then, with another expression of his deep respect, he left us, presumably to see that some sort of meal was prepared for us. As soon as the sound of his steps had died away Nikola leaped to his feet.

"So far so good," he cried. "He does not suspect us you see. We have played our parts to perfection. Tomorrow, if I can only get him into the proper frame of mind, I'll have the rest of the information I want out of him before he can turn round."

For the rest of that day we amused ourselves perambulating the building, walking slowly with dejected bearings whenever we met any of the monks, greeting the various shrines with deepest reverences, prostrating ourselves at the altars, and in every way, so far as lay in our power, creating the impression that, in the practices of our faith, we were without our equals. At five o'clock we participated in the usual evening service held in the great hall, and for the first time saw the monks assembled together. A more disreputable crew, I can unhesitatingly assert, I had never seen before. They were of all ages and of all ranks, but, so far as I could tell, there was not a face amongst them that did not suggest the fact that its owner was steeped to the eyebrows in sensuality and crime. Taken altogether, I very much doubt if, for general blackguardism, their equal could have been found in the length and breadth of Asia. Also I could not help speculating as to what sort of a chance we should stand if our secret should happen to be discovered, and we were compelled to run the gauntlet of the inmates. The service was not a long one, and in something under half an hour we were back in our rooms again. Then Nikola was summoned to an interview with the High Priest, and, while he was away, I wandered downstairs and strolled about the courtyards.

It was the time of the evening meal, and those monks who had already dined, were lolling about smoking, and gossiping over the affairs of the day. What they thought of my presence there I could not tell, but from one or two remarks I heard it struck me that I was not regarded with any too much favour.

At the end of one of the courtyards, that in fact in which we had noticed the large statue of Buddha, there was a well, and round the coping were seated quite a dozen men. Their quaintly coloured garments, their shaven heads and their curiously constructed pipes, backed by the rosy glow of the sunset, constituted a most picturesque and effective group. I crossed towards them, and bowing to the party, seated myself in a place which had just been vacated.

One of those present was an accomplished story-teller, and was in the middle of a lengthy narrative bristling with gods, devils, virtuous men, and reverend ancestors, when I sat down to listen. After he had finished I applauded vigorously, and being desirous of ingratiating myself with the company, called for silence and commenced a tale myself. Fortunately it was received with considerable favour, but I could not help noticing that my success was not very palatable to the previous narrator. He had been watching me ever since I joined the circle, and it struck me as I proceeded with my story that his interest increased. Then, like a flash, the knowledge dawned upon me that I had seen him before. As I remembered the circumstance a cold sweat of fear burst out upon me, my voice shook under my emotion, and in trying to think what I had better do, I lost the thread of my narrative. I saw my listeners look up in surprise, and an expression of malignant satisfaction came into my rival's face. Instantly I pulled myself together and tried to continue as if nothing out of the common had occurred. But it was too late; I had aroused suspicion, and for some reason or another the men had come to the conclusion that all was not right. How bitterly I regretted having joined the circle at all I need not say! But it was no use crying over spilt milk, so after awhile I made an excuse and left them to their own devices, returning to the rooms set apart for the use of Dr. Nikola and myself. Fortunately he was alone. Not knowing, however, who might be about, I did not address him at once, but sat down near the door and waited for him to speak. He very soon did so.

"I have been wanting you," he said rather sharply. "What have you been doing this hour past?"

"Wandering about the building," I answered, "and at the same time discovering something which is the very reverse of pleasant."

"What do you mean," he asked, his eyes—for he had removed his spectacles—glittering like those of a snake.

"I mean that there is a man in this monastery whom I have met before," I said, "and under very unpleasant circumstances."

"Do you think he recognizes you?"

"I hope not," I answered; "but I fear he does."

"Where did you meet him, and why do you say 'unpleasant'?"

"It was in Canton," I answered, "and this fellow tried to break into my house. But I caught him in time, and in the fight that followed he stabbed me in the wrist. I carry the mark to this day. Look at it for yourself. He would have been executed for it had not the magistrate before whom he was brought possessed a personal grudge against me and allowed him to escape."

"Let me look at the mark," said Nikola.

I gave him my left hand, pulling up my sleeve as I did so, that he might have a better view of it. Half way across, a little above the wrist bone, was a long white scar. Nikola gazed at it attentively.

"This is serious," he said. "You will have to be very careful, or that man will carry his news to the High Priest, and then we shall be nicely caught. For the future make it your habit to walk with your hands folded beneath your sleeves, and take care who you let come up beside you."

"I will remember," I answered, and as I spoke the great gongs, calling the monks to the last service of the day, boomed out from the courtyard below. Being determined not to show ourselves lacking in religious zeal we descended to the large hall, which we found already filled with worshippers. Nikola, by virtue of his sanctity, took up his place in a prominent position, hard by where sat the High Priest himself. I was near the western wall, surrounded by a set of the most loathsome and blackguardly ruffians it would be possible to imagine. At first I took but little notice of them, but when a new monk came up and pushed his way in alongside me my suspicions were aroused. It was not long before they were confirmed; the man next to me was the fellow who had looked at me in such a curious fashion when we were seated round the well, and about whom I had spoken to Nikola only a few minutes before. But even if he recognized me he did not allow a sign to escape him to show that he did. Throughout the service he occupied himself completely with his devotions, turned his face neither to the right hand nor to the left, and it was not until we were about to rise from our knees that he came out in his true colours. Then, just as I was half on to my feet, he stumbled against me with such violence that I fell back again and rolled over on to the floor. Then like lightning he sprang forward, seized me by the arm, and tearing back my sleeve looked at the scar upon my wrist. As he did so he allowed a little cry of triumph to escape him. For a moment I lay where I had fallen, too confused and horror-stricken at what had happened to say or

118

do anything, and yet I knew that unless I acted promptly we were ruined indeed.

By this time the hall was more than half empty. I could see Nikola standing at the further end talking earnestly to the High Priest. To interrupt him would be akin to sacrilege; so after I had risen, and when the man had left me and hurried out after the others, I stood at a little distance and waited for him to notice me. As soon as he looked my way I placed three fingers of my right hand upon my forehead, a sign we had agreed to use whenever danger threatened us and it was necessary to act quickly. He saw my meaning, and a moment later, making some excuse, bade the High Priest good-night, and signing to me to follow him, retired to his dormitory.

As soon as we had reached it he turned sharply upon me, his eyes, in his excitement, blazing in his head like live coals.

"What further news have you to tell me?" he asked. "Only that I am discovered," I answered. "While we were at prayers downstairs the man whom I suspected this evening pushed himself in next to me. I took the precaution to keep my hands covered with my sleeves lest he should see the scar he had inflicted. I could not move away from him for obvious reasons, and when the service was over I flattered myself that I had outwitted him. But he was as sharp as I, and just as I was rising from my knees he lurched against me and pushed me down upon the floor. Naturally I put up my hands to save myself, and as I did so he seized upon my wrist."

For some minutes Nikola did not speak. He walked up and down the room like a caged tiger.

"This will put us in a nasty fix," he said at last; "and one mistake at this juncture will ruin everything. He will, of course, go direct to the High Priest in order to reveal his discovery, then that worthy will come to me, and I shall be compelled to produce you. You will be found to be an Englishman, disguised, and as soon as that is discovered we'll see the gleaming of the knives. This has come at a most unfortunate time, for by to-morrow morning, if all had gone well, I should have got the information I wanted, have been told the word that would admit us to the monastery in the mountains, and we could have left this place in safety. However, there is no time to waste talking of what might have been. I must work out some scheme that will save us, and at once. You had better go into the inner apartment and leave me alone."

As he spoke I detected the sound of footsteps on the stairs. I ran into the inner room and drew the heavy curtain across the door. A moment later the High Priest, accompanied by two or three of the principal monks and the man who had discovered me, entered the room. Looking through a hole in the curtain I saw that Nikola had dropped upon his knees and was occupied with his devotions. On observing this the High Priest and his satellites came to a dead stop. Nikola was in no hurry, but kept them waiting for at least ten minutes. Then he rose and turned towards them.

"What does this mean?" he asked sternly; "and how is it that this rabble intrudes upon my privacy? Begone all of you!"

He waved his arm, and the men departed, but none too pleasantly;

"Now, my father," he said to the High Priest, who had watched these proceedings with no small amount of surprise, "what is it that you require of me?"

"Nay, my lord," said the man he addressed, "be not angry with thy servants. There is without doubt some mistake, which will soon be made clear. I have come to thee because it has been asserted by a young priest that he, whom you call your secretary, is not a Chinaman at all, but a certain barbarian Englishman, called by the heathen name of 'Bruce.' I cannot believe that this is so. How long has my lord known the man?"

"It is unseemly that I should be questioned in this fashion," began Nikola angrily. "If the man were what thou sayest, what matter is it to thee or to any one? Yet, lest it breed mischief, I will answer. What thy servant says is false. The man is as true a countryman of thine as the Emperor himself. There is malice in this accusation, and it shall be sifted to the dregs. Let us decide the matter in this way. If it should be as thou sayest, then to-morrow morning I will have the dog out, and he shall answer for his duplicity with his barbarian life. If not, then, I will tear the tongue of that lying knave, thy priest, out of his mouth. To-night I have to offer many prayers, and I am weary, so let it be decided between us in the great hall to-morrow morning."

"It shall be as you say," said the old man. "Do not let there be hard words between us, my lord. Have no fear; if the man be all thou sayest my servant shall surely pay the penalty."

Having said this he bowed himself before Nikola, and then departed from the room. As soon as the sound of his footsteps had ceased upon the stone stairs Nikola came in to me.

"They have gone," he said. "And now we have got to find a way out of this difficulty."

"It would seem impossible," I answered doubtfully.

"Nothing is impossible," Nikola answered. "I hate the word. We've got at least six hours before us in which to do something, and if we want to save our lives we had better look sharp and decide what that something is to be."

Chapter 10

An Exciting Night In The Llamaserai

"There are two points which we must hold in constant remembrance," said Nikola. "The first is that you are *not* a Chinaman, and the other is that if you go before the High Priest to-morrow morning and pose as one, he'll certainly find you out, and then we shall be ruined completely. If you run away I had better run too, for all the good I can get by stopping, but that I am resolved not to do. It has cost me many years' labour, to say nothing of some thousands of British sovereigns, to get as far as I have in this business, and come what may I am determined not to turn back."

"But in what way are we to get out of the difficulty?" I asked dejectedly. "If I can't come before them and brazen the matter out, and I can't remain away for fear of confirming what they already suspect, and I can't leave the monastery without drawing down suspicion on you, I must confess I don't see what *is* to be done. I suppose we couldn't bribe the man to withdraw his charge?"

"Not to be thought of," said Nikola, with conviction. "Our lives would then be simply dependent on his reading of the term 'good faith.' You ought to know what sort of trust we could place in that."

"Could we force him to clear out, and thus let it be supposed that he had brought a false accusation against me, and was afraid to stay and face the consequences?"

"That is not possible either," said Nikola. "He would want to bargain with us, and, to be revenged on us, would turn traitor when we refused his demand. In that case it would be 'pull devil, pull baker,' and the one who could pull the longest would gain the day. No, you had better leave the situation to me. Let me tackle it, and see what is to be done."

I did as he wished, and for nearly half an hour could hear him pacing up and down his room. I did not intrude upon him, or interrupt him in any way. At the end of the time stated he abandoned his sentry-go and came in to me.

"I think I see my way," he said. "But when all is said and done it is almost as desperate as either of the other remedies we thought of. You will have to carry it out, and if you fail—well, Heaven have mercy upon both of us. You have saved my life before, I am going to trust it to you now; but remember this, if you do not carry out my plan exactly as I wish, you will never see me alive again. Give me your best attention, and endeavour to recollect everything I tell you. It is now close on midnight; the gong for early service will sound at half-past five, but it will be daylight an hour before that. By hook or by crook I must get you out of this place within a quarter of an hour, and, even if you have to steal a horse to do it, you must be in Pekin before half-past one. Once there you will find the house of Yoo Laoyeh, who lives at the rear of Legation Street, near the chief gate of the Tartar city."

"But how am I going to get into the city at all?" I asked, amazed that he should have forgotten what struck me as a most hopeless barrier—the wall. "The gates are closed at sundown and are not opened again till sunrise."

"You'll have to climb the wall," he answered.

"But, as you know very well, that's altogether impossible," I said.

"Not a bit of it," he replied. "I will tell you of a place where it is quite practicable. Do you remember the spot where you proposed to Miss Medwin?"

"Perfectly," I answered with a smile. "But how do you know it?"

"My dear fellow, I was within a hundred yards of you the whole time. No, you need not look at me like that. I was not spying upon you. After the fashion of the great Napoleon, I like to be prepared for every emergency, and, thinking I might some day want to get into the city when the gates were shut, I utilized some spare time by taking a look at the wall. You see how useful that chance visit has proved. Well, two bastions from where you were seated that day the stones are larger and more uneven than anywhere else along the whole of that side

123

of the city. To my certain knowledge three men have been in the habit of climbing that portion of the ramparts for the last three years, between midnight and sunrise, smuggling in goods to the city in order to avoid paying the octroi duty, which, as you know, is levied during daylight. When you have got over you will find a sentry posted on the other side; to him you will pay three taels, telling him at the same time that you intend returning in an hour, and that you will pay him the same amount for the privilege of getting out. Having passed the sentry you will proceed into the town, find Yoo Laoyeh, and let him know the fix we are in. You may promise him the sum of £100 cash if he falls in with your suggestions, and you must bring him back with you, willy-nilly, as fast as you can travel. I will meet you at the southern gate. Knock four times, and as you knock, cough. That shall be the signal, and as soon as I hear it I will open the gate. All that must be guarded against inside shall be my care. Everything outside must be yours. Now let us come along, and discover by what means I can get you out."

Together we left the room, descended the stairs, and, crossing the ante-chamber, entered the big hall. The wind which, as I have already said, came in through the narrow windows on either side rustled the long hangings till the place seemed peopled with a thousand silk-clad ghosts. Nikola crossed it swiftly and left by the southern door. I followed close at his heels, and together we passed unobserved through the great courtyard, keeping well in the shadow of the building until we reached the first gate. Fortunately for us this also was unguarded, but we could hear the monk, who was supposed to be watching it, placidly snoring in the room beside it. Slipping the enormous bar aside we opened it quietly, passed through, and, crossing an open strip of green, made for the outer wall. Just, however, as we were about to turn the corner that separated us from it, a sudden sound of voices caused us to hesitate.

"This way," whispered Nikola, seizing my wrist and dragging me to the left. "I can find you another exit. I noticed, yesterday, a big tree growing by the side of the wall."

Leaving the centre gate we turned to our left hand, as I have said, and followed the wall we desired to surmount until we arrived at a large tree whose higher branches more than overspread it.

"This is the very place for our purpose," said Nikola, coming to a halt. "You will have to climb the tree and crawl along the branches until you get on to the wall, then you must let yourself down on the other side and be off to the city as hard as you can go. Good-bye, and may good luck go with you!"

I shook him by the hand and sprang into the branches. Hitherto it had seemed as if I had been acting all this in a wonderfully vivid dream. Now, however, the rough bark of the tree roused me to the reality of my position. I climbed until I came to the level of the wall, then, choosing a thick branch, made my way along it until I stood upon the solid masonry. Once there, only a drop of about twelve feet remained between me and freedom. Bidding Nikola, who was watching me, good-bye, in a whisper, I leant over the wall as far as I was able, grasped the coping with both hands, and then let myself drop.

Once on the ground I ran across the open space towards a cluster of small dwellings. In an enclosure adjoining one of them I could dimly make out a number of ponies running loose, and knowing that if I could only secure one of these and find a saddle and bridle in the residence of its owner, I might be in Pekin in under an hour, I resolved to make the attempt.

Creeping up to the nearest of the houses, I approached the door. Inside I could hear the stertorous breathing of the occupants. A joss-stick burnt before an image near at hand, and though it was well-nigh exhausted by the time I secured it, it still gave me sufficient light to look about me. A moment later I had a saddle and bridle down from a peg and was out among the ponies again.

Securing the most likely animal I saddled him, and as soon as I had done so, mounted and set off towards Pekin as fast as he could take me. The night was dark, but the track was plain; the little beast was more than willing, and as I did not spare him, something less than three-quarters of an hour, counting from the time I had bidden Nikola good-bye, found me dismounting under the great wall of the city.

Having found a convenient spot, I tied up my pony, and when he was made secure set to work and hunted along the wall until I came to the scaling place of which Nikola had told me.

As I reached it a light wind blew from over the plain, and sent the dust eddying about me, otherwise not a sound disturbed the stillness of the night. Then, having made sure that I was unobserved, and that I had chosen the right spot, I began to climb. It was no easy task. The stones were large and uneven. Sometimes I got a good hold, but in many cases I had veritably to cling by my nails. The strain was almost too much for my strength, and when I had been climbing for five minutes, and there still remained as much of the wall ahead, I began to despair of ever getting to the top. But I was not to be beaten; and remembering how much depended upon my getting into the city, I dragged myself wearily on, and at last crawled on to the summit. When I reached it I could see the city spread out on the other side. A little to the left of where I stood was the place, to be for ever sacred in my eyes, where I had proposed to, and been accepted by, my sweetheart, while away to the right was that quarter of the town where at that moment she was in all probability asleep, and, I hoped, dreaming of me. As soon as, I recovered my breath I crossed the wall and descended by the steps on the other side.

I had scarcely reached the bottom before a man rose from a dark corner and confronted me. In the half light I could see that he was a Chinese soldier armed with a long spear. Telling him in a whisper, in answer to his inquiry, that I was a friend, I pressed the money that Nikola had given me for that purpose into his not unwilling hand, and as soon as he drew back, astonished at my munificence, sped past him and darted down the nearest street.

From the place where I had passed the sentry to the thoroughfare where Yoo Laoyeh resided was a distance of about half a mile, and to reach it quickly it was necessary that I should pass the Benfleets' abode. You may imagine what thoughts occupied my brain as I stood in the silent street and regarded it. Under that roof was sleeping the one woman who was all the world to me. I would have given anything I possessed for five minutes' conversation with her; but as that was impossible I turned on my heel and made my way through a by-lane into the street I had been sent to find. The house was not a big one, and at first glance did not strike me very favourably. But the style of building did not matter if I found there the man I wanted. I knocked upon the door—which I discovered was heavily barred—but for some minutes got no response; then, just as I was beginning to wonder in what way I could best manage to attract the attention of those inside, I heard a patter of bare feet on the stone passage, and after much fumbling the door was opened and a man appeared before me. One glance told me that he was not the person I wanted. I inquired if Yoo Laoyeh were at home, but from the answer I received I gathered that he had gone out earlier in the evening, and that he was probably at a neighbouring house playing *fan-tan.*

Having asked the man if he would take me to him, and at the same time offering him a considerable bribe to do so, I was immediately conducted into the street again, down one by-lane, up another, and finally brought to a standstill before one of the largest houses in that quarter. My guide was evidently well known, for when the door was opened the keeper did not attempt to bar our passage, but permitted us to pass through to a fair-sized room at the back. Here quite thirty Chinamen were busily engaged upon their favourite pastime, but though we scanned the rows of faces, the man for whom we were searching was not among the number. As soon as we were convinced of this fact we left that room and proceeded to another, where the same game was also being carried on. Once more, however, we were doomed to disappointment; Laoyeh was not there either.

Being anxious to obtain some news of him my guide interrogated one of the players, who remembered having seen our man about an hour before. He imagined he had then gone into the room we had first visited. We returned there and made further inquiries, only to elicit the fact that he had been seen to leave the house about half an hour before our arrival.

"Have no fear. I will find him for you," said my companion, and we thereupon proceeded down the passage, past the doorkeeper, into the street again. Once more we took up the chase, trying first one house and then another, to bring up eventually in an opium den a little behind the English Legation. The outer room, or that nearest the street, was filled with customers, but our man was not among them. The inner room was not quite so crowded, and here, after all our searching, we discovered the man we wanted. But there was this drawback, he had smoked his usual number of pipes and was now fast asleep.

By this time it was hard upon two o'clock, and at most I dared not remain in the city more than another hour. At the same time it would be a most foolish, if not dangerous, proceeding to attempt to travel with my man in his present condition. If he did nothing else he would probably fall over the wall and break his neck, and then I should either have to leave him behind or remain to answer inconvenient questions; but whatever happened I knew I must carry him out of this house as quickly as possible to some place where I could endeavour to bring him back to his senses. I said as much to the man who had found him for me, and then between us we got him on to his feet, and taking him by either arm led him off to his home. By the time we got him there he had in a small measure recovered from the effects of his smoke. Then we set to work, using every means known to our experience, to bring him round, and by half-past two had so far succeeded as to warrant me in thinking I might set off on my return journey.

"But what does your Excellency require of me?" asked Laoyeh, who was still a bit mystified, though fortunately not so far gone as to be unable to recognize me.

"You are to come with me," I answered, taking good care before I spoke that the other man was well out of hearing, "to the Llamaserai, where Nikola wants you. There is a hundred pounds English to be earned; how, I will tell you as we go."

As soon as he heard Nikola's name and the amount of the reward, he seemed to become himself again. We accordingly left the house and set off together for that part of the wall where I had made my descent into the city. The same soldier was still on guard, and when I had placed the money I had promised him in his hand, he immediately allowed us to pass. Within twenty minutes of leaving Yoo's house we were ready to descend the other side of the wall.

If I had found it difficult to ascend, I discovered that it was doubly difficult to descend. The night was now very dark, and it was well-nigh impossible to see what we were doing. The cracks and crannies which were to serve as resting-places for our feet seemed almost impossible to find, and right glad I was when the business was accomplished and we stood together on *terra firma* at the bottom.

So far my visit to the city had proved eminently successful. But time was slipping by, and there was still the long distance out to the Serai to be overcome. I went over to where the pony stood hitched to the tree, exactly as I had left him, and placed my companion upon his back. He was almost, if not quite, himself now, so urging the little animal into a canter we set off, he riding and I running beside him. In this fashion, running and walking, we came to the southern gate of the great monastery. I had carried out my share of the business, and when once I should have got Laoyeh inside, the direction of the remainder would lie with Nikola.

Having turned the pony loose, his bridle and saddle upon his back, I approached and knocked upon the door, coughing softly as I did so. Then little by little it opened, and we found Nikola standing upon the threshold. He beckoned to us to enter, and without losing a moment we did as we were ordered. Daylight was close at hand, and the unmistakable chill of dawn was in the air. It was very certain that I had returned none too soon.

Having passed through the gate, and fastened it behind us, we made for the second archway on our left. The sentry box—if one might call it by that name—was still deserted, and the guard was snoring as placidly in his little room at the side as when we had crept through nearly four hours before. This courtyard, like its predecessor, was empty; but to show the narrowness of our escape, I may say that as we crossed it we could distinctly hear the jabbering of priests in the dormitories on either hand.

At last we reached the door of the big hall. Opening it carefully we sped across the floor and then up the stairs to our own apartments. Once inside, the door was quickly shut, and we were safe. Then Nikola turned to me, and said—

"Bruce, you have saved me a second time, and I can only say, as I said before, you will not find me ungrateful. But there is no time to lose. Yoo Laoyeh, come in here."

We passed into the inner room, and then Nikola opened a small box he had brought with his other impedimenta. Then bidding the man seat himself upon the floor, he set to work with wonderful dexterity to change his appearance. The operation lasted about a quarter of an hour, and when it was completed Nikola turned to me.

"Change clothes with him, Bruce, as quickly as you can."

When this was done I could hardly believe my own eyes, the likeness was so wonderful. There, standing before me, was an exact reproduction of myself. In height, build, dress, and even in feature, the resemblance was most striking. But Nikola was not satisfied.

"You must be changed too," he said. "We must do the thing thoroughly, or not at all. Sit down."

I did so, and he once more set to work. By the time I left his hands I was as unlike my real self as a man could well be. No one could have recognized me, and in that case it was most unlikely that our secret would be discovered.

On the way from Pekin I had clearly explained to Laoyeh the part he would be called upon to play. Now Nikola gave the final touches to his education, and then all was completed.

"But, look here," I cried, as a thought struck me; "we have forgotten one thing—the scar upon my arm."

"I had omitted that," said Nikola. "And it is just those little bits of forgetfulness that hang people."

Then taking a long strip of native cloth from a chair he constructed a sling, which he placed round my neck. My left arm was placed in rough splints, which he procured from his invaluable medicine chest, and after it had been bandaged I felt I might also defy detection, as far as my wrist was concerned.

Half an hour later the great gong sounded for morning worship, and in a few moments we knew that the courtyards and halls would be filled with men. Acting under Nikola's instructions I descended to the hall alone, and choosing my opportunity slipped in and mingled with the throng. I was not the only cripple, for there were half a dozen others with their arms in slings. Nor was the fact that I was a stranger likely to attract any undue attention, inasmuch as there were mendicants and people of all sorts and descriptions passing into the Serai directly the gates were opened at daylight.

I had not been in the hall very long before I saw Nikola hobble in on his stick and take his place beside the High Priest. Then the service commenced. When it was at an end it was evident that something unusual was going to take place, for the monks and their guests remained where they were, instead of leaving the hall as usual. Then the High Priest mounted the small platform at the further end and seated himself in the chair of justice. Nikola followed and took his place beside him, and presently two tall monks appeared bringing with them the man who had brought the accusation against me on the previous evening. He seemed pretty certain of being able to prove his case, and I could not help smiling as I watched his confident air. First the old High Priest, who it must be remembered was almost blind with age, addressed him. He said something in reply, and then Nikola spoke. His voice was scarcely as loud as usual, yet every word rang across the hall.

"Liar and traitor!" he said. "You have brought this charge against my faithful servant for some devilish reason of your own. But old as I am I will meet it, and evil be upon you if it be proved that what you say is false."

He then turned to a monk standing beside him and said something to him; the man bowed, and leaving the platform disappeared in the direction of our staircase. Presently he returned with Laoyeh, whose head was bent, and whose hands were folded across his breast. He climbed the steps, and, when he had done so, accuser and accused confronted each other from either end of the platform.

Then it was that I saw the cleverness of Nikola's scheme. He had arranged that the trial should take place after the morning service for the reason that, at that tune, the big hall would not be thoroughly lighted. As it proved, it was still wrapped in more than semi-darkness, and by the promptness with which he commenced business it was evident that he was resolved to dispose of the matter in hand before it would be possible for any one to see too clearly.

First the man who brought the accusation against me was ordered to repeat his tale. In reply he gave a detailed description of our meeting in Canton and led up, with a few unimportant reservations, to the stab he had given me upon the wrist. He then unhesitatingly asserted the fact that I was a *kueidzu,* or foreign devil, and dared the man who was taking my place to disprove it. When he had finished, Nikola turned to the High Priest and said—

"My father, thou hast heard all that this wicked man hath said. He accuses my servant yonder—he himself being a thief and a would-be murderer by his own confession—of being one

131

of those barbarians whom we all hate and despise. I have found my man faithful and true in all his dealings, yet if he is a foreign devil, as this fellow asserts, then he shall be punished. On the other hand, if this rogue shall be proved to be in the wrong, and to have lied for the sake of gain, then it shall be my request to thee that I be allowed to deal with him according to the powers with which thou knowest I am invested. I have no fear; judge therefore between us."

When he had finished the old man rose and hobbled forward on his stick; he looked steadfastly from one to the other of the two men, and then, addressing Laoyeh, said—

"Come thou with me "; and took him into a small room leading out of the big hall.

For nearly half an hour we sat in silence, wondering what the upshot of it all would be. I watched Nikola, who sat during the whole of the time with his chin resting on his hand, staring straight before him.

At last our period of waiting was at an end. We heard the tapping of the High Priest's stick upon the floor, and presently he ascended the platform again. Laoyeh followed him. Reaching his chair the old man signed for silence, and as soon as he had obtained it, said—

"I have examined this man, and can swear that the charge this fellow has brought against him is without truth in every particular. Let justice be done."

Then facing Nikola he continued—

"The rogue yonder waits for thee to do with him as thou wilt."

Nikola rose slowly from his chair and faced the unhappy man.

"Now, dog!" he cried. "By the words of thine own High Priest I have to deal with thee. Is it for this that thou earnest into the world. Thou hast dared to malign this my servant, and thy superior has sworn to it. Draw nearer to me."

The man approached a few paces, and it was easily seen that he was afraid. Then for nearly a minute Nikola gazed fixedly at him, and I cannot remember ever to have seen those terrible eyes look so fierce. If you can imagine a rabbit fascinated by a serpent you will have some notion of how the man faced his persecutor. Slowly, inch by inch, Nikola raised his right hand until it pointed to a spot on the wall a little above the other's head. Then it began to descend again, and as it did so the fellow's head went down also until he stood almost in a stooping posture.

"You see," said Nikola, "you are in my power. You cannot move unless I bid you do so."

"I cannot move," echoed the man almost unconsciously.

"Try how you will, you cannot stand upright," said Nikola.

"I cannot stand upright," repeated the man in the same monotonous voice, and as he spoke I saw large drops of perspiration fall from his face upon the floor. You may be sure that every eye in that large hall was riveted upon them, and even the High Priest craned forward in his chair in order that he might not lose a word.

"Look into my face," said Nikola, and his words cut the air like a sharp knife.

The man lifted his eyes and did as he was ordered, but without raising his head.

"Now leave this place," said Nikola, "and until this time tomorrow you cannot stand upright like your fellow-men. It is my command, and you cannot disobey. Let that help you to remember that for the future my servants must be sacred. Go!"

He pointed with his right hand to the doors at the end of the hall, and, bent double, the man went down the aisle between the rows of gaping monks out into the courtyard and the streaming sunshine. The High Priest had risen to his feet, and calling up a monk who stood beside him, said—

"Follow him, and be certain that he leaves the Serai."

Then approaching Nikola he said—

"My master, I see that, without a doubt, thou art he whom we were told to expect. In what way can thy servant prove of service to thee?"

"Grant me an interview and I will tell you," said Nikola.

"If my lord will follow me," said the old man, "we can talk in private." Next moment they disappeared into the room where the High Priest had conducted the examination of Laoyeh. Thereupon the congregation dispersed.

As soon as the hall was empty I seized my opportunity and went upstairs to our own apartment. There I discovered Laoyeh. According to Nikola's instructions we changed clothes again, and when he was himself once more, I gave him the peddler's dress which Nikola had prepared for this occasion, and also the reward which had been promised him. Then bidding him good-bye, I bade him get out of the monastery as quickly as he could.

It was nearly an hour before Nikola joined me. When he did he could hardly conceal his exultation.

"Bruce," he said, almost forgetting his usual caution in the excitement of the moment, "I have discovered everything! I have got the chart, and I have learnt the password. I know where the monastery is, and at daybreak to-morrow morning we'll set out in search of it."

Chapter 11

En Route To Thibet

Daylight was scarcely born in the sky next morning before Nikola roused me from my slumbers.

"Wake up," he said; "for in half an hour we must be starting. I have already given orders for the ponies to be saddled, and as we have a long stage before us we must not keep them waiting."

Within a quarter of an hour of his calling me I was dressed and ready. A breakfast of rice was served to us by one of the monks, and when we had eaten it we descended to the great hall. The High Priest was waiting there for us, and after a short conversation with Nikola he led us down the steps into the courtyard, where, beneath the shadow of the great statue of Buddha, we took an impressive farewell of him.

Having thanked him for his hospitality, we made our way towards the outer gate, to find our ponies and servants standing ready to receive us. The gate was thrown open, and in single file we proceeded through it. Then it clanged to behind us, and when it had done so we had said good-bye to the Great Llamaserai.

During the first day's ride nothing occurred worth chronicling. We reached a small village at mid-day, camped there, and after a brief rest, continued our journey, arriving at the fortified town of Ho-Yang-Lo just as dusk was falling. Having been directed to the principal inn, we rode up to it, and engaged rooms for the night. Our first day's stage had been one of thirty-six miles, and we felt that we had well earned a rest.

It was not until the evening meal was eaten, and Nikola and I had retired to our own private room, that I found an opportunity of asking what he thought of the success which had attended our efforts so far.

"To tell you the truth," he said, "I must confess that I am surprised that we have been as successful as we have."

"Well, that man's recognizing me was unfortunate, I admit; but still——"

"Oh, I don't mean that at all," said Nikola. "I regard that as quite an outside chance. And after all it proved a golden opportunity in the end. What does surprise me, however, is that I should have been accepted so blindly for the Priest of Hankow."

"That is certainly strange," I answered. "But there is one thing which astonishes me even more: that is, how it comes about that, as the stick was being searched for by the Chinese in Australia who knew of your intentions, it should fail to be evident to the society in China that you are the man who stole it?"

"My dear fellow," said Nikola, laying his hand upon my arm, "you don't surely imagine that in such a business as the present, in which I have sunk, well, if nothing else, your £10,000, I should have left anything to chance. No, Bruce. Chance and Dr. Nikola do not often act in concert. When I obtained that stick from Wetherell I took care that the fact should not be known outside the circle of a few men whom I felt perfectly certain I could trust. As soon as it was in my possession I offered a large reward for it in Sydney, and I took care that the news of this reward should reach the ears of the Chinamen who were on the look-out for it. Then, on the plea that I was still searching for it, I returned to China, with what result you know. What does puzzle me, however, is the fact that the society has not yet found out that it has been deceived. It must eventually come to this conclusion, and it can't be very long before it does. Let us hope that by that time we shall be back in civilization once more."

I knocked the ashes out of my pipe, and rolling over on my blankets, looked Nikola straight in the face.

"By the time you have got to the end of this business," I said, "your information, presuming all the time that you *do* get it, will have cost you close on £40,000—very possibly more; you will have endangered your own life, to say nothing of mine, and have run the risk of torture and all other sorts of horrors. Do you think it is worth it?"

"My dear Bruce, I would risk twice as much to attain my ends. If I did not think it worth it I should not have embarked upon it at all. You little know the value of my quest. With the knowledge I shall gain I shall revolutionize the whole science of medicine. There will be only one doctor in the world, and he will be Dr. Nikola! Think of that. If I desired fame, what greater reputation could I have. If money, there is wealth untold in this scheme for me. If I wish to benefit my fellow-man, how can I do it better than by unravelling the tangled skein of Life and Death? It is also plain that you have not grasped my character yet. I tell you this, if it became necessary for me, for a purpose I had in view, to find and kill a certain fly, I would follow that fly into the utmost parts of Asia, and spend all I possessed in the world upon the chase; but one thing is very certain, *I would kill that fly.* How much more then in a matter which is as important as life itself to me?"

As I looked at him I had to confess to myself that I had not the least doubt but that he would do all he said.

"There is a proverb," continued Nikola, "to the effect that 'Whatever is worth doing, is worth doing well.' That has been my motto through life, and I hope I shall continue to live up to it. But time is getting on; let us turn in; we have a long day's ride before us to-morrow."

We blew out the light and composed ourselves for the night, but it was hours before sleep visited my eyelids. Thoughts on almost every conceivable subject passed in and out of my brain. One moment I was in the playing-fields of my old familiar English school; the next I was *ratching* round the Horn in an ice-bound clipper, with a scurvy-ridden crew in the forecastle, and a trio of drunken miscreants upon the quarter-deck; the next I was in the southern seas, some tropic island abeam, able to hear the thunder of the surf upon the reef, and to see palm-clad hill on palm-clad hill rearing their lovely heads up to the azure sky. Then my thoughts came back to China, and as a natural sequence, to Pekin. I enacted again that half-hour on the wall, and seemed once more to feel the pressure of a certain tiny hand in mine, and to see those frank sweet eyes gazing into my face with all the love and trust imaginable. Gladys was my promised wife, and here I lay on the road to Thibet, disguised as a Chinaman, in a filthy native inn, in the company of a man who would stop at nothing and who was feared by everybody who knew him. It was long past midnight before I fell asleep, and then it seemed as if my eyes had not been closed five minutes before Nikola, who, as usual, appeared to require no sleep at all, was up and preparing to go on; indeed, the sun was hardly risen above the horizon before our breakfast was dispatched, and we were ready for the saddle.

Prior to starting Nikola went off to speak to the man who kept the inn. While he was away I amused myself by riding round to look at the other side of the house. It was of the ordinary Chinese pattern, not much dirtier and not much cleaner. A broad verandah surrounded it on two sides, and at the rear was a sort of narrow terrace, on which, as I turned the corner, two men were standing. As soon as they saw me they were for retreating into the house, but before they were able to accomplish this manoeuvre I had had a good look at them.

The taller of the pair I had never seen before, but his companion's face was somehow familiar to me. While I was wondering where I had encountered it, a *niafoo* came round the building to inform me that Nikola was ready to be off, so touching up my pony I returned to the front to find the cavalcade in the act of starting.

As usual Nikola took the lead, I followed him at a respectful distance, and the servants were behind me again. In this fashion we made our way down the track and across a stream towards the range of mountains that could just be discerned on the northern horizon. All round us the country was bare and uncultivated, with here and there a mud-hut, in colour not unlike the plain upon which it stood.

By midday we had reached the range of mountains just mentioned, and were following a well-made track through gloomy but somewhat picturesque scenery. With the exception of a few camel teams laden with coal passing down to Pekin, and here and there a travelling hawker, we met but few people. In this region the villages are far apart, and do not bear any too good a reputation.

That night we camped at an inn on the mountain top, and next morning made our descent into the valley on the other side. By the time darkness fell we had proceeded some thirty odd miles along it. The country was quickly changing, becoming more and more rocky, and the ascents and descents more precipitous. For this reason, at the next halting-place we were compelled to part with our ponies, and to purchase in their stead half a dozen tiny, but exceedingly muscular, donkeys.

On the third night after our entry into the hills and the fourth from Pekin, we halted at a small monastery standing in an exposed position on the hill top. As we rode up to it the sun was declining behind the mountains to the westward. There was no need for any password, as we were invited to enter almost before we had knocked upon the gate. The place was occupied by an abbot and six priests, all of whom were devotees of Shamanism. The building itself was but a poor one, consisting of an outer court, a draughty central hall, and four small rooms adjoining it. At the entrance to the central hall we were received by the abbot, a villainously dirty little fellow of middle age, who conducted us to the rooms we were to occupy. They were small and mean, very much out of repair, and, as a result, exceedingly draughty. But if a view, such as would be found in few parts of the world, could compensate for physical discomfort, we should have been able to consider ourselves domiciled in luxury. From one window we could look across the range of mountains, over valley and peak, into the very eye of the setting sun. From another we could gaze down, nearly three hundred feet, sheer drop, into the valley, and perceive the track we had followed that morning, winding its way along, while, through a narrow gully to our left we could distinguish the stretch of plain, nearly fifty miles distant, where we had camped two nights before.

As the sun dropped, a chilly wind sprang up and tore round the building, screaming through the cracks and crevices with a noise that might have been likened to the shrieks of a thousand souls in torment. The flame of the peculiar lamp with which our room was furnished rose and fell in unison with the blasts, throwing the strangest shadows upon the walls and ceiling. This eccentric light, combined with the stealthy movements of the coarse-robed, shaven monks, as they passed and repassed our door, did not, as may be expected, conduce to our cheerfulness, so that it may not be a matter for surprise that when I sat down with Nikola to our evening meal, it was with a greater feeling of loneliness, and a greater amount of home-sickness in my heart, than I had felt at all since the journey commenced.

When our repast was finished we lit our pipes and sat smoking for half an hour. Then, being unable to stand the silence of the room any longer—for Nikola had a fit of the blues, and was consequently but a poor companion—I left our side of the house and went out into the courtyard before the central hall. Just as I reached it a loud knocking sounded upon the outer gate. On hearing it two of the monks crossed the yard to open it, and, when they had swung the heavy doors back, a small party of men, mounted on donkeys, rode into the square. Thinking the arrival of a party of travellers would at least serve to distract my thoughts, I went down to watch them unload.

As I approached them I discovered that they were five in party, the principals numbering three, the remaining two being coolies. Their profession I was unable to guess; they were all armed, and, as far as I could tell, carried no merchandise with them. When they had dismounted the abbot came down to receive them, and after a little talk conducted them to the guest chambers on the other side of the hall opposite to our quarters.

For some time after the leaders had retired to their rooms I remained where I was, watching the coolies unharness; then, just as the last pack-saddle was placed upon the ground, one of the owners left the house and approached the group. He had come within a few paces of where I stood before he became aware of my presence; then he stooped, and, as if to excuse his visit, opened the pack-saddle lying nearest him. I noticed that he did not take anything from it, and that all the time he was examining it he did not once turn his face in my direction; therefore, when he wheeled quickly round and hurried back to the house, without speaking to either of his men, I felt that I had every right to suppose he did not wish me to become aware of his identity.

This set me thinking, and the more I thought the more desirous I became of finding out who my gentleman might be. I waited in the courtyard for nearly a quarter of an hour after the animals had been picketed, and the pack-saddles and harness had been carried away, but he did not put in another appearance. Seeing this, I returned to the buildings, and set my brain to work to try and discover what I wanted so much to know. It was a long time before I could hit on any plan; then an idea came to me and I left the room again and went round to the back of the buildings, hoping, if possible, to find a window through which I could look in upon the new arrivals as they sat at supper; but it was easier, I discovered, to talk of such a window than actually to find it.

The back of the monastery was built flush with the edge of the cliff, the rampart wall joining the building at the angle of our room. If only, therefore, I could manage to pass along the wall, and thus reach a small window which I guessed must look out on to a tiny court, situated between the rearmost wall of the central hall and that on the left of our room, I thought I might discover what I wanted to know. But to do this would necessitate a long and dangerous climb in the dark, which I was not at all anxious to attempt until I had satisfied myself that there was no other way of obtaining the information I required.

It might very well be asked here why I was so anxious to convince myself as to the man's identity. But one instant's reflection will show that in such a situation as ours we could not afford to run a single risk. The man had allowed me to see that he did not wish me to become aware of his personality. That in itself was sufficient to excite my suspicion and to warrant my taking any steps to satisfy myself that he was not likely to prove an enemy. As I have said before, we were carrying our lives in our hands, and one little precaution neglected might ruin all.

Before venturing on the climb just mentioned, I determined to go round to the other side of the house and endeavour to look in through one of the windows there. I did so, and was relieved to find that by putting my hands on the rough stone window-sills, and bracing my feet against a buttress in the angle of the wall, I could raise myself sufficiently to catch a glimpse of the room.

I accordingly pulled myself up and looked in, but, to my astonishment and chagrin, there were only two people present, and neither of them was the man I wanted.

I lowered myself to the ground again and listened, hoping to hear the sound of a third person entering the room, but though I remained there nearly twenty minutes I could not distinguish what I wanted. That the man was a member of the same party I was perfectly convinced, but why was he not with them now? This absence on his part only increased my suspicion and made me the more anxious to catch a glimpse of him.

Seating myself on the stone steps of the central hall, I roughly traced in my own mind a ground plan of the building, as far as I was familiar with it. The central hall was, of course, empty; we occupied the rooms on the right of it, the second party those on the left; of these their coolies had the front room, while the two men I have just referred to had taken possession of the rearmost one. A moment's reasoning convinced me that there must be a third, which did not look out on the open courtyard, but must have its window in the small court, formed by the angles of the wall at the rear. If, therefore, I wanted to look into it I must undertake the climb I had first projected, and, what was more, must set about it immediately, for if I did not do so his lamp would in all probability be extinguished, and in that case I might as well spare myself the trouble and the danger.

I returned to my own side of the house, and, having convinced myself that there was no one about, mounted the wall a little to the right of where I had been standing when I heard the men knock upon the gate.

If you would estimate the difficulty and danger of what I was about to attempt, you must remember that the wall at the top was scarcely more than eighteen inches wide. On one hand it had the buildings for support, the side of which rose above my head for more than a dozen feet, and permitted no sort of hold on its smooth surface, while, on the other hand, I had a sheer drop into the valley below, a fall of fully three hundred feet.

At the summit of the mountain the wind was blowing a perfect hurricane, but so long as I was behind the building I was not subjected to its full pressure; when, however, I arrived at the courtyard, where I could see the light of the window I was so anxious to reach, it was as much as I could do to keep my footing. Clinging to everything that could offer a support, and never venturing a step till I was certain that it was safe, I descended from the wall, approached the window, and looked in. This time I was not destined to be disappointed. The man I wanted was lying upon a bed-place in the corner, smoking a long pipe.

His face was turned towards me, and directly I looked at it I remembered where I had seen him. He was one of the principal, and, at the same time, one of the most interested members of the society who had visited the house to which we had been conducted by Laohwan, in Shanghai.

As I realized this fact a cold sweat came over me. This was the same man whom we had seen at the rest-house two nights before. Was he following us? That he had recognized me, in spite of my disguise, I felt certain. If so, in whose employ was he, and what was his object? I remained watching him for upwards of an hour, hoping some one would come in, and that I should overhear something that would tell me how to act. Then, just as I was about to turn away, deeming it useless to wait any longer, the taller of the pair I had seen in the other room entered and sat down.

"Success has attended us. At last we have laid our hands on them," said the new-comer. "They do not suspect, and by to-morrow evening we shall meet Quong Yan Miun at the ford, tell him all, and then our part of the work will be at an end."

"But we must have the stick, come what may," said the man upon the bed. "It would be death for us to go back to Pekin without it."

"We shall receive much honour if we capture it," chuckled the other. "And then these foreign devils will suffer torture till they die."

"A lesson to them not to defy the Great Ones of the Mountains," returned his friend. "I wish that we could be there to see it!"

"It is said that they have many new ways of torture, of which we cannot even dream, up there in the mountains," continued the first man. "Why may we not go forward to see what befalls them?"

"Because we could not enter even if we did go on," returned the man I had recognized; "nor for myself do I want to. But these foreign devils have stolen the password and imitated the Priest of Hankow, and if it had not been for Laoyeh, who liked Chinese gold better than foreign devils' secrets, and so betrayed them, we should never have found them out at all."

Then with significant emphasis he added—

143

"But they will die for it, and their fate will be a warning to any who shall come after them. And now tell me, where do we meet Quong Yan Miun?"

"At the crossing of the river in the mountains, at sundown tomorrow evening."

"And is it certain that we shall know him? There may be many crossing."

"He will be riding a camel, and sitting upon a red saddle embroidered with silver. Moreover, it is said that he has but one eye, and that his left hand, which was cut off by the mandarin Li, is still nailed to the gateway at I-chang."

"Does he expect our coming?"

"By no means. Once in every month he is sent down by the Great Ones of the Mountains to receive messages and alms from the outside world. Our instructions are not to tarry until this letter be delivered into his hands."

As he spoke he took from his pocket a small roll of paper carefully tied up. Having replaced it, he turned again to his companion.

"Now leave me," he said. "I am tired, and would sleep. Tomorrow there be great doings on hand."

The second man left the room, and next moment the lamp was extinguished.

As soon as all was dark I crept softly across the yard, mounted the wall—not without a tremor, as I thought of what my fate would be if I should overbalance, and retraced my steps round the house. Once safely in the courtyard I made all the haste I could back to my room.

I fully expected to find Nikola asleep; my surprise, therefore, may be imagined when I discovered him seated on the floor working out Euclid's forty-third problem with a piece of charcoal upon the stones. He looked up as I entered, and, without moving a muscle of his face, said quietly:

"What have you discovered?"

I seated myself beside him and furnished him with a complete *resume* of what I had overheard that evening.

When I had finished he sat looking at the wall. I could see, however, that he was thinking deeply. Then he changed his position, and with his piece of charcoal began to draw figure eights inside each other upon the floor. By the time the smallest was the size of a halfpenny he had arrived at a conclusion.

"It is evident that we are in a tight place," he said coolly, "and if I were to sacrifice you here I could probably save myself and go forward with nothing to fear. It's a funny thing that I should think so much of a man as to be willing to save his life at the expense of my own, but in this case I intend doing so. You have no desire to be tortured, I presume?"

"I have a well-founded objection to it," I said.

"In that case we must hit upon some scheme which will enable us to avert such a catastrophe. If these fellows arrive at the ford before us they will have the first chance of doing business with the messenger. Our endeavour must be to get there before they do, and yet to send them back to Pekin satisfied that they have fulfilled their mission. How to do this is the problem we have to work out."

"But how *are* we to do it?" I inquired.

"Let me think for a few minutes," he answered, "and I'll see if I can find out."

I waited for fully five minutes. Then Nikola said:

"The problem resolves itself into this. By hook or crook we must delay this man and his party on the road for at least three hours. Then one of us must go on to the ford and meet the man from the monastery. To him must be handed the letter I received from the High Priest at the Llamaserai, and when he has been sent back with it to his superiors there must be another man, accoutred exactly like himself, to take his place. This man, who will have to be myself, will receive our friends, take their letters and dispatch them back to Pekin with a message that their warning shall be attended to. After that it will be touch-and-go with us. But I'm not afraid to go forward, and I pay you the compliment of saying that I don't believe you are!"

"Well, upon my word, Dr. Nikola," I answered candidly, quite carried away by the boldness of his scheme, "of all the men I've ever met you're the coolest, and since you take it in this way I will go on with you and carry it through if it costs me my life."

"I thank you," said Nikola quietly. "I thought I wasn't deceived in you. Now we must arrange the manner in which these different schemes are to be worked. To begin with, we must leave here at least an hour before our friends in the other rooms. Once on the way I must push forward as fast as I can go in order to secure a camel and saddle of the kind described. Then we have got to discover some means of delaying them upon the road. How can that be accomplished?"

"Couldn't we induce the villagers along the path to rise against them?"

"It would cost too much; and then there would be the chance of their turning traitor, like our friend Laoyeh. No; we must think of something else."

He recommended drawing eights upon the floor. By the time he had perfected the thirtieth—for I counted them—he had worked it out to his satisfaction.

"By twelve o'clock to-morrow at the very latest," he said, "that is, if my information be correct, we ought to be at an inn in the mountains twenty miles from here. It is the only dwelling between this place and the ford, and they must perforce call at it. I shall instruct one of my men, whom I will leave behind for that purpose, to see that their animals are watered at a certain trough. If they drink what I give him to pour in, they will go about five miles and then drop. If they don't drink I shall see that he brings about another result."

"If you can depend on him, that should do the trick. But what about Laoyeh?"

"I shall deal with him myself," said Nikola with grim earnestness; "and when I've done I think he will regret having been so imprudent as to break faith with me."

He said no more, but I could not help entertaining a feeling of satisfaction that I was not the man in question. From what I have seen of Nikola's character, I can say that I would rather quarrel with any other half dozen people in the world, whoever they might be, than risk his displeasure.

"Now," I said, when he had finished, "as they've turned in we shouldn't be long in following their example."

"But before we do so," he answered, "I think you had better find the coolies and see that they thoroughly understand that we start at three o'clock. Moreover, bid them hold their tongues."

I complied with his request, and half an hour later was wrapped in my blankets and fast asleep.

Chapter 12

Through The Mountains

At ten minutes to three I was out of bed, fully dressed and prepared for the start. Nikola had roused the coolies before calling me, and they were already busy with their preparations. At three precisely a bowl of rice was brought to us by one of the monks, and by a quarter past we were on our donkeys in the courtyard ready to be off.

So far the only person aroused, in addition to our own party, was the monk who cooked our breakfast; him Nikola largely rewarded, and, in return for his generosity, the gates were opened without disturbing the household. We filed out and picked our way down the rocky path into the valley. Arriving at the bottom we continued our journey, ascending and descending according to the nature of the path. Every hour the country was growing more and more mountainous, and by midday we could plainly discern snow upon the highest peaks.

At half-past twelve we reached the inn where it had been decided that one of our retinue should be left behind to hocus the animals of our pursuers. For this work we had chosen a man whom we had the best of reasons for being able to trust. A sufficient excuse was invented to satisfy his scruples, and when we said good-bye to him it was with instructions to follow us as soon as he had done the work and could discover a convenient opportunity. That the man would do his best to accomplish his errand, we had not the slightest doubt, for the reward promised him was large enough to obviate the necessity of his doing any more work as long as he should live. Therefore when we left the inn, after baiting our animals for a short time, it was to feel comparatively certain that the success of our scheme was assured.

As soon as the caravansera was hidden by the corner of the mountain Nikola called me up to him.

"In a few moments," he said, "I am going to push forward to a village which I am told lies off the track a few miles to the northward. I hear that they have camels for sale there, and it will be hard if I cannot purchase one, and with it a silver-plated red saddle, before dusk. You must continue your journey to the ford, where you will in all probability find the messenger awaiting you. Give him this letter from the High Priest of the Llamaserai, warning the Great *Ones* of the Mountains of my coming, and bestow upon him this tip." Here he handed me a number of gold pieces. "After that be sure to hasten his departure as much as you can, for we must run no risk of his meeting those who are behind us. I turn off here, so press forward yourself with all speed, and good luck go with you."

"But when I have dispatched the messenger back to the monastery, what am I to do?"

"Wait till he is out of sight and then follow in his track for about half a mile. Having done so, find a convenient spot, camp and wait for me. Do you understand?"

I answered that I understood perfectly. Then ordering one coolie to follow him, with a wave of his hand, he turned off the track and in less than five minutes was lost to my sight. For nearly three hours I rode on, turning over and over in my mind the plan I had arranged for conducting the interview that lay before me. The chief point I had to remember was that I was a courier from the Society, sent from Pekin to warn the monastery that one of the Great Three was approaching. Upon my success in carrying out this mission would very much depend the reception accorded to Nikola, therefore the story I was about to tell must necessarily be plausible in every particular.

By five o'clock, and just as the sun was sinking behind the highest peaks, the valley began to widen out, and the track became more plain. I followed it along at a medium pace, and then, having turned a corner, saw the smooth waters of the river before me.

As I did so I felt a cold chill pass over me; the success of our expedition seemed to rest upon my shoulders, to depend upon my presence of mind and the plausibility of my tale. If by any chance the man should suspect that I was not all I pretended to be, he might decide to wait, and then, with the help of such men as he might have with him, would detain me a prisoner. In that case, those behind us would catch us up, and I should be proved to be an impostor. Then, if I were not killed upon the spot, I should find myself carried on to the monastery, to become a subject for those experiments in torture, of which I had heard mention made the previous night.

When I reached it I discovered that the river at this particular ford was about eighty yards in width and scarcely more than two feet in depth. On either bank rose precipitous cliffs, reaching, even in the lowest places, to more than two hundred feet. To the right, that is, facing the north, the channel flowed between solid granite walls, but where I stood it had evenly sloping banks. I rode to the water's edge, and, seeing no one on the other side, dismounted from my donkey and seated myself upon the sand. I was relieved to find that there were no pilgrims about; but I became more anxious when I saw that the man whom I was to meet had not yet put in an appearance. If he delayed his arrival for very long I should be placed in a nasty position, for in that case our pursuers would come up, discover me, and then I should be hopelessly lost.

But I need not have worried myself, for I had not long to wait. Within half an hour of my arrival at the ford a man mounted on a camel, rode out of the defile on the other side and approached the water's edge. He was tall, was dressed in some light-brown material, rode a well-bred camel, and when he turned round I could see that his saddle was red and ornamented with silver. Calling my men together I bade them wait for me where they were, and then, taking my donkey by the head, rode him into the stream.

So small was the animal that the water was well above the saddle flaps when I reached the deepest part. But in spite of much snorting and endeavours to turn back I persuaded him to go on, and we finally reached the other side in safety. The messenger from the monastery had dismounted from his camel by this time, and was pacing up and down the shore. As I came closer to him I saw that he had but one arm, and that one of his eyes was missing.

Dismounting from my donkey on the bank, I approached him, at the same time bowing low.

"I was told that I should find here a messenger from the Great Ones of the Mountains," I said. "Are you he whom I seek?"

"From whom come you?" he asked, answering my question by asking another.

"I come from the High Priest of the Llamaserai at Pekin," I answered, "and I am the bearer of important tidings. I was told that I should find a man here who would carry forward the letter I bring, without a moment's delay."

"Let me see the letter," said the man. "If it is sealed with the right seal I will do what you ask, not otherwise."

I gave him the letter and he turned it over and over, scrutinizing it carefully.

"This is the High Priest's seal," he said at last, "and I am satisfied; but I cannot return at once, as it is my duty to remain here until dusk has fallen."

"Of that I am quite aware," I answered. "But you will see that this is a special case, and to meet it I am to pay you this gold, that is provided you will go forward and warn those from whom you come of my master's approach."

When I had given him the bribe he counted it carefully and deposited it in his pocket.

"I will remain until the shadows fall," he said "and if no pilgrims have arrived by that time I will set off."

Having arranged it in this fashion, we seated ourselves on the sandy beach, and after we had lit our pipes, smoked stolidly for half an hour. During that time my feelings were not to be envied. I did not enjoy my smoke, for I was being tortured on the rack of suspense. For aught I knew our man might have failed in drugging the ponies of the pursuing party. In that case they would probably suspect us of an attempt to outwit them, and might put in an appearance at any moment.

The sun sank lower and lower behind the hill, till finally he disappeared altogether. Long shadows fell from the cliffs across the water, the evening wind sprang up and moaned among the rocks, but still there was no sign of any cavalcade upon the opposite bank. If only our rivals did not put in an appearance for another quarter of an hour we should be saved.

In addition to this suspense I had another anxiety. Supposing Nikola had not succeeded in obtaining an animal and saddle of the kind he wanted, and should be prevented from reaching the ford in time to receive the men he was expecting, what would happen then? But I would not let my mind dwell upon such a contingency. And yet for most positive reasons I dared not attempt to hurry the messenger, who was still sitting stolidly smoking. To let him think that I was anxious to get rid of him would only be to excite his suspicions, and, those once aroused, he would in all probability determine to remain at the ford. In that case I might as well walk into the river and drown myself without further waste of time.

One by one the stars came out and began to twinkle in the cloudless heavens, such stars as one never sees anywhere save in the East. The wind was rising, and in another half hour it would be too dark to see.

At last my companion rose and shook himself.

"I see no pilgrims," he said, "and it is cold by the water. I shall depart. Is it your pleasure to come with me or will you remain?"

"I have no will," I answered. "I must perforce wait here till the caravan bringing my master arrives. Then I shall follow you. Do not wait for me."

He did not need to be bidden twice, but approaching his camel, mounted, and then with a curt nod to me set off up the path.

As soon as he had disappeared I walked down to the water's edge and called to my men to come over, which they did. When they had landed, I bade them follow me, and, forsaking the ford, we set off at a brisk pace up the path.

A hundred yards from the river the track we were following turned abruptly to the right hand and wound through a narrow gorge. This, however, we did not enter, as I deemed it wisest to settle in a sheltered spot on the left. I rode ahead, and reconnoitred, and having ascertained that it could not be seen from the path, bade them pitch our camp there. Within ten minutes of our arrival the donkeys were picketed, the tents erected, and the camp fires lighted. Then, leaving the men to the preparation of the evening meal, I returned to the track and hurried along it in the direction of the ford.

When I was within fifty yards of the turning, which I knew would bring me within full sight of the river, I heard a low whistle. Next moment a man mounted on a camel came into view, and pulled up alongside me. In spite of the half dark I could see that the rider was dressed exactly like the man to whom I had talked at the ford; he had also one arm, and his right eye was closed.

"Bear to your left hand," he said, leaning down from his camel to speak to me; "there you will find some big rocks, and behind them you must hide yourself. Have your revolver ready to your hand, and if anything should happen, and I should call to you for assistance, come to me at once."

"Did you have much difficulty in procuring your camel?" I asked, hardly able to believe that the man was Nikola.

"None whatever," he answered; "but the clothes and saddle were a little more difficult. However, I got them at last, and now do you think I look at all like the man I am here to represent?"

"One or two things are different," I replied; "but you need have no fear; they'll not suspect."

"Let us hope not," said Nikola. "Where are the men?"

"Camped back yonder," I answered, "in a little gully to the left of the gorge."

"That's well; now creep down to the rocks and take your place. But sure not to forget what I have told you."

I made my way down as he ordered and little by little crept along to where three big boulders stood out upon the sands. Between these I settled myself, and to my delight found I had an almost uninterrupted view of the ford. As I looked across the water I made out a small party coming down the slope on to the sand on the other side. Without losing time they plunged in, and so quiet was the night I could even hear the splashing made by the animals and distinguish between the first noise on the bank, and the sullen thud as they advanced into deeper water. Then I heard a hoarse call, and a moment later Nikola rode across the sand on his camel.

In two or three minutes the fording party had reached the bank, scarcely more than ten paces from where I lay. So close were they indeed that I could hear the breathing of the tired animals quite distinctly and the sigh of relief with which they hailed the dismounting of their masters. The man who was in command approached Nikola and, after a little preamble, said:

"We were delayed on the road by the sickness of our animals, or we should have been here earlier. Tell us, we pray, if any other travellers have passed this way?"

"But one party," said the spurious messenger with a chuckle; "and by this time they are lost among the mountains. They grudged me alms and I did not tell them the true path. Ere this time to-morrow the vultures will have torn the flesh from their bones."

"How many in number were they?" asked the man who had first spoken.

"Five," answered Nikola; "and may the devils of the mountains take possession of them! And now who be ye?"

"We have come from Pekin," answered the spokesman of the party, "and we bring letters from the High Priest of the Llamaserai to the Great Ones of the Mountains. There be two barbarians who have stolen their way into our society, murdered him who was to be one of the Three, and substituted themselves in his place. The symbol of the Three, which was stolen by a foreign devil many years ago, is in their possession; and that was the party who passed this ford on their way to the mountains, and whom thou sawest."

"They will go no farther," said Nikola, when they had finished, with another grim laugh; "and the hearts that would know our secrets will be tit-bits for the young eagles. What is it that ye want of me?"

"There is this letter of warning to be carried forward," said the man; and as he spoke he produced from his pocket the roll of paper I had seen in his possession the previous night. He handed it to Nikola, who placed it inside his wadded coat, and then proceeded towards his camel, which he mounted. When it had risen to its feet he turned to the small party who were watching him, and said:

"Turn back on your path. Camp not near the ford, for the spirits of the lost pass up and down in the still hours of the night, and it is death for those who hear them."

His warning was not without effect, for as soon as he had ridden off I noticed with considerable satisfaction that the party lost no time in retracing their steps across the river. I watched them for some time, and only when they were dimly outlined against the stars on the brow of the hill did I move. Then, knowing that they must be making haste to be out of the valley, I slipped from my hiding-place and made my way up the path towards the gully where we had fixed our camp.

When I reached the firelight I saw that Nikola had dismounted from his camel and had entered his own tent. I found him removing his disguise and preparing to change back into his own garments.

"We have come out of that scrape very neatly," he said; "and I can only add, Bruce, that it is owing to your foresight and intelligence that we have done so. Had you not had the wit to try to obtain a glimpse of that man the other night, we should in all probability have been caught in a trap from which there would have been no escaping. As it is we have not only got rid of our enemy but have improved our position into the bargain. If we make as good progress in the future as we have done in the past we should be inside the monastery by tomorrow evening."

"I hope we shall," I answered; "but from what we have gone through of late I am induced to think that it could be wiser not to contemplate stocking our poultry-yard before we have seen that our incubator is in good forking order."

"You are quite right, we won't."

Half an hour later our evening meal was served, and when it was eaten we sat round the camp fire smoking and talking, the dancing flames lighting up the rocks around us, and the great stars winking grimly down at us from overhead. The night was very still; save the grunting of the picketed donkeys, the spluttering of the flames of the fire, the occasional cry of some night bird, and once the howl of a jackal among the rocks, scarcely a sound was to be heard. It cannot be considered extraordinary, therefore, if my thoughts turned to the girl I loved. I wondered if she were thinking of me, and if so, what she imagined I was doing. Our journey to the monastery was nearly at an end. How long we should remain there when we had once got inside I had not the very vaguest notion; but, if the luck which had followed us so far still held good, we ought soon to be able to complete our errand there and return with all speed to the coast. Then, I told myself, I would seek out my darling and, with her brother's permission, make her my wife. What I would do after that was for the Fates to decide. But of one thing I was convinced, and that was that as long as I lived I would never willingly set foot in China again.

Next morning, a little after daylight, we broke camp, packed the animals, mounted, and set off. For the first ten miles or so the track was a comparatively plain one, leading along a valley, the entrance to which was the gorge I had seen on the previous night. Then circling round the side of the mountain by a precipitous path we came out on to a long tableland, whence a lovely view could be obtained. The camel we had turned loose earlier in the day to roam the country, or to find its way back to its former owner, as might seem to it best. It was well that we did so, for at the elevation to which we had now ascended, travelling with it would have proved most difficult, if not altogether impossible. Not once but several times we had to dismount and clamber from rock to rock, making our way through ravines, and across chasms as best we could. On many occasions it looked as if it would be necessary for us to abandon even the surefooted animals we had brought with us, but in each case patience and perseverance triumphed over difficulties, and we were enabled to push on with them again.

By midday we had lost sight of the track altogether; the air had become bitterly cold, and it looked as if snow might fall at any minute. At half-past three a few flakes did descend, and by the time we found a camping-place, under an overhanging cliff, the ground was completely covered.

Being provided with plenty of warm clothing ourselves we were not so badly off, but for our poor coolies, whom nothing we had been able to say or do, before we set out, would induce to provide themselves with anything different to their ordinary attire, it was a matter of serious concern. Something had to be done for them. So choosing a hollow spot in the cliff into which we could all huddle, we collected a supply of brushwood and lit a bonfire at the mouth. Into this circle of warmth we led and picketed our donkeys, hoping to be able to keep them snug so that they should have sufficient strength left to continue their journey next day.

Every moment the snow was falling faster, and by the time we turned into our blankets it was nearly four inches deep around the camp. When we woke in the morning the whole contour of the country was changed. Where it had been bare and sterile the day before, we now had before us a plain of dazzling white. Unfortunately the intense cold had proved too much for one of our donkeys, for when we went to inspect them, we found him lying dead upon the ground. One of the smaller coolies was not in a much better state. Seeing this, Nikola immediately gave him a few drops of some liquid from that marvellous medicine-chest, without which, as I have already said, he never travelled. Whatever its constituents may have been it certainly revived the man for a time, and by the time we began our march again he was able to hobble along beside us. Within an hour of setting out, however, he was down again, and in half an hour he was dead, and we had buried him beneath the snow.

Our route now, by reason of the snow, was purely a matter of conjecture, for no track of any sort could be seen. As we could not turn back, however, and it was a dangerous matter to proceed without knowing in what direction to steer, our position might have been reckoned a fairly dangerous one. By the middle of the afternoon another of our coolies dropped, and, seeing this, Nikola decided to camp.

Choosing the most sheltered spot we could discover, we cleared away the snow and erected our tents, and, when this was done, lit a fire and picketed the remaining donkeys. The sick coolie we made as comfortable as possible with all the clothing we could spare, but the trouble was of little avail, for at nightfall he too reached the end of his journey.

By this time I must confess my own spirits had sunk down to the lowest depths. Nikola, however, was still undismayed.

"The death of these men," he said, "is a thing much to be regretted, but we must not let it break us down altogether. What do you say if we take that fellow out and bury him in the snow at once? There is still light enough if we are quick about it."

Having no more desire than he to spend the night in the company of the poor man's dead body, we lifted it up and carried it out to where a great drift of snow showed some fifty paces from our tent door. Here we deposited it and went back to the camp, leaving the softly falling flakes to cover him quite as effectually as we could have done. But that evening two more unpleasant facts revealed themselves to us. Our two remaining donkeys were unable to stand the rigour of the climate any longer, and were on the verge of dying. Seeing this, Nikola left the tent again, and taking his revolver with him, put an end to their sufferings. When they dropped he cut their throats, and then returned to the tent.

"What did you do that for?" I asked, at a loss to understand his last action.

"If you want an explanation," he said quietly, "examine the state of our larder, and then review our position. We are here on the tops of these mountains; one track is like another; where the monastery is I cannot tell you; and now, to add to our sorrows, our provisions are running short. Donkeys are not venison, but they are better than cold snow. And now you know why I shot them."

Accordingly, next morning before we began our journey, we cut up all that was worth carrying with us of the poor beasts. It was well that we did so, for our search for the monastery was no more successful on this occasion than it had been on the previous day. To add to the hopelessness of it all I was beginning to feel ill, while the one remaining coolie staggered on after us more like a galvanized corpse than a living man.

Sometimes in my dreams I live that dreadful time over again. I see the snow-covered country with its yawning precipices, gently sloping valleys, and towering heights; I picture our weary, heart-sick trio, struggling on and on, sinking into the white shroud at every step, Nikola always in advance, myself toiling after him, and the last coolie lagging in the rear. Round us the snow whirls and eddies, and overhead some great bird soars, his pinions casting a black shadow on the otherwise speckless white. Then the dream invariably changes, and I find myself waking with a certain nameless but haunting terror upon me, for which I cannot account. But to return to my narrative.

An hour before sundown the coolie dropped, and once more we had to camp. If I live to be a hundred I shall not forget a single particular connected with that ghastly night. We were so weak by this time that it was a matter of impossibility for us to erect a tent. A drowsiness that there seemed no withstanding had laid its finger upon us. Only the coolie could keep awake, and he chattered incoherently to himself in his delirium.

"Bruce," said Nikola about eight o'clock, coming round the fire to where I sat, "this will never do. That poor fellow over yonder will be dead in half an hour, and if you don't mind what you are about you will soon follow suit. I'm going to set to work to keep you awake."

So saying, this extraordinary individual produced his medicine-chest, and opened it by the fire. From inside the cover he produced a tiny draught-board and a box of men.

"May I have the pleasure of giving you a game?" he asked, as politely as if we were comparative strangers meeting in a London club. Half awake and half asleep, I nodded, and began to arrange my men. Then, when all was ready, we commenced to play, and before three moves had been executed, I had caught Nikola's enthusiasm and was wide awake.

Whether I played it well or ill I cannot remember. I only know that Nikola worked out his plans, prepared strategies and traps for me, and not only that, but executed them, too, as if he had not a thought of anything else on his mind. Only stopping to throw wood upon the fire, and once to soothe the coolie just before he died, we played on till daylight. Then, after a hasty breakfast, we abandoned everything we had, save the medicine-chest, our few remaining provisions, and such small articles as we could stow about our persons, and started off on what we both believed must certainly prove our last march.

How strange are the workings of Fate! As we left the brow of that hill, and prepared to descend into the valley, we discerned before us, on the other side of the valley, a great stone building. It was the monastery, in search of which we had come so far and braved so much.

Chapter 13

The Monastery

We stood and looked across the valley, hardly able to believe that we had at last arrived at the place of which we had heard so much. There it stood gaunt and lonely, on the edge of the ravine, a dark grey collection of roofs and towers, and surrounded by a lofty wall. But, though we could see it plainly enough before us, the chief question was "How were we to reach it?" The cañon, to employ an American term, stretched to right and left of us, as far as the eye could reach, in unbroken grandeur. Certainly, on the side upon which we stood, the cliff sloped enough for an experienced mountaineer to clamber down, but across the ravine it rose a sheer precipice for fully 1,500 feet, and though I examined it carefully I could not see a single place where even a goat could find a footing.

"It would take us a week to go round," said Nikola, when he had examined it with his usual care; "and starving as we are we should be dead before we got half way."

"Then what are we to do?"

"Climb down into the valley, I suppose. It's Hobson's choice."

"It will be a terrible business," I said.

"You will find death up here equally undesirable," he answered. "The worst of it is, however, I don't see how we are going to reach it when we *do* get down there. But as it is within the sphere of practical politics, as they say, that we may break our necks on the way down, we had better postpone further argument until we know that we have arrived at the bottom with our lives. Come along then."

For the next ten minutes we occupied ourselves searching the cliff for the best climbing place. That once discovered we crawled over the edge and began our descent. For the first fifty yards or so it was comparatively easy work; we had nothing to do but to drop from rock to rock. Then matters became more difficult. An unbroken face of cliff, with only one small foothold in nearly forty feet, had to be negotiated. The wall at Pekin was not to be compared with it for difficulty, and, as I knew to my cost, I had found that quite difficult enough. How we were to manage this seemed to me incomprehensible. But as usual Nikola was equal to the occasion.

"Take off your coat," he said, "and give it to me."

I did as he ordered me, whereupon he divested himself of his own, and then tied the sleeves of the two garments together. This done we crawled along to the opposite end of the ledge, where grew one of the stunted trees which provided the only show of vegetation to be seen along the whole face of the cliff, and tied the end of the rope he had thus made, to a long and thick root which had straggled over the face of the cliff in the hope of finding a holding place. Thus we obtained an additional three feet, making in all nearly fifteen feet, which, when we had added our own length, should carry us down to the ledge with a foot to spare.

As soon as these preparations were completed, we tossed up (strange relic of civilization!) for the honour of going first and testing its strength, and, of course, the position fell to Nikola, whom Fate willed should be first in everything. Before setting off he carefully examined the strap by which his treasured medicine-chest was fastened round his neck, then with a nod of farewell to me knelt down upon the edge of the cliff, took the rope in his hands and began his descent. I have spent more enjoyable moments in my life than watching the strain upon that root. Of the coats themselves I had little fear; they were of the best silk, and, save where the sleeves joined the body, were woven in one piece. However the root held, and presently I heard Nikola calling to me to follow him. Not without a feeling of trepidation I lowered myself and went down hand over hand. Though the rope was a comparatively short one, it seemed centuries before I was anywhere near Nikola. Another three feet would find me on the ledge, and I was just congratulating myself on my cleverness when there was an ominous tearing noise on the cliff top, and the next moment I was falling backwards into midair. I gave myself up for lost, but fortunately the catastrophe was not as serious as it might have been, for with that presence of mind which never deserted him Nikola braced himself against the wall and clutched the rope as it slid by. The result of his action was that the force of my fall was broken, and instead of falling on to the little plateau below, and probably breaking my neck, or at least an arm or leg, I swung against the cliff and then slipped easily to the ground.

"Are you hurt?" cried Nikola from his perch above.

"More frightened than hurt," I replied. "Now, how are you going to get down?"

Without vouchsafing any reply Nikola turned his face to the rock, went down upon his knees once more, and then clutching at the ledge lowered himself and finally let go. He landed safely beside me, and having ascertained that his medicine-chest was uninjured, went quietly across to where our coats had fallen and disengaged them from the broken root. Then having handed me mine he donned his own and suggested that we should continue our downward journey without more ado. I believe if Nikola were to fall by accident into the pit of Tophet, and by the exercise of superhuman ingenuity succeeded in scrambling out again, he would calmly seat himself on the brink of the crater and set to work to discover of what chemical substances the scum upon his garments was composed! I can assert with truth that in the whole of my experience of him I never once saw him really disconcerted.

Our climb from the plateau to the bottom of the valley—though still sufficiently dangerous to render it necessary that we should exercise the greatest caution—was not so difficult. At last we arrived at the foot, and, having looked up at the towering heights on either side of us, began to wonder what we had better do next.

We had not long to wait, however, for it appears our arrival had been observed. The bottom of the valley was covered with soft turf, dotted here and there with enormous rocks. We had just arranged to proceed in a westerly direction, and were in the act of setting out, when our ears were assailed by a curious noise. It was more like the sound of a badly blown Alpine horn than anything else, and seemed to be echoed from side to side of the path. Then a voice coming from somewhere close to us, but whence we could not tell, said slowly:

"Who are ye who thus approach the dwelling in the cliff?"

"I am he whom ye have been told to expect," said Nikola.

"Welcome!" said the same passionless voice. Then, after a pause: "Go forward to yonder open space and wait."

All the time that the voice was speaking I had been carefully listening in the hope of being able to discover whence it came, but my exertions were useless. One moment it seemed to sound from my right, the next from my left. It had also a quaint metallic ring that made it still more difficult to detect its origin. To properly explain my meaning, I might say that it was like the echo of a voice the original of which could not be heard. The effect produced was most peculiar.

When the voice had finished Nikola moved forward in the direction indicated, and I followed him.

Arriving at the place, we stood in the centre of the open space and waited. For nearly ten minutes we looked about us wondering what would happen next. There was nothing to be seen in the valley save the green grass and the big rocks, and nothing to be heard but the icy wind sighing through the grass and the occasional note of a bird. Then from among the rocks to our right appeared one of the most extraordinary figures I have ever seen in my life. He was little more than three feet in height, his shoulders were abnormally broad, his legs bowed so that he could only walk on the sides of his feet, while his head was so big as to be out of all proportion to his body. He was attired in Chinese dress, even to the extent of a pigtail and a little round hat. Waddling towards us he said in a shrill falsetto:

"Will your Excellencies be honourably pleased to follow me?"

Thereupon he turned upon his heel and preceded us up the valley for nearly a hundred yards. Then, wheeling round to see that we were close behind him, he marched towards what looked like a hole in the cliff and disappeared within. We followed to find him standing in a large cave, bowing on the sand as if in welcome. On either side in rows were at least a dozen dwarfs, dressed in exactly the same fashion, and every one as small and ugly as himself. They held torches in their hands, and as soon as they saw that we were following, they set off up the cave, headed by the little fellow who had come to meet us.

When we had penetrated into what seemed the bowels of the earth, we left the narrow passage and found ourselves confronted by a broad stone staircase which wound upwards in spiral form. The procession of dwarfs again preceded us, still without noise. It was a weird performance, and had it not been for the reek of the torches, and the fluttering of bats' wings as the brutes were disturbed by the flames and smoke, I should have been inclined to imagine it part of some extraordinary dream; indeed, more than once I felt an impulse to touch the stone wall in order to convince myself by its rough surface that I really was awake. I could see that Nikola was fully alive to all that was passing, and I noticed that he had adopted a demeanour consistent with the aged and important position he was supposed to be filling. Up and up the stairs wound, twisting and twining this way and that, till it almost made me giddy trying to remember how far we had come; indeed, my legs were nearly giving way under me, when we came to a halt before a large door at the top of the stairs. This was thrown open, and our party filed through. From the level of the doorway a dozen more steps conducted us to the floor above, and here we came to a second stop. On looking about us we discovered that we were in an enormous hall of almost cathedral proportions. The raftered roof towered up for more than a hundred feet above our heads; to right and left were arches of strange design, while at the further end was an exquisite window, the glass of which was stained blood-red. The whole place was wrapt in semi-darkness, and though it had the appearance of a place of worship, I could distinguish no altar or anything to signify that it was used for sacred purposes.

As we reached the top the dwarf, who had met us in the valley and headed the procession up the stairs, signed to his followers to fall back on either hand and then led the way to a small square of masonry at the top of two steps and placed in the centre of the hall. Arriving there, he signed to us to take up our positions upon it, and himself mounted guard beside us.

For fully ten minutes we remained standing there, looking towards the blood-red window, and waiting for what would happen next. The silence was most unpleasant, and I had to exercise all my powers of self-control to prevent myself from allowing some sign of nervousness to escape me.

Then, without any warning, a sound of softest music greeted our ears, which gradually rose from the faintest pianissimo to the crashing chords of a barbaric march. It continued for nearly five minutes, until two doors, one on either side of what might be termed the chancel, opened, and a procession of men passed out. I call them men for the reason that I have no right to presume that they were anything else, but there was nothing in their appearance to support that theory. Each was attired in a long, black gown which reached to his feet, his hands were hidden in enormous sleeves, and his head was wrapped in a thick veil, thrown back to cover the poll and shoulders, with two round holes left for the eyes.

One after another they filed out and took up their positions in regular order on either side of us, all facing towards the window.

When the last had entered, and the doors were closed again, service commenced. The semi-darkness, through which the great red window glared like an evil eye, the rows of weird, black figures, the mysterious wailing chant and the recollection of the extraordinary character I had heard given to the place and its inmates, only increased the feeling of awe that possessed me.

When for nearly a quarter of an hour the monks had knelt at their devotions, the muffled notes of a great bell broke upon our ears. Then with one accord they rose to their feet again and filed solemnly out by the doors through which they had entered. When the last had disappeared we were left alone again in the same unearthly silence.

"What on earth does all this mean?" said Nikola in a whisper. "Why doesn't somebody come out to receive us?"

"There is a charnel-house air about the place," I answered, "that is the very reverse of pleasant."

"Hush!" said Nikola; "some one is coming."

As he spoke, a curtain in the chancel was drawn aside, and a man, dressed in the same fashion as those we had seen at their devotions a few minutes since, came down the steps towards us. When he reached the dais upon which we stood, he bowed, and beckoned to us with his finger to follow him. This we did, up the steps by which he had descended, and past the curtain. Here we found another flight of steps leading to a long corridor, on either side of which were many small cells. The only light obtainable came from the torch which our guide had taken from a bracket on leaving the chancel and now carried in his hand.

Without stopping, the monk led us along the whole length of the corridor, then turned to his right hand, descended three more steps, and having drawn back another curtain, beckoned to us to pass him into a narrow but lofty room. It was plainly furnished with a table, a couple of stools, and a rough bed, and was lighted by a narrow slit in the wall about three inches wide by twenty-five deep.

When we were both inside, our guide turned, and, approaching me, pointed first to myself and then to the room, as if signifying that this was for my use, then taking Nikola by the arm, he led him through another doorway in the corner to an inner apartment, which was evidently designed for his occupation. Presently he emerged again by himself, and went out still without speaking a word. A moment later Nikola appeared at his doorway and invited me to inspect his abode. It was like mine in every particular, even to the bracket for a torch upon the wall.

"We are fairly inside now," said Nikola, "and we shall either find out what we want to know within a very short space of time, or be sent to explore the mysteries of another world."

"It's within the bounds of possibility that we shall do both," I answered.

"One thing, Bruce, before we go any further," he said, not heeding my remark, "you must remember that this place is not like an ordinary Shamanist or Buddhist monastery where things are carried on slipshod fashion. Here every man practises the most rigid self-denial possible, and, among other things, I have no doubt the meals will prove inadequate. We shall have to reconcile ourselves to many peculiar customs, and all the time we must keep our eyes wide open so that we may make the most of every chance that offers."

"I don't mind the customs," I answered, "but I am sorry to hear about the meals, for to tell you the honest truth, at the present moment I am simply starving."

"It can't be helped," replied Nikola. "Even if we don't get anything till to-morrow evening we shall have to grin and bear it."

I groaned and went back to my room. It must have been nearly midday by this time, and we had eaten nothing since daybreak. I seated myself on my bed, and tried to reconcile myself to our position. I thought for some time, then a fit of drowsiness came over me, and before very long I was fast asleep.

For nearly two hours I must have remained unconscious of what was going on around me. When I woke my hunger was even greater than before. I rose from my bed, and went in to look at Nikola, only to find that extraordinary man occupied in his favourite way—working out abstruse problems on the floor. I did not disturb him, but returned to my own apartment, and fell to pacing the floor like a caged beast. I told myself that if I did not get a meal very soon I should do something desperate.

My hunger, however, was destined to be appeased before long. Just about sundown I heard the noise of footsteps in the corridor, and presently a bare-footed monk, dressed all in black, and wearing the same terrifying head-dress we had first seen in the great hall, made his appearance, carrying a large bowl in his hands. This he conveyed through my room and placed on Nikola's table.

When he entered, he found the latter upon his knees engaged in his devotions, and I began to reproach myself for having allowed him to catch me doing anything else.

The man had hardly left again, indeed, the sound of his footsteps had not died away on the stone steps, before I was in the inner room.

"Dinner is served," said Nikola, and went across to the bowl upon the table. To my dismay it contained little more than a pint of the thinnest soup mortal man ever set eyes on. In this ungenerous fluid floated a few grains of rice, but anything more substantial there was none. There was neither spoon nor bread, so how we were to drink it, unless we tilted the bowl up and poured it down our throats, I could not imagine. However, Nikola solved the difficulty by taking from his medicine-chest a small travelling cup, which he placed in my hand. Thereupon I set to work. Seeing that Nikola himself took scarcely more than a cupful, I remonstrated with him, but in vain. He said he did not want it, and that settled the matter. I accordingly finished what remained, and when I had done so felt as hungry as ever. If this were to be the fare of the monastery, I argued, by the time we left it, if leave it we did, I should be reduced to a skeleton.

When I had finished my meal, the long streak of light which had been under the window when we arrived, and had gradually crossed the floor, was now some feet up the opposite wall. A little later it vanished altogether. The room was soon in total darkness, and I can assure you my spirits were none of the best. I returned to Nikola's apartment not in the most cheerful of humours.

"This is very pleasant," I said ironically. "Are they never going to receive us properly?"

"All in good time," he answered quietly. "We shall have enough excitement to last us a lifetime presently, and I don't doubt that we shall be in some danger too."

"I don't mind the danger," I said; "it is this awful waiting that harasses my nerves."

"Well, you won't have long to wait. If I mistake not there is somebody coming for us now,"

"How do you know that?" I asked. "I can't hear anybody."

"Still they are coming," said Nikola. "If I were you I should go back into my room and be ready to receive them when they arrive."

I took the hint, and returned to my apartment, where I waited with all the patience I could command.

How Nikola knew that some one was coming to fetch us I cannot tell, but this much is certain, within five minutes of his having warned me I heard a man come down the steps, then a bright light appeared upon the wall, and a moment later the same dwarf who had ushered us into the monastery entered my room carrying a torch in his hand. Seeing that he desired speech with Nikola, I held up my hand to him in warning, and then, assuming an air of the deepest reverence, signed him to remain where he was while I proceeded into the inner room. Nikola was on the alert, and bade me call the man to him. This I did, and next moment the dwarf stood before him.

"I am sent, oh stranger," said the latter, "to summon thee to an audience with the Great Ones of the Mountains."

"I am prepared," said Nikola solemnly. "Let us go."

Thereupon the dwarf turned himself about and led the way out into the corridor. I had no desire to be left behind, so I followed close at Nikola's heels.

We ascended first a long flight of steps, threaded the same corridor by which we had entered, mounted another flight of stairs, crossed a large hall, and finally reached a small ante-chamber. Here we were told to wait while the dwarf passed through a curtain and spoke to some one within. When he emerged again he drew back the covering of the doorway and signed to us to enter. We complied with his request, to discover a rather larger apartment, which was guarded by a monk in the usual dress. He received us with a bow, and also without speaking, conducted us to another room, the door of which was guarded by yet another monk.

All this had a most depressing effect upon my nerves, and by the time we reached the last monk I was ready to jump away from my own shadow. I make these confessions, in the first place, because having set my hand to the tale, I think I have no right to withhold anything connected with my adventures, and in the second, because I don't want to pose as a more courageous man than I really was. I have faced danger as many times as most men, and I don't think my worst enemy could accuse me of cowardice, but I feel bound to confess that on this occasion I *was* nervous. And who would not have been?

On reaching the last ante-room Nikola passed in ahead of me, without looking to right or left, his head bent, and his whole attitude suggestive of the deepest piety. Here we were told to wait. The monk disappeared, and for nearly five minutes did not put in an appearance again. When he did he pointed to a door on the opposite side of the apartment, and requested that we would lose no time in entering.

We complied with his request to find ourselves in a large room, the hangings of which were all of the deepest black. By the light of the torches, fixed in brackets on the walls, we could distinguish two men seated in quaintly carved chairs on a sort of dais at the further end. They were dressed after the same fashion as the monks, and for this reason it was quite impossible to discover whether they were young or old. As soon as we got inside I came stiffly to attention alongside the door, while Nikola advanced and stood before the silent couple on the dais. For some moments no one spoke. Then the man on the right rose, and turning towards Nikola said:

"Who are ye, and by what right do ye thus brave our solitude?"

"I am He of Hankow, of whom thou hast been informed," answered Nikola humbly, with a low reverence. "And I have come because thou didst command."

"What proof have we of that?" inquired the first speaker.

"There is the letter sent forward by your messenger from the High Priest of the Llamaserai in Pekin, saying that I was coming," replied Nikola, "and I have this symbol that ye sent to me."

Here he exhibited the stick he had procured from Wetherell, and held it up that the other might see.

"And if this be true, what business have ye with us?"

"I am here that I may do the bidding of the living and of the dead."

"It is well," said the first speaker and sat down again.

For five minutes or so there was another silence, during which no one spoke, and no one moved. I stood on one side of the door, the monk who had admitted us on the other; Nikola was before the dais, and on it, rigid and motionless, the two black figures I have before described. When the silence had lasted the time I have mentioned I began to feel that if some one did not speak soon I should have to do so myself. The suspense was terrible, and yet Nikola stood firm, never moving a muscle or showing a sign of embarrassment.

Then the man who had not yet spoken said quietly:

"Hast thou prepared thyself for the office that awaits thee?"

"If it should fall out as ye intend," said Nikola, "I am prepared."

"Art thou certain that thou hast no fear?"

"Of that I am certain," he replied.

"And what knowledge hast thou of such things as will pertain to thy office?" To my surprise Nikola answered humbly:

"I have no knowledge, but as thou knowest I have given my mind to the study of many things which are usually hid from the brain of man."

"It is well," answered this second man, after the manner of the first.

There was another silence, and then the man who had first addressed Nikola said with an air of authority:

"To-morrow night we will test thy knowledge and thy courage. For the present prepare thyself and wait."

Thereupon the monk at the doorway beckoned to Nikola to follow him. He did so, and I passed out of the room at his heels. Then we were conducted back to our cells and left alone for the night.

As soon as our guide had departed I went in to Nikola.

"What do you think of our interview?" I inquired.

"That its successor to-morrow evening will prove of some real importance to us," he answered. "Our adventure begins to grow interesting."

"But are you prepared for all the questions they will ask?"

"I cannot say," said Nikola. "I am remembering what I have been taught and leaving the rest to Fate. The luck which has attended us hitherto ought surely to carry us on to the end."

"Well, let us hope nothing will go wrong," I continued. "But I must confess I am not happy. I have seen more cheerful places than this monastery, and as far as diet is concerned, commend me to the cheapest Whitechapel restaurant."

"Help me through to the end, and you shall live in luxury for the rest of your days."

We talked for a little while and then retired to bed. For one day we had surely had enough excitement!

Next day we rose early, breakfasted on a small portion of rice, received no visitors, and did not leave our rooms all day. Only the monk who had brought us our food on the previous evening visited us, and, as on that occasion, he had nothing to say for himself. Our evening meal was served at sundown, and consisted of the same meagre soup as before. Then darkness fell, and about the same time as on the previous evening the dwarf appeared to conduct us to the rendezvous.

Chapter 14

An Ordeal

When we left our rooms on this occasion we turned to the right hand instead of to the left, and proceeded to a long corridor running below that in which our cells were situated. Whereabouts in the monastery this particular passage was placed, and how its bearings lay with regard to the staircase by which we had ascended from the valley on the previous day, I could not discover. Like all the others, however, it was innocent of daylight, but was lighted by enormous torches, which again were upheld by iron brackets driven into the walls. Once during our march an opportunity was vouchsafed me of examining these walls for myself, when to my astonishment I discovered that they were not hewn out of the rock as I had supposed, but were built of dressed stone of a description, remarkably resembling granite. This being so, I realized, for the first time, that the cells and the corridors were built by human hands, but how long it could have taken the builders to complete such an enormous task was a calculation altogether beyond my powers. But to return to my narrative.

From the corridor just described we passed down another flight of steps, then across a narrow landing, after which came another staircase. As we reached it our ears were assailed by a noise resembling distant thunder.

"What sound is that?" asked Nikola of our guide.

The dwarf did not answer in words, but, leading us along a side passage, held his torch above his head, and bade us look.

For a moment the dancing flame prevented us from seeing anything. Then our eyes became accustomed to the light, and to our amazement we discovered that we were standing on the very brink of an enormous precipice. In the abyss, the wind, which must have come in through some passage from the open air, tore and shrieked with a most dismal noise, while across the way, not more than twelve yards distant, fell the waters of a magnificent cataract. Picture to yourself that great volume of water crashing and roaring down through the darkness into the very bowels of the earth. The fall must have been tremendous, for no spray came up to us. All we could see was a mass of black water rushing past us. We stood and looked, open-mouthed, and when our wonder and curiosity were satisfied as much as it ever would be, turned and followed our guide back to the place where we had been standing when we had first heard the noise. At the other end of this corridor or landing, whichever you may please to term it, was a large stone archway, resembling a tunnel more than anything else, and at its mouth stood a monk. The dwarf went forward to him and said something in a low voice, whereupon he took a torch from the wall at his side and signed to us to follow him. The dwarf returned to the higher regions, while we plunged deeper still below the surface of the earth. Whether we were really as far down as we imagined, or whether the dampness was caused by some leakage from the cataract we had just seen, I cannot say; at any rate, the walls and floors were all streaming wet.

The passage, or tunnel, as I have more fittingly termed it, was a long one, measuring at least fifty feet from entrance to exit. When we had passed through it we stood in the biggest cave I have yet had the good fortune to behold; indeed, so large was it that in the half-dark it was with the utmost difficulty I could see the other side. Our guide led us across the first transept into the main aisle and then left us. No sign of furniture of any kind—either stool, altar, or dais—was to be seen, and as far as we could judge there was not a living soul within call. The only sound to be heard was the faint dripping of water, which seemed to come from every part of the cave.

"This is eerie enough to suit any one," I whispered to Nikola. "I hope the performance will soon commence."

"Hush!" he said. "Be careful what you say, for you don't know who may overhear you."

He had hardly spoken before the first mysterious incident of the evening occurred. We were standing facing that part of the cavern which had been on our right when we entered. The light was better in that particular spot than anywhere else, and

172

I am prepared to swear that at that instant, to the best of my belief, there was not a human being between ourselves and the wall. Yet as we looked a shadow seemed to rise out of the ground before us; it came closer, and as it came it took human shape. The trick was a clever one and its working puzzles me to this day. Of course the man may have made his appearance from behind a pillar, specially arranged for the purpose, or he may have risen from a trap-door in the floor, though personally I consider both these things unlikely; the fact however remains, come he did.

"By your own desire, and of no force applied by human beings," he said, addressing Nikola, "thou art here asking that the wisdom of our order may be revealed to thee. There is still time to draw back if thou wouldst."

"I have no desire to draw back," Nikola answered firmly.

"So be it," said the man. "Then follow me."

Nikola moved forward, and I was about to accompany him when the man ahead of us turned, and pointing to me said: "Come no farther! It is not meet that thou shouldst see what is now to be revealed."

Nikola faced me and said quietly, "Remain."

Having given this order he followed the other along the cave and presently disappeared from my sight.

For some minutes I stood where they had left me, listening to the dripping of the water in the distant parts of the cave, watching the bats as they flitted swiftly up and down the gloomy aisles, and wondering into what mysteries Nikola was about to be initiated. The silence was most oppressive, and every moment that I waited it seemed to be growing worse. To say that I was disappointed at being thus shelved at the most important point in our adventure would scarcely express my feelings. Besides, I wanted to be at Nikola's right hand should any trouble occur.

As I waited the desire to know more of what he was doing grew upon me. I felt that come what might I must be present at the interview to which he had been summoned. No one, I argued, would be any the wiser, and even if by chance they should discover that I had followed them, I felt I could trust to my own impudence and powers of invention to explain my presence there. My mind was no sooner made up than I set off down the cave in the direction in which they had disappeared. Arriving at the further end I discovered another small passage, from which led still another flight of steps. Softly I picked my way down them, at the same time trying to reason out in my own mind how deep in the mountain we were, but as usual I could come to no satisfactory conclusion.

When I arrived at the bottom of the steps, I stood in a peculiar sort of crypt, supported by pillars, and surrounded on all sides by tiers of niches, or shelves, cut, after the fashion of the Roman catacombs, in the solid rock. This dismal place was lighted by three torches, and by their assistance I was able to discern in each niche a swaddled-up human figure. Not without a feeling of awe I left the steps by which I had descended and began to hunt about among the pillars for a doorway through which I might pass into the room below, where Nikola was engaged with the Great Ones of the Mountains. But though I searched for upwards of ten minutes, not a sign of any such entrance could I discover. I was now in a curious position. I had left my station in the larger cave and, in spite of orders to the contrary, had followed to witness what was not intended for my eyes; in that case, supposing the door at the top were shut, and I could find no other exit, I should be caught like a rat in a trap. To make matters worse, I should have disobeyed the strict command of the man who had summoned Nikola, and I should also have incurred the blame of Nikola himself. Remembering how rigorously he had dealt with those who had offended him before, I resolved in my own mind to turn back while I had the chance. But just as I was about to do so, something curious about the base of one of the pillars, to the right of where I stood, caught my eye. It was either a crack magnified by the uncertain light of the torches, or it was a doorway cleverly constructed in the stonework, and which had been improperly closed. I approached it, and, inserting the blade of my knife, pulled. It opened immediately, revealing the fact that the entire pillar was hollow, and what was more important to me, that it contained a short wooden ladder which led down into yet another crypt.

In an instant my resolution to return to the upper cave was forgotten. An opportunity of discovering their business was presented to me, and come what might I was going to make the most of it. Pulling the door open to its full extent I crept in and went softly down the ladder. By the time I reached the bottom I was in total darkness. For a moment I was at a loss to understand the reason of this, as I could plainly hear voices; but by dint of feeling I discovered that the place in which I stood was a sort of ante-chamber to a room beyond, the door of which was only partially shut. My sandals made no noise on the stone floor, and I was therefore able to creep up to the entrance of the inner room without exciting attention. What a sight it was that met my eyes!

The apartment itself was not more than fifty feet long by thirty wide. But instead of being like all the other places through which I had passed, an ordinary cave, this one was floored and wainscotted with woodwork now black with age. How high it was I could not guess, for the walls went up and up until I lost them in the darkness. Of furniture the room boasted but little; there was, however, a long and queer-shaped table at the further end, another near the door, and a tripod brazier on the left-hand side. The latter contained a mass of live coal, and, as there was some sort of forced draught behind it, it roared like a blacksmith's forge.

Nikola, when I entered, was holding what looked like a phial in his left hand. The black-hooded men I had expected to find there I could not see, but standing by his side were two dressed in a totally different fashion.

The taller of the pair was a middle-aged man, almost bald, boasting a pleasant, but slightly Semitic cast of countenance, and wearing a short black beard. His companion, evidently the chief, differed from him in almost every particular. To begin with, he was the oldest man I have ever seen in my life able to move about. He was small and shrivelled almost beyond belief, his skin was as yellow as parchment, and his bones, whenever he moved, looked as if they must certainly cut through their coverings. His countenance bore unmistakable traces of having once been extremely handsome, and was now full of intellectual beauty; at the same time, however, I could not help feeling certain that it was not the face of an Asiatic. Like his companion, he also wore a beard, but in his case it was long and snow-white, which added materially to his venerable appearance.

"My son," he was saying, addressing himself to Nikola, "hitherto thou hast seen the extent to which the particular powers of which we have been speaking can be cultivated by a life of continual prayer and self-denial. Now thou wilt learn to what extent our sect has benefited by earthly wisdom. Remember always that from time immemorial there have been those among us who have given up their lives to the study of the frailties and imperfections of this human frame. The wonders of medicine and all the arts of healing have come down to us from years that date from before the apotheosis of the ever-blessed Buddha. Day and night, generation after generation, century after century in these caves those of our faith have been studying and adding to the knowledge which our forefathers possessed. Remote as we are from it, every fresh discovery of the Western or Eastern world is known to us, and to the implements with which our forefathers worked we have added everything helpful that man has invented since. In the whole world there are none who hold the secret of life and death in their hands as we do. Wouldst thou have an example? There is a case at present in the monastery."

As he spoke he struck a gong hanging upon the wall, and almost before the sound had died away a monk appeared to answer it. The old fellow said something to him, and immediately he retired by the way he had come. Five minutes later he reappeared, followed by another monk. Between them they bore a stretcher, on which lay a human figure. The old man signed to them to place him in the centre of the room, which they did, and retired.

As soon as they had departed Nikola was invited to examine the person upon the stretcher. He did so, almost forgetting, in his excitement, his role of an old man.

For nearly five minutes he bent over the patient, who lay like a log, then he rose and turned to his companions.

"A complete case of paralysis," he said.

"You are assured in your own mind that it is complete?" inquired the old man.

"Perfectly assured," said Nikola.

"Then pay heed, for you are about to witness the power which the wisdom of all the ages has given us."

Turning to his companion he took from his hand a small iron ladle. This he placed upon the brazier, pouring into it about a tablespoonful of the mixture contained in the phial, which, when I first looked, Nikola had been holding in his hand. As the ladle became heated, the liquid, whatever it may have been, threw off a tiny vapour, the smell of which reminded me somewhat of a mixture of sandal-wood and camphor.

By the time this potion was ready for use the second man had divested the patient of his garments. What remained of the medicine was thereupon forced into his mouth, that and his nostrils were bound up, and after he had lost consciousness, which he did in less than a minute, he was anointed from head to toe with some penetrating unguent. Just as the liquid, when heating on the brazier, had done, this ointment threw off a vapour, which hung about the body, rising into the air to the height of about three inches. For something like five minutes this exhalation continued, then it began to die away, and as soon as it had done so the unguent was again applied, after which the two men kneaded the body in somewhat the same fashion as that adopted by masseurs. So far the colour of the man's skin had been a sort of zinc white, now it gradually assumed the appearance of that of a healthy man. Once more the massage treatment was begun, and when it was finished the limbs began to twitch in a spasmodic fashion. At the end of half an hour the bandage was removed from the mouth and nostrils, also the plugs from the ears, and the man, who had hitherto lain like one asleep, opened his eyes.

"Move thy arms," said the old man with an air of command.

The patient promptly did as he was commanded.

"Bend thy legs."

He complied with the order.

"Stand upon thy feet."

He rose from the stretcher and stood before them, apparently as strong and hearty a man as one could wish to see.

"To-morrow this treatment shall be repeated, and the day following thou shalt be cured. Now go and give thanks," said the old man with impressive sternness. Then turning to Nikola, he continued—

"Thou hast seen our powers. Could any man in the world without these walls do as much?"

"Nay, they are ignorant as earthworms," said Nikola. "But I praise Buddha for the man's relief."

"Praise to whom praise is due," answered the old fellow. "And now, having seen so much, it is fitting that thou shouldst go further, and to do so it is necessary that we put aside the curtain that divides man's life from death. Art thou afraid?"

"Nay," said Nikola, "I have no fear."

"It is well said," remarked the elder man, and again he struck the gong.

The monk having appeared in answer he gave him an order and the man immediately withdrew. When he returned, he and his companion brought with them another stretcher, upon which was placed the dead body of a man. The monk having withdrawn the old priest said to Nikola—

"Gaze upon this person, my son; his earthly pilgrimage is over; he died of old age to-day. He was one of our lay brethren, and a devout and holy man. It is meet that he should conduct thee, of whose piety we have heard so much, into our great inner land of knowledge. Examine him for thyself, and be sure that the spirit of life has really passed out of him."

Nikola bent over the bier and did as he was requested. At the end of his examination he said quietly—

"It is even as thou sayest; the brother's life is departed from him."

"Thou art convinced of the truth of thy words?" inquired the second man.

"I am convinced," said Nikola.

"Then I will once more show thee what our science can do."

With the assistance of his colleague he brought what looked like a large electric battery and placed it at the dead man's feet. The priest connected certain wires with the body, and, having taken a handle in either hand, placed himself in position, and shut his eyes. Though I craned my head round to see, I could not tell what he did. But this much is certain, after a few moments he swayed himself backwards and forwards, seemed to breathe with difficulty, and finally became almost rigid. Then came a long pause, lasting perhaps three minutes, at the end of which time he opened his eyes, raised his right arm, and pointed with his forefinger at the dead man's face. As he did so, to my horror, I saw the eyes open! Again he seemed to pray, then he pointed at the right arm, whereupon the dead man lifted it and folded it upon his breast, then at his left, which followed suit. When both the white hands were in this position he turned to Nikola and said—

"Is there aught in thy learning can give thee the power to do that?"

"There is nothing," said Nikola, who I could see was as much amazed as I was.

"But our power does not end there," said the old man.

"Oh, wonderful father! what further canst thou teach me?" asked Nikola. The man did not answer, but again closed his eyes for a few moments. Then, still holding the handles but pointing them towards the dead man, he cried in a loud voice—

"Ye who are dead, arise!"

And then—but I do not expect you will believe me when I tell it—that man who had been ten hours dead, rose little by little from his bier and at last stood before us. I continued to watch what happened. I saw Nikola start forward as if carried out of himself. I saw the second man extend his arm to hold him back, and then the corpse fell in a heap upon the floor. The two men instantly sprang forward, lifted it up, and placed it upon the stretcher again.

"Art thou satisfied?" inquired the old man.

"I am filled with wonder. Is it possible that I can see more?" said Nikola.

"Thou wouldst see more?" asked the chief of the Two in a sepulchral tone. "Then, as a last proof of our power, before thou takest upon thee the final vows of our order, when all our secrets must be revealed to thee, thou shalt penetrate the Land of Shadows, and see, as far as is possible for human eyes, the dead leaders of our order, of all ages, stand before you."

With that he took from a bag hanging round his waist a handful of what looked like dried herbs. These he threw upon the fire, and almost instantly the room was filled with a dense smoke. For some few seconds I could distinguish nothing, then it drew slowly off, and little by little I seemed to see with an extraordinary clearness. Whether it was that I was hypnotized, and fancied I saw what I am about to describe, or whether it really happened as I say, I shall never know. One thing, however, is certain—the room was filled with the shadowy figures of men. They were of all ages, and apparently of all nations. Some were Chinese, some were Cingalese, some were Thibetans, while one or two were certainly Aryans, and for all I knew to the contrary, might have been English. The room was filled with them, but there was something plainly unsubstantial about them. They moved to and fro without sound, yet with regular movements. I watched them, and as I watched, a terror, such as I had never known in my life before, came over me. I felt that if I did not get out of the room at once I should fall upon the floor in a fit. In this state I made my way towards the door by which I had entered, fled up the ladder, through the crypt, and then across the cave to the place where I had stood when Nikola had left me, and then fell fainting upon the floor.

How long I remained in this swoon I cannot tell, but when I came to myself again I was still alone.

It must have been quite an hour later when Nikola joined me. The monk who had brought us into the hall accompanied him, and led us towards the tunnel. There the dwarf received us and conducted us back to our apartments.

Once there, Nikola, without vouchsafing me a word, retired into the inner room. I was too dazed, and, I will confess, too frightened by what I had seen to feel equal to interviewing him, so I left him alone.

Presently, however, he came into my room, and crossing to where I sat on my bed, placed his hand kindly upon my shoulder. I looked up into his face, which was paler than I had ever seen it before.

"Bruce," he said, not without a little touch of regret in his voice, "how was it that you did not do what you were told?"

"It was my cursed curiosity," I said bitterly. "But do not think I am not sorry. I would give all I possess in the world not to have seen what I saw in that room."

"But you *have* seen, and nothing will ever take away that knowledge from you. You will carry it with you to the grave."

"The grave," I answered bitterly. "What hope is there even in the grave after what we have seen tonight? Oh, for Heaven's sake, Nikola, let us get out of this place to-night if possible."

"So you are afraid, are you?" he answered with a strange expression on his face. "I did not think you would turn coward, Bruce."

"In this I *am* a coward," I answered. "Give me something to do, something human to fight, some tangible danger to face, and I am your man! But I am not fit to fight against the invisible."

"Come, come, cheer up!" said Nikola. "Things are progressing splendidly with us. Our identity has not been questioned; we have been received by the heads of the sect as the people we pretend to be, and tomorrow I am to be raised to the rank of one of the Three. The remaining secrets will then be revealed to me, and when I have discovered all I want to know, we will go back to civilization once more. Think of what I may have achieved by this time to-morrow. I tell you, Bruce, such an opportunity might never come to a Western man again. It will be invaluable to me. Think of this, and then it will help your pluck to go through with it to the end!"

"If I am not asked to see such things as I saw tonight, it may," I answered, "but not unless."

"You must do me the credit to remember you were not asked to see them."

"I know that, and I have paid severely for my disobedience."

"Then let us say no more about it. Remember, Bruce, I trust you."

"You need have no fear," I said, after a pause, lasting a few moments. "Even if I could get out of it, for your sake I would go through with it, come what might."

"I thank you for that assurance. Good-night."

So saying, Nikola retired to his room, and I laid myself down upon my bed, but, you may be sure, it was not to sleep.

Chapter 15

How Nikola Was Installed

As soon as I woke next morning I went into Nikola's room. To my surprise he was not there. Nor did he put in an appearance until nearly an hour later. When he did, I could see that he was completely exhausted, though he tried hard not to show it.

"What have you been doing?" I asked, meeting him on the threshold with a question.

"Qualifying myself for my position by being initiated into more mysteries," he answered. "Bruce, if you could have seen all that I have done since midnight tonight, I verily believe it would be impossible for you ever to be a happy man again. When I tell you that what I have witnessed has even frightened me, you will realize something of what I mean."

"What have you seen?"

"I have been shown the flesh on the mummified bodies of men who died nearly a thousand years ago made soft and healthy as that of a little child; I have seen such surgery as the greatest operator in Europe would consider impossible; I have been shown a new anaesthetic that does not deprive the patient of his senses, and yet renders him impervious to pain; and I have seen other things, such that I dare not describe them even to you."

"And you were not tempted to draw back?"

"Only once," answered Nikola candidly. "For nearly a minute, I will confess, I hesitated, but eventually I forced myself to go on. That once accomplished, the rest was easy. But I must not stay talking here. To-day is going to be a big day with us. I shall go and lie down in order to recoup my energies. Call me if I am wanted, but otherwise do not disturb me."

He went into the inner room, laid himself down upon his bed, and for nearly two hours slept as peacefully as a little child.

The morning meal was served soon after sunrise, but I did not wake him for it; indeed, it was not until nearly midday that he made his appearance again. When he did, we discussed our position more fully, weighed the pros and cons more carefully, and speculated still further as to what the result of our adventure would be. Somehow a vague feeling of impending disaster had taken possession of me. I could not rid myself of the belief that before the day was over we should find our success in some way reversed. I told Nikola as much, but he only laughed, and uttered his usual reply to the effect that, disaster or no disaster, he was not going to give in, but would go through with it to the bitter end, whatever the upshot might be.

About two o'clock in the afternoon a dwarf put in an appearance, and intimated that Nikola's presence was required in the great hall. He immediately left the cell, and remained away until dusk. When he returned he looked more like a ghost than a man, but even then, tired as he undoubtedly was, his iron will would not acknowledge such a thing as fatigue. Barely vouchsafing me a word he passed into the inner room, to occupy himself there until nearly eight o'clock making notes and writing up a concise account of all that he had seen. I sat on my bed watching the dancing of his torch flame upon the wall, and feeling about as miserable as it would be possible for a man to be. Why I should have been so depressed I cannot say. But it was certain that everything served to bring back to me my present position. I thought of my old English school, and wondered if I had been told then what was to happen to me in later life whether I should have believed it. I thought of Gladys, my pretty sweetheart, and asked myself if I should ever see her again; and I was just in the act of drawing the locket she had given me from beneath my robe, when my ear caught the sound of a footstep on the stones outside. Next moment the same uncanny dwarf who had summoned us on the previous evening made his appearance. Without a word he pointed to the door of the inner room. I supposed the action to signify that those in authority wished Nikola to come to them, and went in and told him so. He immediately put away his paper and pencil, and signed to me to leave his room ahead of him. The dwarf preceded us, I came next, and Nikola following me. In this fashion we made our way up one corridor and down another,

183

ascended and descended innumerable stairs, and at last reached the tunnel of the great cavern, the same in which we had passed through such adventures on the preceding night. On this occasion the door was guarded by fully a dozen monks, who formed into two lines to let us pass.

If the cave had been bare of ornament when we visited it the previous night, it was now altogether different. Hundreds of torches flamed from brackets upon the walls, distributed their ruddy glare upon the walls and ceiling, and were reflected, as in a million diamonds, in the stalactites hanging from the roof.

At the further end of the great cavern was a large and beautifully decorated triple throne, and opposite it, but half-way down the hall, a dais covered with a rich crimson cloth bordered with heavy bullion fringe. As we entered we were greeted with the same mysterious music we had heard on the day of our arrival. It grew louder and louder until we reached the dais, and then, just as Nikola took up his place at the front, and I mine a little behind him, began to die slowly away again. When it had ceased to sound a great bell in the roof above our heads struck three. The noise it made was almost deafening. It seemed to fill the entire cave, then, like the music above mentioned, to die slowly away again. Once more the same number of strokes were repeated, and once more the sound died away. When it could no longer be heard, curtains at the further end were drawn back, and the monks commenced to file slowly in from either side, just as they had done at the first service after our arrival. There must have been nearly four hundred of them; they were all dressed in black and all wore the same peculiar head-covering I have described elsewhere.

When they had taken their places on either side of the dais upon which we stood, the curtain which covered the doorway, through which I had followed Nikola down into the subterranean chamber the night before, was drawn aside and another procession entered. First came the dwarfs, to the number of thirty, each carrying a lighted torch in his hand; following them were nearly a hundred monks, in white, swinging censers, then a dozen grey-bearded priests in black, but without the head-covering, after which the two men who were the heads of this extraordinary sect.

184

Reaching the throne the procession divided itself into two parts, each half taking up its position in the form of a crescent on either side. The two heads seated themselves beneath the canopy, and exactly at the moment of their doing so the great bell boomed forth again. As its echo died away all the monks who had hitherto been kneeling rose to their feet and with one accord took up the hymn of their sect. Though the music and words were barbaric in the extreme, there was something about the effect produced that stirred the heart beyond description. The hymn ceased as suddenly as it had begun, and then, from among the white-robed monks beside the throne, a man stepped forth with a paper in his hand. In a loud voice he proclaimed the fact that it had pleased the two Great Ones of the Mountains to fill the vacancy which had so long existed in the triumvirate. For that reason they had summoned to their presence a man who bore a reputation for wisdom and holiness second to none. Him they now saw before them. He had rendered good service to the Society, he had been proved to be a just man, and now it only remained for him to state whether he was willing to take upon himself the responsibilities of the office to which he had been called. Having finished his speech, the man retired to his place again. Then four of the monks in white, two from either side of the throne, walked slowly down the aisle towards Nikola, and, bidding him follow them, escorted him in procession to the room behind the curtain. While he was absent from the cave no one moved or spoke.

At the end of something like ten minutes the small procession filed out again, Nikola coming last. He was now attired in all the grand robes of his office. His tall, spare form and venerable disguise became them wonderfully well, and when he once more stood upon the dais before me I could not help thinking I had never in my life seen a more imposing figure.

Again the great bell tolled out, and when the sound had ceased, the man who had first spoken stepped forward and in a loud voice bade it be known to all present that the ex-priest of Hankow was prepared to take upon himself the duties and responsibilities of his office. As he retired to his place again two monks came forward and escorted Nikola up the centre aisle towards the triple throne. Arriving at the foot the two Great Ones threw off the veils they had hitherto been wearing, and came down to meet him. Having each extended a hand, they were about to escort him to his place when there was a commotion at the end of the hall.

In a flash, though so far the sound only consisted of excited whispering, all my forebodings rushed back upon me, and my heart seemed to stand still. The Chief of the Three dropped Nikola's hand, and, turning to one of the monks beside him, bade him go down the hall and discover what this unseemly interruption might mean.

The man went, and was absent for some few minutes. When he returned it was to report that there was a stranger in the monastery who craved immediate speech with the Two on a matter concerning the election about to take place.

He was ordered to enter, and in a few minutes a travel-stained, soiled and bedraggled Chinaman made his appearance and humbly approached the throne. His four followers remained clustered round the door at the further end.

"Who art thou, and what is thy business here?" asked the old man in a voice that rang like a trumpet call. "Thinkest thou that thou wilt be permitted to disturb us in this unseemly fashion?"

"I humbly sue for pardon. But I have good reason, my father!" returned the man, with a reverence that nearly touched the ground.

"Let us hear it then, and be speedy. What is thy name, and whence comest thou?"

"*I am the Chief Priest of the temple of Hankow, and I come asking for justice,*" said the man, and as he said it a great murmur of astonishment ran through the hall. I saw Nikola step back a pace and then stand quite still. If it were the truth this man was telling we were lost beyond hope of redemption.

"Thou foolish man to come to us with so false a story!" said the elder of the Two. "Knowest thou not that the Priest of Hankow stands before thee?"

"It is false!" said the man. "I come to warn you that that man is an impostor. He is no priest, but a foreign devil who captured me and sent me out of the way while he took my place."

"Then how didst thou get here?" asked the chief of the sect.

"I escaped," said the man, "from among those whom he paid to keep me, and made my way to Tientsin, thence to Pekin, and so on here."

"O my father!" said Nikola, just as quietly as if nothing unusual were happening, "wilt thou allow such a cunningly-devised tale to do me evil in thy eyes? Did I not bring with me a letter from the High Priest of the Llamaserai, making known to thee that I am he whom thou didst expect? Wilt thou then put me to shame before the world?"

The old man did not answer.

"I, too, have a letter from the High Priest," said the new arrival eagerly. Whereupon he produced a document and handed it to the second of the Two.

"Peace! peace! We will retire and consider upon this matter," said the old man. Then turning to the monks beside him he said sternly: "See that neither of these men escape." After which he retired with his colleague to the inner room, whence they had appeared at the beginning of the ceremony.

In perfect silence we awaited their return, and during the time they were absent, I noticed a curious fact that I had remarked once or twice in my life before. Though all day I had been dreading the approach of some catastrophe, when it came, and I had to look it fairly in the face, all my fears vanished like mist before the sun. My nervousness left me like a discarded cloak, and so certain seemed our fate that I found I could meet it with almost a smile.

At the end of about twenty minutes there was a stir near the door, and presently the Two returned and mounted their thrones. It was the old man who spoke.

"We have considered the letters," he said, "and in our wisdom we have concluded that it would be wisest to postpone our judgment for awhile. This matter must be further inquired into." Then turning to Nikola, he continued: "Take off those vestments. If thou art innocent they shall be restored to thee, and thou shall wear them with honour to thyself and the respect of all our order; but if thou art guilty, prepare for death, for no human soul shall save thee." Nikola immediately divested himself of his gorgeous robes, and handed them to the monks who stood ready to receive them.

"Thou wilt now," said the old man, "be conducted back to the cells thou hast hitherto occupied. To-night at a later hour this matter will be considered again."

Nikola bowed with his peculiar grace, and then came back to where I stood, after which, escorted by a double number of monks, we returned to our rooms and were left alone, not however before we had noted the fact that armed guards were placed at the gate at the top of the steps leading into the main corridor.

When I had made sure that no one was near enough to eavesdrop, I went into Nikola's room, expecting to find him cast down by the failure of his scheme. I was about to offer him my condolences, but he stopped me by holding up his hand.

"Of course," he said, "I regret exceedingly that our adventure should have ended like this. We must not grumble, however, for we have the satisfaction of knowing that we have played our cards like men. We have lost on the odd trick, that is all."

"And what is the upshot of it all to be?"

"Very simple, I should say. If we don't find a way to escape we shall pay the penalty of our rashness with our lives. I don't know that I mind so much for myself, though I should very much like to have had an opportunity of putting into practice a few of the things I have learnt here; but I certainly do regret for your sake."

"That is very good of you."

"Oh, make no mistake, I am thinking of that poor little girl in Pekin who believes so implicitly in you."

"For Heaven's sake don't speak of her or I shall turn coward! Are you certain that there is no way of escape?"

"To be frank with you I do not see one. You may be sure, however, that I shall use all my ingenuity to-night to make my case good, though I have no hope that I shall be successful. This man, you see, holds all the cards, and we are playing a lone hand against the bank. But there, I suppose it is no use thinking about the matter until after the trial to-night."

The hours wore slowly on, and every moment I expected to hear the tramp of feet upon the stones outside summoning us to the investigation. They came at last, and two monks entered my room, and bade me fetch my master. When I had done so we were marched in single file up the stairs and along the corridor, this time to a higher level instead of descending as on previous occasions.

Arriving on a broad landing we were received by an armed guard of monks. One of them ordered us to follow him, and in response we passed through a doorway and entered a large room, at the end of which two people were seated at a table; behind them and on either side were rows of monks, and between guards at the further end, the man who had brought the accusation against us.

At a signal from a monk, who was evidently in command of the guard, I was separated from Nikola, and then the trial commenced.

First the newcomer recited his tale. He described how in the village of Tsan-Chu he had been met and betrayed by two men, who, having secured his person, had carried him out to sea, and imprisoned him aboard a junk. His first captors, it was understood, were Englishmen, but he was finally delivered into the care of a Chinaman, who had conveyed him to Along Bay. From this place he managed to effect his escape, and after great hardships reached Tientsin. On arrival there he made inquiries which induced him to push on to Pekin. Making his way to the Llamaserai, and being able to convince the High Priest of his identity, he had learned to his astonishment that he was being impersonated, and that the man who was filling his place had preceded him to Thibet.

On the strength of this discovery he obtained men and donkeys, and came on to the monastery as fast as he could travel.

At the end of his evidence he was closely questioned by both of the great men, but his testimony was sound and could not be shaken. Then his attendants were called up and gave their evidence, after which Nikola was invited to make his case good.

He accepted the invitation with alacrity, and, reviewing all that his rival had said, pointed out the manifest absurdities with which it abounded, ridiculed what he called its inconsistency, implored his judges not to be led away by an artfully contrived tale, and brought his remarks to a conclusion by stating, what was perfectly true, though hardly in the manner he intended, that he had no doubt at all as to their decision. A more masterly speech it would have been difficult to imagine. His keen instinct had detected the one weak spot in his enemy's story, and his brilliant oratory helped him to make the most of it. His points told, and to my astonishment I saw that he had already influenced his judges in his favour. If only we could go on as we had begun, we might yet come successfully out of the affair. But we were reckoning without our host.

"Since thou sayest that thou art the priest of the temple of Hankow," said the younger of the two great men, addressing Nikola, "it is certain that thou must be well acquainted with the temple. In the first hall is a tablet presented by a Taotai of the province: what is the inscription upon it?"

"'With the gods be the decision as to what is best for man,'" said Nikola without hesitation.

I saw that the real priest was surprised beyond measure at this ready answer.

"And upon the steps that lead up to it, what is carved?"

"'Let peace be with all men!'" said Nikola, again without stopping. The judge turned to the other man.

"There is nothing there," he said; and my heart went down like lead.

"Now I know," said the old man, turning to Nikola, "that you are not what you pretend. There are no steps; therefore there can be nothing written upon them."

Then turning to the guards about him he said—

"Convey these men back to the room whence they came. See that they be well guarded, and at daybreak to-morrow morning let them be hurled from the battlements down into the valley below."

Nikola bowed, but said never a word. Then, escorted by our guards, we returned to our room. When we had arrived there, and the monks had left us to take up their places at the top of the steps outside, I sat myself down on my bed and covered my face with my hands. So this was what it had all come to. It was for this I had met Nikola in Shanghai; to be hurled from the battlements, the fate for which we had braved so many dangers.

Chapter 16

A Terrible Experience

Hour after hour I sat upon my bed-place, my mind completely overwhelmed by the consideration of our terrible position. We were caught like rats in a trap, and, as far as I could see, the only thing left for us to do now was to continue our resemblance to those animals by dying game. For fear lest my pluck should give way I would not think of Gladys at all, and when I found I could no longer keep my thoughts away from her, I went into the adjoining room to see what Nikola was doing. To my surprise I found him pacing quietly up and down, just as calm and collected as if he were waiting for dinner in a London drawing-room. "Well, Bruce," he said, as I entered, "it looks as if another three hours will see the curtain rung down upon our comedy."

"Tragedy, I should call it," I answered bitterly.

"Isn't it rather difficult to define where one begins and the other ends?" he asked, as if desirous of starting an argument. "Plato says——"

"Oh, confound Piato!" I answered sharply. "What I want to know is how you are going to prevent our being put to death at daybreak."

"I have no intention that we shall be," said Nikola.

"But how are you going to prevent it?" I inquired.

"I have not the remotest notion," he answered, "but all the same I *do* intend to prevent it. The unfortunate part of it is that we are left so much in the dark, and have no idea where the execution will take place. If that were once settled we could arrange things more definitely. However, do not bother yourself about it; go to bed and leave it to me."

I went back into my own room and laid myself down upon my bed as he commanded. One thought followed another, and

191

presently, however singular it may seem, I fell fast asleep. I dreamt that I was once more walking upon the wall in Pekin with my sweetheart. I saw her dear face looking up into mine and I felt the pressure of her little hand upon my arm. Then suddenly from over the parapet of the wall in front of us appeared the man who had discovered my identity in the Llamaserai; he was brandishing a knife, and I was in the act of springing forward to seize him when I felt my shoulder rudely shaken, and woke up to discover a man leaning over me.

One glance told me that it was one of the monks who had conducted us to the room, and on seeing that I was awake he signed to me to get up. By this time a second had brought Nikola from his room, and as soon as we were ready we were marched out into the corridor, where we found about a dozen men assembled.

"It seems a pity to have disturbed us so early," said Nikola, as we fell into our places and began to march up the long passage, "especially as I was just perfecting a most admirable scheme which I feel sure would have saved us."

"You are too late now," I answered bitterly.

"So it would appear," said Nikola, and strode on without further comment.

To attempt to describe to you my feelings during that march through those silent corridors, would be impossible. Indeed, I hardly like to think of it myself. What the time was I had no idea, nor could I tell to what place we were being conducted. We ascended one stair and descended another, passed through large and small caves and threaded endless corridors, till I lost all count of our direction. At last, however, we came to a halt at the foot of the smallest staircase I had yet seen in the monastery. We waited for a few moments, then ascended it and arrived at a narrow landing, at the end of which was a large door. Here our procession once more halted. Finally the doors were unbarred and thrown open, and an icy blast rushed in. Outside we could see the battlements, which were built on the sheer side of the cliff. It was broad daylight, and bitterly cold. Snow lay upon the roof-tops, but the air was transparently clear; indeed when we passed outside we could plainly distinguish the mountains across the valley where we had lost our coolies and donkeys only a week or so before.

192

Once in the sunshine our guides beat their torches against the wall till the flames were extinguished, and then stood at attention. From their preparations it was evident that the arrival of some person of importance was momentarily expected.

All this time my heart was beating like a wheat-flail against my ribs, and, try how I would to prevent them, my teeth were chattering in my head like castanets. As our gaolers had brought us up here it was evident we were going to be thrown over the cliff, as had been first proposed. I glanced round me to see if it would be possible to make a fight for it, but one glimpse showed me how utterly futile such an attempt would be.

While I was arguing this out in my own mind our guards had somewhat relaxed their stiffness; then they came suddenly to attention, and next moment, evidently with a signal from the other side, we were marched to a spot further along the battlements.

Here the two great men of the monastery were awaiting us, and as soon as we made our appearance they signed to our guides to bring us closer to them. The old man was the first to speak.

"Men of the West! ye have heard your sentence," he said in a low and solemn voice. "Ye have brought it upon yourselves; have ye anything to urge why the decree should not be executed."

I looked at Nikola, but he only shook his head. Hard as I tried I could not discover sufficient reason myself, so I followed his example.

"Then let it be so," said the old man, who had noticed our hesitation; "there is nought to be done save to carry out the work. Prepare ye for death."

We were then ordered to stand back, and, until I heard another commotion on the stairs, I was at a loss to understand why we were not immediately disposed of. Then a second procession of monks appeared upon the battlements escorting a third prisoner. He was a tall, burly fellow, and from the way in which he was dressed and shaved I gathered had been a monk. He made his appearance with evident reluctance, and when he arrived at the top of the steps had to be dragged up to face the

Two. Their interview was short, and even more to the point than our own.

"Thou hast murdered one of thy brethren," said the old man, still in the same sepulchral tone in which he had addressed us. "Hast thou anything to say why the sentence of death passed upon thee should not be carried into effect?"

In answer the man first blustered, then became stolid, and finally howled outright. I watched him with a curiosity which at any other time I should have deemed impossible. Then, at a signal from the old man, four stalwart monks rushed forward, and, having seized him, dragged him to the edge of the battlements. The poor wretch struggled and screamed, but he was like a child in the hands of those who held him. Closer and closer they drew to the edge. Then there was an interval of fierce struggling, a momentary pause, a wild cry, and next moment the man had disappeared over the edge, falling in a sheer drop quite fifteen hundred feet into the valley below. As he vanished from our sight my heart seemed to stand still. The poor wretch's cry still rang in my ears, and in another minute I knew it would be our turn.

I looked up at the blue sky above our heads, across which white clouds were flying before the breeze; I looked across the valley to where the snow-capped peaks showed on the other side, then at the battlements of the monastery, and last at the crowd of black figures surrounding us. In a flash all my past life seemed to rise before my eyes. I saw myself a little boy again walking in an English garden with my pretty mother, with my play-fellows at school, at sea, on the Australian goldfields, and so on through almost every phase of my life up to the moment of our arrival at the place where we now stood. I looked at Nikola, but his pale face showed no sign of emotion. I will stake my life that he was as cool at that awful moment as when I first saw him in Shanghai. Presently the old man came forward again.

"If ye have ought to say—any last request to make—there is still time to do it," he said.

"I have a request to make," answered Nikola. "Since we *must* die, is it not a waste of good material to cast us over that cliff? I have heard it said that my skull is an extraordinary one, while my companion here boasts such a body as I would give worlds to anatomise. I have no desire to die, as you may suppose; but if nothing will satisfy you save to kill us, pray let us die in the interests of science."

Whether they had really intended to kill us, I cannot say, but this singular request of my companion's did not seem to cause as much astonishment as I had expected it would do. He consulted with his colleague, and then turned to Nikola again.

"Thou art a brave man," he said.

"One must reconcile oneself to the inevitable," said Nikola coolly. "Have you any objection to urge?"

"We will give it consideration," said the old man. "The lives of both of you are spared for the time being."

Thereupon our guards were called up, and we were once more marched back to our room. Arriving there, and when the monks had departed to take up their positions at the top of the staircase as before, Nikola said:—

"If we escape from this place, you will never be able to assert that science has done nothing for you. At least it has saved your life."

"But if they are going to scoop your brains out and to practise their butchery on me," I said with an attempt at jocularity I was far from feeling, "I must say I fail to see how it is going to benefit us."

"Let me explain," said Nikola. "If they are going to use us in the manner you describe, they cannot do so before to-morrow morning, for I happen to know that their operating room is undergoing alterations, and, as I am a conscientious surgeon myself, I should be very loath to spoil my specimens by any undue hurry. So you see we have at any rate all to-night to perfect our plan of escape."

"But have you a plan?" I asked anxiously.

"There is one maturing somewhere in the back of my head," said Nikola.

"And you think it will come to anything?"

"That is beyond my power to tell," he answered; "but I will go so far as to add that the chances are in our favour."

Nothing would induce him to say more, and presently he went back into his own room, where he began to busy himself with his precious medicine-chest, which I saw he had taken care to hide.

"My little friend," he said, patting and fondling it as a father would do his favourite son, "I almost thought we were destined to part company; now it remains for you to save your master's life."

Then turning to me he bade me leave him alone, and in obedience to his wish I went back to my own room.

How we survived the anxiety of that day I cannot think; such another period of waiting I never remember. One moment I felt confident that Nikola would carry out his plan, and that we should get away to the coast in safety; the next I could not see how it could possibly succeed, the odds being so heavy against us.

Almost punctually our midday meal was served to us, then the ray of light upon the floor began to lengthen, reached the opposite wall, climbed it, and finally disappeared altogether.

About seven o'clock Nikola came in to me.

"Look here, Bruce," he said with unusual animation, "I've been thinking this matter out, and I believe I've hit on a plan that will save us if anything can. In half an hour the monk will arrive with our last meal. He will place the bowl upon the floor over there, and will then turn his back on you while he puts his torch in the bracket upon the wall yonder. We will have a sponge, saturated with a little anaesthetic I have here, ready for him, and directly he turns I will get him by the throat and throttle him while you clap it over his nose. Once he's unconscious you must slip on his dress, and go out again and make your way up the steps. There are two men stationed on the other side, and the door between us and them is locked. I have noticed that the man who brings us our food simply knocks upon it and it is opened. You will do as he does, thus, and as you pass out will drop this gold coin as if by accident." (Here he gave me some money.) "One of the men will be certain to stoop to pick it up; as he goes down you must manage by hook or crook to seize and choke the other. I shall be behind you, and I will attend to his companion."

"'It seems a desperate scheme."

"We are desperate men!" said Nikola.

"And when we have secured them?" I asked.

"I shall put on one of their robes," this intrepid man answered, "and we will then make our escape as quickly as

196

possible. Luck must do the rest for us. Are you prepared to attempt so much?"

"To get out of this place I would attempt anything," I answered.

"Very good then," he said. "We must now wait for the appearance of the man. Let us hope it won't be long before he comes."

For nearly three-quarters of an hour we waited without hearing any sound of the monk. The minutes seemed long as years, and I don't think I ever felt more relieved in my life than I did when I heard the door at the top of the stairs open, and detected the sound of sandalled feet coming down the steps.

"Are you ready?" whispered Nikola, putting the sponge down near me, and returning to his own room.

"Quite ready," I answered.

The man came nearer, the glare of his torch preceding him. At last he entered, carrying a light in one hand and a large bowl in the other. The latter he put down upon the floor, and, having done so, turned to place the torch in the socket fastened to the wall. He had hardly lifted his arm, however, before I saw Nikola creep out of the adjoining room. Closer and closer he approached the unsuspecting monk, and then, having measured his distance, with a great spring threw himself upon the man and clutched him by the throat. I pulled his legs from under him, and down he dropped upon the floor, with Nikola's fingers still tightening on his throat. Then, when the sponge had been applied, little by little, his struggles ceased, and presently he lay in Nikola's arms as helpless as if he were dead.

"That is one man accounted for," said Nikola quietly, as he laid the body upon the floor; "now for the others. Slip on this fellow's dress as quickly as you can."

I did as he bade me, and in a few seconds had placed the peculiar black covering over the upper part of my face and head, and was ready to carry out the rest of the scheme. In the face of this excitement I felt as happy as a child; it was the creepy, crawly, supernatural, business that shook my nerve. When it came to straightforward matter-of-fact fighting I was not afraid of anything.

Carrying the money in my hand as we had arranged, I left the room and proceeded up the steps, Nikola following half a dozen yards or so behind me, but keeping in the shadow. Arriving at the gate I rapped upon it with my knuckles, and it was immediately opened. Two men were leaning on either side of it, and as I passed through, I took care that the one on the right should see the money in my hand. As if by accident I dropped it, and it rolled away beyond his feet. Instantly he stooped and made a grab for it. Seeing this I wheeled round upon the other man, and before he could divine my intention had him by the throat. But though I had him at a disadvantage, he proved no easy capture. In stature he must have stood nearly six feet, was broad in proportion, and, like all the men in the place, in most perfect training. However, I held on to him for my life, and presently we were struggling upon the floor. For some strange reason, what I cannot tell, that fight seemed to be the most enjoyable three minutes I have ever spent in the whole of my existence.

Over and over we rolled upon the stone floor, my hand still fixed upon his throat to prevent him from crying out.

At last throwing my leg over him I seated myself upon his chest, and then—having nothing else to do it with—I drew back my right arm, and let him have three blows with the whole strength of my fist.

Written in black and white it looks a trifle bloodthirsty, but you must remember we were fighting for our lives, and if by any chance he gave the alarm, nothing on earth could save us from death. I had therefore to make the most of the only opportunity I possessed of silencing him.

As soon as he was unconscious, I looked round for Nikola. He was kneeling by the body of the other man who was lying, face downwards upon the floor, as if dead.

"I would give five pounds," whispered Nikola, as he rose to his feet, "for this man's skull. Just look at it; it goes up at the back of his head like a tom cat! It is my luck all over to come across such a specimen when I can't make use of it."

As he spoke he ran his first finger and thumb caressingly up and down the man's poll.

"I've got a bottle in my museum in Port Said," he said regretfully, "which would take him beautifully."

Then he picked up the sponge which he had used upon the last man, and went across to my adversary. For thirty seconds or thereabouts he held it upon his nose and mouth; then, throwing it into a corner, divested the man of his garments, and attired himself in them.

"Now," he said, when he had made his toilet to his own satisfaction, "we must be off. They change the guard at midnight, and it is already twenty minutes past eleven."

So saying, he led the way down the corridor, I following at his heels. We had not reached the end of it, however, before Nikola bade me wait for him while he went back. When he rejoined me, I asked him in a whisper what he had been doing.

"Nothing very much," he answered. "I wanted to convince myself as to, a curious malformation of the occipital bone in that man's skull. I am sorry to have kept you waiting, but I might never have had another chance of examining such a complete case."

Having given this explanation, this extraordinary votary of science condescended to continue his escape. Leaving the long corridor, now so familiar to us, we turned to our left hand, ascended a flight of steps, followed another small passage, and then came to a standstill at a spot where four roads met.

"Where on earth are we?" inquired Nikola, looking round him. "This place reminds me of the Hampton Court maze."

"Hark! What is that booming noise?"

We listened, and by doing so discovered that we were near the subterranean waterfall we had seen on the occasion of our first visit to the large cave.

"We are altogether out of our course," I said.

"On the other hand," answered Nikola, "we are not close enough to it yet."

"What do you mean?" I asked.

"My dear Bruce," he said, "tell me this: Why are we in this place? Did we not come here to obtain possession of their secrets? Well, as we are saying good-bye to them to-night for good and all, do you suppose, after adventuring so much, I am going empty handed? If you think so, you are very much in error. Why, to do that would be to have failed altogether in our journey; and though Nikola often boasts, you must admit he seldom fails to do what he undertakes. Don't say any more, but come along with me."

199

Turning into a passage on his right, he led the way down some more steps. Here the torches were almost at their last flicker.

"If we don't look sharp," said Nikola, "we shall have to carry out our errand in the dark, and that will be undesirable for more reasons than one."

From the place where we now stood we could hear the roar of the waterfall quite distinctly, and could just make out, further to our left, the entrance to the great cave. To our delight there were no guards to be seen, so we were able to pass in unmolested. Taking what remained of a torch from a socket near the door, we entered together. A more uncanny place than that great cave, as it revealed itself to us by the light of our solitary torch, no man can imagine. Innumerable bats fluttered about the aisles, their wings filling the air with ghostly whisperings, while dominating all was that peculiar charnel-house smell that I had noticed on the occasion of our previous visit, and which no words could properly describe.

"The entrance to the catacombs is at this end," said Nikola, leading the way up the central aisle. "Let us find it."

I followed him, and together we made towards that part of the cave furthest from the doors. The entrance once found, we had only to follow the steps, and pass down into the crypt I have before described. By the light of our torch we could discern the swathed-up figures in the niches. Nikola, however, had small attention to spare for them—he was too busily occupied endeavouring to discover the spring in the central pillar to think of anything else. When he found it he pressed it, and the door opened. Then down the ladder we crept into the anteroom where I had waited on that awful night. I can tell you one thing, and it is the sober truth—I would far rather have engaged a dozen of the strongest monks in that monastery singlehanded, than have followed my chief into that room. But he would not let me draw back, and so we pushed on together. All around us were the mysterious treasures of the monastery, with every sort of implement for every sort of chemistry known to the fertile brain of man. At the further end was a large wooden door, exquisitely carved. This was padlocked in three places, and looked as if it would offer a stubborn resistance to any one who might attempt to break it. But Nikola was a man hard to beat, and he solved the difficulty in a very simple fashion. Unfastening his loose upper garment, he unstrapped his invaluable medicine-chest, and placed it on the floor; then, choosing a small but sharp surgeon's saw, he fell to work upon the wood surrounding the staple. In less than ten minutes he had cut out the padlocks, and the door swung open. Then, with all the speed we were masters of, we set to work to hunt for the things we wanted. It contained small phials, antique parchment prescriptions, a thousand sorts of drugs, and finally, in an iron coffer, a small book written in Sanscrit and most quaintly bound. This Nikola stowed away in one of his many voluminous pockets, and, as soon as he had made a selection of the other things, announced that it was time for us to turn back. Just as he came to this conclusion, the torch, which had all the time been burning lower and lower, gave a final flicker, and went out altogether. We were left in the dark in this awful cave.

"This is most unfortunate," said Nikola. Then, after a pause, "However, as it can't be cured, we must make the best of it."

I answered nothing, but waited for my leader to propose some plan. At the end of a few moments the darkness seemed to make little or no difference to Nikola. He took me by the hand, and led me straight through the cave into the antechamber.

"Look-out!" he said; "here is the ladder."

And, true enough, as he spoke my shins made its acquaintance. Strange is the force of habit; the pain was sharp, and though I was buried in the centre of a mountain, surrounded by the dead men of a dozen centuries, I employed exactly the same epithet to express my feelings as I should have done, had a passing taxi splashed my boots opposite the Mansion House.

Leaving the lower regions, we climbed the ladder, and reached the crypt, passed up the stairs into the great cave, made our way across that, and then, Nikola still leading, found the tunnel, and passed through it as safely as if we had been lighted by a hundred linkmen.

"Our next endeavour must be to discover how we are to get out of the building itself," said Nikola, as we reached the four cross passages; "and as I have no notion how the land lies, it looks rather more serious. Let us try this passage first."

As quickly as was possible under the circumstances we made our way up the stairs indicated, passed the great waterfall, sped along two or three corridors, were several times nearly observed, and at last, after innumerable try-backs, reached the great hall where we had been received on the day of our arrival.

Almost at the same instant there was a clamour in the monastery, followed by the ringing of the deep-toned bell; then the shouting of many voices, and the tramping of hundreds of feet.

"They are after us!" said Nikola. "Our flight has been discovered. Now, if we cannot find a way out, we are done for completely."

The noise was every moment coming closer, and any instant we might expect our pursuers to come into view. Like rats in a strange barn, who hear the approach of a terrier, we dashed this way and that in our endeavours to discover an exit. At last we came upon the steps leading from the great hall into the valley below. Down these we flew as fast as we could go, every moment risking a fall which would inevitably break our necks. Almost too giddy to stand, we at last reached the bottom, to find the door shut, and guarded by a stalwart monk. To throw ourselves upon him was the work of an instant. He lifted his heavy staff, and aimed a blow at me; but I dodged it in time, and got in at him before he could recover. Drawing back my arm, I hit him with all the strength at my command. His head struck the floor with a crash, and he did not move again.

Nikola bent over him, and assured himself that the sleep was genuine. Then he signed to me to give him the key, and when the door was unfastened we passed through it, and closed it after us, locking it on the other side. Then down the valley we ran as fast as our legs would carry us.

Chapter 17

Conclusion

As I have said, we were no sooner through the gates than we took to our heels and fled down the valley for our lives. For my own part I was so thankful to be out of that awful place, to be once more breathing the fresh air of Heaven, that I felt as if I could go on running for ever. Fortunately the night was pitch dark, with a high wind blowing. The darkness prevented our pursuers from seeing the direction we had taken, while the noise of the wind effectually deadened any sound we might make that would otherwise have betrayed our whereabouts.

For upwards of an hour we sped along the bottom of the valley in this fashion, paying no heed where we went and caring for nothing but to put as great a distance as possible between ourselves and our pursuers. At last I could go no further, so I stopped and threw myself upon the ground. Nikola immediately came to a standstill, glanced round him suspiciously, and then sat down beside me.

"So much for our first visit to the great monastery of Thibet," he said as casually as if he were bidding good-bye to a chance acquaintance.

"Do you think we have given them the slip?" I queried, looking anxiously up the dark valley through which we had come.

"By no means," he answered. "Remember we are still hemmed in by the precipices, and at most we cannot be more than five miles from their doors. We shall have to proceed very warily for the next week or so, and to do that we must make the most of every minute of darkness."

We were both silent for a little while. I was occupied trying to recover my breath, Nikola in distributing more comfortably about his person the parchments, etc., he had brought away with him.

"Shall we be going on again?" I asked, as soon as I thought I could go on. "I've no desire to fall into their hands, I can assure you. Which way is it to be now?"

"Straight on," he answered, springing to his feet. "We must follow the valley down and see where it will bring us out. It would be hopeless to attempt to scale the cliffs."

Without further talk we set off, not to stop again until we had added another four miles or perhaps five to our flight. By this time it was close upon daybreak, the chilliest, dreariest, greyest dawn in all my experience. With the appearance of the light the wind died down, but it still moaned among the rocks and through the high grass in the most dreary and dispiriting fashion. Half an hour later the sun rose, and then Nikola once more called a halt.

"We must hide ourselves somewhere," he said, "and travel on again as soon as darkness falls. Look about you for a place where we shall not be likely to be seen."

For some time it seemed as if we should be unable to discover any such spot, but at last we hit upon one that was just suited to our purpose. It was a small enclosure sheltered by big boulders and situated on a rocky plateau high up the hill-side. To this place of refuge we scrambled, and then with armfuls of grass, which we collected from the immediate neighbourhood, endeavoured to make ourselves as comfortable as possible until night should once more descend upon us. It was not a cheery camp. To make matters worse we were quite destitute of food, and already the pangs of hunger were beginning to obtrude themselves upon us.

"If we ever do get back to civilization," said Nikola, after we had been sitting there some time, "I suppose this business will rank as one of the greatest exploits of your life?"

"I have no desire ever to undertake such another," I replied truthfully. "This trip has more than satisfied my craving for the adventurous."

"Wait till you've been settled in a sleepy English village for a couple of years," he said with a laugh. "By that time I wouldn't mind wagering you'll be ready for anything that turns up. I wonder what you would think if I told you that, dangerous as this one has been, it is as nothing to another in which I was concerned about six years since. Then I was occupied trying to discover——"

I am sorry to have to confess that it is beyond my power to narrate what his adventure was, where it occurred, or indeed anything connected with it, for while he was talking I fell into a sound sleep, from which I did not wake until nearly three hours later.

When I opened my eyes the sun was still shining brightly, the wind had dropped, and the air was as quiet as the night had been noisy and tempestuous. I looked round for Nikola, but to my surprise he was not occupying the place where he had been sitting when I fell asleep, nor indeed was he inside the enclosure at all. Alarmed lest anything untoward might have befallen him, I was in the act of going in search of him when he reappeared creeping between the rocks upon his hands and knees. I was about to express my delight at his return, but he signed to me to be silent, and a moment later reached my side.

"Keep as still as you can," he whispered; "they're after us."

"How close are they?" I asked, with a sudden sinking in my heart.

"Not a hundred yards away," he answered, and as he spoke he bent his head forward to listen.

A moment later I could hear them for myself, coming along the valley to our left. Their voices sounded quite plain and distinct, and for this reason I judged that they could not have been more than fifty yards from us. Now came the great question, Would they discover us or not? Under the influence of the awful suspense I scarcely breathed. One thing I was firmly resolved upon—if they did detect our hiding-place I would fight to the last gasp rather than let them capture me and carry me back to that awful monastery. The sweat stood in great beads upon my forehead as I listened. It was evident they were searching among the rocks at the base of the cliff. Not being able to find us there, would they try higher up? Fortune, however, favoured us. Either they gave us credit for greater speed than we possessed, or they did not notice the hiding-place among the rocks; at any rate, they passed on without molesting us. The change from absolute danger to comparative safety was almost overpowering, and even the stoical Nikola heaved a sigh of relief as the sound of their voices died gradually away.

That night, as soon as it was dark, we left the place where we had hidden ourselves and proceeded down the valley, keeping a watchful eye open for any sign of our foes. But our lucky star was still in the ascendant, and we saw nothing of them. Towards daylight we left the valley and entered a large basin, if it may be so described, formed by a number of lofty hills. On the bottom of the bowl thus fashioned was a considerable village. Halting on an eminence above it, Nikola looked round him.

"We shall have to find a hiding-place on the hills somewhere hereabouts," he said; "but before we do so we must have food."

"And a change of dress," I answered, for it must be remembered that we were still clad in the monkish robes we had worn when we left the monastery.

"Quite so," he answered: "first the food and the dress, then the hiding-place."

Without more ado he signed to me to follow him, and together we left the hillock and proceeded towards the village. It was not a large place, nor, from all appearances, was it a very wealthy one; it contained scarcely more than fifty houses, the majority of which were of the usual Thibetan type, that is to say, built of loose stones, roofed with split pine shingles, and as draughty and leaky as it is possible for houses to be. The family reside in one room, the other—for in few cases are there more than two—being occupied by the cows, pigs, dogs, fowls, and other domestic animals.

As we approached the first house Nikola bade me remain where I was while he went forward to see what he could procure. For many reasons I did not care very much about this arrangement, but I knew him too well by this time to waste my breath arguing. He left me and crept forward. It was bitterly cold, and while he was absent and I was standing still, I felt as if I were being frozen into a solid block of ice. What our altitude could have been I am not in a position to tell, but if one could estimate it by the keenness of the air, it must have been something considerable.

Nikola was absent for nearly twenty minutes. At last, however, he returned, bringing with him a quantity of clothing, including two typical Thibetan hats, a couple of thick blankets, and, what was better than all, a quantity of food. The latter consisted of half a dozen coarse cakes, a hunk of a peculiar sort of bread, and a number of new-laid eggs, also a large bowl of milk. As to payment he informed me that he had left a small gold piece, believing that that would be the most effectual means of silencing the owner's tongue. Seating ourselves in the shelter of a large rock, we set to work to stow away as much of the food as we could possibly consume. Then dividing the clothing into two bundles we set off across the valley in an easterly direction.

By daylight we had put a considerable distance between us and the village, and were installed in a small cave, half-way up a rugged hill. Below us was a copse of mountain pines and, across the valley, a cliff, not unlike that down which we had climbed to reach the monastery. We had discarded our monkish robes by this time, and, for greater security, had buried them in a safe place beneath a tree. In our new rigs, with the tall felt hats upon our heads, we might very well have passed for typical Thibetans.

Feeling that our present hiding-place was not likely to be discovered, we laid ourselves down to sleep. How long we slumbered, I cannot say; I only know that for some reason or other I woke in a fright to hear a noise in the valley beneath us. I listened for a few moments to make sure, and then shook Nikola, who was still sleeping soundly.

"What is it?" he cried, as he sat up. "Why do you wake me?"

"Because we're in danger again," I answered. "What is that noise in the valley?"

He listened for a moment.

"I can hear nothing," he said.

Then just as he was about to speak again there came a new sound that brought us both to our feet like lightning—*the baying of dogs.* Now, as we both knew, the only dogs in that district are of the formidable Deggi breed, standing about as high as Shetland ponies, as strong as mastiffs, and as fierce as they are powerful. If our enemies were pursuing us with these brutes our case was indeed an unenviable one.

"Get up!" cried Nikola. "They are hunting us down with the dogs. Up the hill for your life!"

The words were scarcely out of his mouth before we were racing up the hill like hares. Up and up we went, scrambling from rock to rock and bank to bank till my legs felt as if they could go no further. Though it was but little over a hundred yards from our hiding-place into the wood at the summit it seemed like miles. When we reached it we threw ourselves down exhausted upon a bed of pine needles, but only for a minute, then we were up and on our way again as hard as ever. Through the thicket we dashed, conscious of nothing but a desire to get away from those horrible dogs. The wood was a thick one, but prudence told us it could offer no possible refuge for us. Every step we took was leaving a record to guide them, and we dared not hesitate or delay a second longer than was absolutely necessary.

At last we reached the far side of the wood. Here, to our surprise, the country began to slope downwards again into a second valley. From the skirt of the timber where we stood, for nearly a mile, it was all open, with not a bush or a rock to serve as cover. We were in a pretty fix. To wheel round would be to meet our pursuers face to face; to turn to either hand would be equally as bad, while to go on would only be to show ourselves in the open, and after that to be run to earth like foxes in the second valley. But there was no time to stop or to think, so for good or ill we took to our heels again and set off down the slope. We were not half-way across the open, however, before we heard the dogs break cover behind us, and a moment later, the excited shouting of men, who had seen us ahead of them, and were encouraging the hounds to run us down.

If we had run fast before we literally flew now. The dogs were gaining on us at every stride, and unless something unexpected happened to save us we could look upon ourselves in the light of men as good as dead. Only fifty yards separated us from the cover that bounded the moor, if I may so describe it, on the other side. If the worst came to the worst, and we could reach the timber at the bottom, we could climb a tree there and sell our lives as dearly as possible with our revolvers.

Putting on a final spurt we gained the wood and plunged into the undergrowth. The nearest dog—there were three of these gigantic brutes—was scarcely twenty yards behind us. Suddenly Nikola, who was in front, stopped as if shot, threw up his arms and fell straight backwards. Seeing him do this I stopped too, but only just in the nick of time. A moment later I should have been over a precipice into the swift-flowing river that ran below. By the time I realized this the first dog was upon us. Nikola supported himself on his elbow, and, as coolly as if he were picking off a pigeon, shot him dead. The second fell to my share; the third proved somewhat more troublesome. Seeing the fate of his companions, he stopped short and crouched among the bushes, growling savagely.

"Kill him!" cried Nikola, with one of the only signs of excitement I had ever known him show. I fired again, but must have missed him, for he rushed in at me, and had I not thrown up my arm would have seized me by the throat. Then Nikola fired—I felt the bullet whiz past my ear—and before I could think the great beast had fallen back upon the ground and was twisting and twining in his death agony.

"Quick!" cried Nikola, springing to his feet once more. "There's not a moment to be lost. Throw the dogs into the stream."

Without wasting time we set to work, and in less than half a minute all three animals had disappeared into the river. As the last went over the side we heard the foremost of our pursuers enter the wood. Another moment and we should have been too late.

"There's nothing for it," cried Nikola, "but for us to follow the dogs' example. They'll hunt about wondering which way the brutes have gone, and by that time we ought to be some distance down stream."

"Come on then," I said, and, without more deliberation, took a header. It was a dive of at least sixty feet, but not so unpleasant as our position would have been upon the bank had we remained. Nikola followed me, and before our enemies could have gained the river side we had swept round the bend and were out of their sight. But though we had for the moment given them the slip our position was still by no means an enviable one. The water was as cold as ice and the current ran like a mill sluice, while the depth could not have been much under fifty feet, though I could only judge this by the shelving of the banks. For nearly ten minutes we swam on side by side in silence. The voices of our pursuers grew more and more faint until we could no longer hear them. The horror of that swim I must leave you to imagine. The icy coldness of the water seemed to eat into the very marrow of my bones, and every moment I expected to feel an attack of cramp. One thing soon became evident, the stream was running more and more swiftly. Suddenly Nikola turned his head and shouted, "Make for the bank!"

I endeavoured to do so, but the whole force of the current was against me. Vainly I battled. The stream bore me further and further from my goal, till at last I was swept beyond the ford and down between two precipitous banks where landing was impossible. It was then that I realized Nikola's reason for calling to me. For a hundred yards or so ahead I could see the river, then only blue sky and white cloud. For obvious reasons it could not have come to a standstill, so this sudden break-off could have but one meaning—*a fall!* With incredible swiftness the water bore me on, now spinning me round and round like a teetotum, now carrying me this way, now that, but all the time bringing me closer to the abyss.

Ten yards further, and I could hear the sullen boom of the falling waters, and as I heard it I saw that the bank of the fall was studded with a fringe of large rocks. If I did not wish to be hurled over into eternity, I knew I must catch one of these rocks, and cling to it with all my strength. Strange to say, even in that moment of despair, my presence of mind did not desert me. I chose my rock, and concentrated all my energies upon the work of reaching it. Fortunately the current helped me, and with hardly an effort on my part, I was carried towards it. Throwing up my arms I clutched at it, but the stone was slippery, and I missed my hold. I tried again with the same result. Then, just as I was on the very brink of the precipice, my fingers caught in a projecting ledge, and I was able to stay myself. The weight of the water upon my back was terrific, but with the strength of a dozen men I clung on, and little by little lifted myself up. I was fighting for dear life, for Gladys, for all that made life worth living, and that gave me superhuman strength. At last I managed to lift myself sufficiently to get a purchase on the rock with my knees. After that it was all plain sailing, and in less time almost than it takes to tell, I was lying stretched out upon the rock, safe, but exhausted almost to the point of death.

When I had somewhat recovered my strength, I opened my eyes and looked over the edge. Such a sight I never want to see again. Picture a river, as wide as the Thames at London Bridge, walled in between two steep banks, pouring its water down into a rocky pool almost half a mile below. The thunder of the fall was deafening, while from the lake at the foot rose a dense mist, changing, where the sun caught it, to every colour of the rainbow. Fascinated by this truly awful picture, and the narrowness of my own escape from death, I could scarcely withdraw my eyes. When I did it was to look across at the right-hand bank. Nikola stood there waving to me. Cheered by his presence, I began to cast about me for a means of reaching him, but the prospect was by no means a cheerful one. Several rocks there certainly were, and near the bank they were close enough to enable an active man to jump from one to the other. Unfortunately, however, between the one on which I lay and the next was a yawning gulf of something like eight feet. To reach it seemed impossible. I dared not risk the leap, and yet if I did not jump, what was to become of me? I was just beginning to despair again, when I saw Nikola point up stream and disappear.

For something like a quarter of an hour I saw no more of him, then he reappeared a hundred yards or so further up the bank, and as he did so he pointed into mid-stream. I looked, and immediately realized his intention. He had discovered a large log and had sent it afloat in the hope that it would be of service to me. Closer and closer it came, steering directly for where I knelt. As it drew alongside I leant over, and, catching at a small branch which decorated it, attempted to drag it athwart the channel. My strength, however, was uncertain, and had the effect of bringing the current to bear on the other end. It immediately spun swiftly round, went from me like an express train, and next moment disappeared over the brink into the abyss below, nearly dragging me with it. Once more Nikola signalled to me and disappeared into the wood. Half an hour later another log made its appearance. This time I was more fortunate, and managed, with considerable manoeuvring and coaxing, to get it jambed by the current between the two rocks.

The most perilous part of the whole undertaking was now about to commence. I had to cross on this frail bridge to the next stone. With my heart in my mouth I crawled over my own rock, and then having given a final look round, and tested it as well as I was able, seated myself astride of the log. The rush of the water against my legs was tremendous, and I soon found I should have all my time taken up endeavouring to preserve my balance. But with infinite caution I continued to advance until at last I reached the opposite rock. All the time I had never dared to look over the brink; had I done so I believe my nerve would have deserted me, and I should then have lost my balance and perished for good and all.

When the journey was accomplished, and I was safely established on the second rock, I rested for a few minutes, and then, standing up, measured my distance as carefully as possible, and jumped on to the third. The rest was easy, and in a few moments I was lying quite overcome among the bracken at Nikola's feet. As soon as I was safe, my pluck, presence of mind, nerve, or whatever you like to call it, gave way completely, and I found myself trembling like a little child.

"You have had a narrow escape," said Nikola.

"When I saw that you could not make the bank up yonder, I made up my mind it was all over with you. However, all's well that ends well, and now we've got to find out what we had better do next."

"What do you advise?" I asked, my teeth chattering in my head like castanets.

"That we find a sheltered spot somewhere hereabouts, light a fire and dry our things, then get down to the river below the falls, construct a raft, and travel upon it till we come to a village. There, if possible, we will buy donkeys, and, if all goes well, pursue our journey to the coast by another route."

"But don't you think our enemies will have warned the inhabitants of the villages hereabouts to be on the look-out for us?"

"We must chance that. Now let us find a place to light a fire. You are nearly frozen."

Half a mile or so further on we discovered the spot we wanted, lit our fire and dried our things. All this time I was in agony—one moment as cold as ice, the next in a burning fever. Nikola prescribed for me from his medicine chest, which, with the things he had obtained from the monastery, he still carried with him, and then we laid ourselves down to sleep.

From that time forward I have no recollection of anything that occurred till I woke to find myself snugly ensconced in a comfortable but simply furnished bedroom. Where I was, or how I got there, I could no more tell than I could fly. I endeavoured to get up in order to look out of the window, but I found I was too weak to manage it, so I laid myself down again, and as I did so made another startling discovery—*my pigtail was gone!*

For nearly half an hour I was occupied endeavouring to puzzle this out. Then I heard a footstep in the passage outside, and a moment later a dignified priest entered the room and asked me in French how I felt. I answered that I thought I was much better, though still very weak, and went on to state that I should feel obliged if he would tell me where I was, and how I had got there.

"You are in the French mission at Ya-Chow-Fu," he said. "You were brought here a fortnight ago by an Englishman, who, from what we could gather, had found you higher up the river suffering from a severe attack of rheumatic fever."

"And where is this—this Englishman now?"

"That I cannot say. He left us a week ago to proceed on a botanizing excursion, I believe, further west. When he bade us farewell he gave me a sum of money which I am to devote, as soon as you are fit to move, to chartering a boat and coolies to convey you to I-chang, where you will be able to obtain a steamer for Shanghai."

"And did he not leave any message to say whether I should see him again, and if so, where?"

"I have a note in my pocket for you now." Thus reminded, the worthy priest produced a letter which he handed to me. I opened it as soon as he had departed, and eagerly scanned its contents. It ran as follows:

"Dear Bruce—By the time you receive this I hope you will be on the high road to health again. After your little experiment on the top of the falls you became seriously ill with rheumatic fever. A nice business I had conveying you down stream on a raft, but, as you see, I accomplished it, and got you into the French Mission at Ya-Chow-Fu safely. I am writing this note to bid you good-bye for the present, as I think it is better we should henceforth travel by different routes. I may, however, run across you in I-chang. One caution before I go—figure for the future as a European, and keep your eyes wide open for treachery. The society has branches everywhere, and by this time I expect they will have been warned. Remember, they will be sure to try to get back the things we've taken, and also will attempt to punish us for our intrusion. I thank you for your companionship, and for the loyalty you have extended to me throughout our journey. I think I am paying you the greatest compliment when I say that I could have wished for no better companion.—Yours,

"Nikola."

That was all.

A week later I bade my hospitable host, who had engaged a boat and trustworthy crew for me, good-bye, and set off on my long down-river journey. I reached I-chang—where I was to abandon my boat and take a passage to Shanghai—safely, and without any further adventure.

On learning that there would not be a river steamer leaving until the following day, I went ashore, discovered an inn, and engaged a room. But though I waited all the evening, and as late as I could next day, Nikola did not put in an appearance. Accordingly at four o'clock I boarded the steamer *Kiang-Yung,* and in due course reached Shanghai.

How thankful I was to again set foot in that place, no one will ever know. I could have gone down on my knees and kissed the very ground in gratitude. Was I not back again in civilization, free to find my sweetheart, and, if she were still of the same mind, to make her my wife? Was not my health thoroughly restored to me? and last, but not least, was there not a sum of £10,000 reposing at my bankers to my credit? That day I determined to see Barkston and McAndrew, and the next to leave for Tientsin in search of my darling. But I was not destined to make the journey after all.

Calling at the club, I inquired for George Barkston. He happened to be in the building and greeted me in the hall with all the surprise imaginable.

214

"By Jove, Bruce!" he cried. "This is really most wonderful. I was only speaking of you this morning, and here you turn up like——"

"'Like a bad penny,' you were going to say."

"Not a bit of it. Like the Wandering Jew would be more to the point. But don't let us stand here. Come along with me. I'm going to take you to my bungalow to tiffin."

"But my dear fellow, I——"

"I know all about that," he cried. "However, you've just got to come along with me. I've got a bit of news for you."

As nothing would induce him to tell me what it was, we chartered 'rickshaws, and set off for his residence.

When we reached it I was ordered to wait in the hall while he went in search of his wife. Having made some inquiries, he led me to the drawing-room, opened the door, and bade me go inside. Though inwardly wondering what all this mystery might mean, I followed his instructions.

A lady was sitting in an easy chair near the window, sewing. *That lady was Gladys!*

"Wilfred!" she cried, jumping to her feet, and turning quite pale, for she could scarcely believe her eyes.

"Gladys!" I answered, taking her in my arms, and kissing her with all the enthusiasm of a long-parted lover.

"I cannot realize it yet," she said, when the first transports were over. "Why did you not let me know you were coming to Shanghai?"

"Because I had no notion that you were here," I answered.

"But did you not call on Mr. Williams in Tientsin? and did he not give you my letter?"

"I have not been to Tientsin, nor have I seen Mr. Williams. I have come straight down the Yangtze-Kiang from the west."

"Oh, I am so glad—so thankful to have you back. We have been separated such a long, long time."

"And you still love me, Gladys?"

"Can you doubt it, dear? I love you more fondly than ever. Does not the warmth of my greeting now convince you of that?"

"Of course it does," I cried. "I only wanted to have the assurance from your own dear lips. But now tell me, how do you

215

come to be in Shanghai, and in George Barkston's house, of all other places?"

"Well, that would make too long a story to tell *in extenso* just now. We must reserve the bulk of it. Suffice it that my brother and sister have been transferred to a new post in Japan, and while they are getting their house in Tokyo ready, I came down here to stay with Mrs. Barkston, who is an old school friend. I expect them here in about a week's time to fetch me."

"And now the most important of all questions. When are we to be married?"

She hung her pretty head and blushed so sweetly that I had to take her in my arms again and kiss her. I pressed my question, however, and it was finally agreed that we should refer the matter to her brother-in-law on his arrival the following week.

To bring my long story to a close, let me say that we were married three weeks after my return to Shanghai, in the English church, and that we ran across to Japan for our honeymoon. It may be thought that with my marriage my connection with the Chinese nation came to an end. Unfortunately that was not so. Two days after our arrival in Nagasaki two curious incidents occurred that brought in their train a host of unpleasant suspicions. My wife and I had retired to rest for the night, and were both sleeping soundly, when we were awakened by a loud cry of fire. To my horror I discovered that our room was ablaze. I forced the door, and having done so, seized my wife, threw a blanket over her, and made a rush with her outside. How the fire had originated no one could tell, but it was fortunate we were roused in time, otherwise we should certainly have both lost our lives. As it was most of our belongings perished in the flames. A kindly Englishman, resident in the neighbourhood, seeing our plight, took pity on us, and insisted that we should make use of his house until we decided on our future movements. We remained with him for two days, and it was on that following our arrival at his abode that the second circumstance occurred to cause me uneasiness.

We had been out shopping in the morning and returned just in time for tiffin, which when we arrived was already on the table. While we were washing our hands before sitting down to it, our host's little terrier, who was possessed of a thieving disposition, clambered up and helped himself. By the time we returned (the owner of the bungalow, you must understand, lunched at his office, and did not come home till evening) he had eaten half the dish and spoiled the rest. We preferred to make our meal off biscuits and butter rather than call the servants and put them to the trouble of cooking more. An hour later the dog was dead, poisoned, as we should have been had we partaken of the curry. The new cook, who we discovered later was a Chinaman, had meanwhile decamped and could not again be found.

That evening when returning home in the dusk, a knife was thrown from a window across the street, narrowly grazed my throat, and buried itself in the woodwork of the house I was passing at the time. Without more ado I booked two passages aboard a mail steamer and next day set sail with my wife for England.

Arriving in London I took a small furnished house in a quiet part of Kensington, and settled myself down while I looked about me for a small property in the country.

Now to narrate one last surprise before I say good-bye. One afternoon I went up to town to consult a land agent about a place I had seen advertised, and was walking down the Strand, when I felt a hand placed upon my shoulder. I wheeled round to *find myself face to face with Nikola.* He was dressed in frock coat and top hat, but was otherwise the same as ever.

"Dr. Nikola!" I cried in amazement.

"Yes, Dr. Nikola," he answered quietly, without any show of emotion. "Are you glad to see me?"

"Very glad indeed," I replied; "but at first I can hardly believe it. I thought most probably you were still in China."

"China became too hot to hold me," he said with a laugh. "But I shall go out there again as soon as this trouble blows over. In the meantime I am off to St. Petersburg on important business. Where are you staying? and how is your wife?"

"I am staying in Kensington," I replied; "and I am glad to say that my wife is in the best of health."

"I needn't ask if you are happy; your face tells me that. Now can you spare me half an hour?"

"With every pleasure."

"Then come along to Charing Cross; I want to talk to you. This is my taxi."

He led me to a cab which was waiting alongside the pavement, and when I had seated myself in it, stepped in and took his place beside me.

"This is better than Thibet, is it not?" he said, as we drove along.

"Very much better," I answered with a laugh. "But how wonderful it seems that we should be meeting here in this prosaic fashion after all we have been through together. There is one thing I have never been able to understand: what became of you after you left me at Ya-Chow-Fu?"

"I went off on another track to divert the attention of the men who were after us."

"You think we were followed then?"

"I am certain of it, worse luck. And what's more they are after us now. I have had six attempts made upon my life in the last three months. But they have not managed to catch me yet. Why, you will hardly believe it, *but there are two Chinamen following you down the Strand even now.* Dusk has fallen, and you might walk down a side street and thus give them the opportunity they want. That was partly why I picked you up."

"The devil! Then my suspicions were correct after all. The hotel we stayed at in Nagasaki was fired the first night we were in it, a dish of curry intended for us was poisoned two days later, while I was nearly struck with a knife two days after that again. Yesterday I saw a Chinaman near our house in Kensington, but though I thought he appeared to be watching my house I may have been mistaken in his intentions."

"What was he like? Was he dressed in English clothes? and was half his left ear missing?"

"You are describing the man exactly."

"Quong Ma. Then look out. If that gentleman has his eye upon you I should advise you to leave. He'll stick to you like wax until he gets his opportunity, and then he'll strike. Be advised by me, take time by the forelock and clear out of England while you have the chance. They want the things we took, and they want revenge To get both they'll follow us to the ends of the earth."

"And now one very important question: have the things you took proved of sufficient value to repay you for all your trouble and expense?"

"Of more than sufficient value. I'm going to see a French chemist in St. Petersburg about that anaesthetic now. In less than a year I shall enlighten this old country, I think, in a fashion it will not forget. Wait and see!"

As he said this we entered the station-yard, and a minute or so later were standing alongside the Continental express. Time was almost up, and intending passengers were already being warned to take their seats. Nikola saw his baggage placed hi the van and then returned to me and held out his hand.

"Good-bye, Bruce," he said. "We shall probably never meet again. You served me well, and I wish you every happiness. One last word of caution, however, beware of that fellow with half an ear, and don't give him a chance to strike. Farewell, and think sometimes of Dr. Nikola!"

I shook hands with him, the guard fluttered his flag, the engine whistled, and the train steamed out of the station. I waved my hand in token of good-bye, and since then I have never heard or seen anything of Dr. Nikola, the most extraordinary man I have ever come in contact with.

When the last carriage was out of sight, I went into the station-yard intending to get a taxi, but when I had beckoned one up a man brushed past me and appropriated it. *To my horror it was the Chinaman with half an ear I had seen outside my house the day before.*

Waiting until he had left the station-yard, I made my way down to the Embankment and took the Underground Railway for Earl's Court, driving home as fast as I could go from there. On the threshold of my residence my servant greeted me with the information that a Chinaman had just called to see me. I waited to hear no more, but packed my things, and within a couple of hours my wife and I had left London for a tiny country town in the Midlands. Here at least we thought we should be safe; but as it turned out we were no more secure there than in London or Nagasaki, for that week the hotel in which we stayed caught fire in the middle of the night, and for the second time since our wedding we only just managed to escape with our lives.

Next day we migrated to a still smaller place in Devonshire, near Torquay. Our enemies still pursued us, however, for we had not been there a month before a most daring burglary was committed in my rooms in broad daylight, and when my wife and I returned from an excursion to a neighbouring village, it was to find our trunks rifled, and our belongings strewn about our rooms. The most extraordinary part of the affair, however, was the fact that nothing, save a small Chinese knife, was missing.

The county police were soon to the fore, but the only suspicious character they could think of was a certain Celestial with half an ear, who had been observed in the hamlet the day before, and even he could not be discovered when they wanted him.

On hearing that last piece of news I had a consultation with my wife, told her of Nikola's warning, and asked her advice.

As a result we left the hotel, much to the chagrin of the proprietor, that night, and departed for Southampton, where we shipped for New York the following day. Judge of our feelings on reading in an afternoon paper, purchased on board previous to sailing, that the occupants of our bed had been found in the morning with their throats cut from ear to ear.

In New York things became even more dangerous than in England, and four distinct attempts were made upon my life. We accordingly crossed the continent to San Francisco, only to leave it in a hurry three days later for the usual reason.

Where we are now, my dear Craigie, as I said in my Introduction, I cannot even tell *you.* Let me tell you one thing, however, and that is, though we have been here six months, we have seen no more of the half-eared Chinaman, nor indeed any of his sinister race. We live our own lives, and have our own interests, and now that my son is born, we are as happy as any two mortals under similar circumstances can expect to be. I love and honour my wife above all living women, and for that reason, if for no other, I shall never regret the circumstances that brought about my meeting with that extraordinary individual, Dr. Nikola.

Now, old friend, you know my story. It has taken a long time to tell—let us hope that you will think it worth the trouble. If you do, I am amply repaid. Good-bye!

THE END

Attribution and License

The text of this eBook is from The Gutenberg Project Australia at
http://gutenberg.net.au/ebooks06/0601621h.html,
which is made available at no cost and with almost no restrictions whatsoever. You may copy it, give it away or re-use it, under the terms of the Project Gutenberg of Australia License which may be viewed online at http://gutenberg.net.au/licence.html , which is a Creative Commons 3.0 license.
To contact Project Gutenberg of Australia go to http://gutenberg.net.au .

The cover image is "Hanging scroll, ink on silk. Size 111.4 x 56 cm (height x width). Created circa year 960 by artist Li Cheng (c. 919 - c. 967 AD). Painting is located in the Nelson-Atkins Museum of Art, Kansas City, Missouri." The image was downloaded from Wikimedia Commons at
http://commons.wikimedia.org/wiki/File:Li_Cheng_Buddhist_Temple_in_Moutain_All.jpg, which says "This work is in the public domain in the United States, and those countries with a copyright term of life of the author plus 100 years or less." It has been re-sized, not in proportion, to fit the eBook cover.

www.feedbooks.com
Food for the mind

Printed in Great Britain
by Amazon.co.uk, Ltd.,
Marston Gate.